THE DEVIL'S HALF

THE DEVIL'S HALF

Ovid Williams Pierce

1968

DOUBLEDAY & COMPANY, INC., GARDEN CITY, NEW YORK

All of the characters in this book
are fictitious, and any resemblance
to actual persons, living or dead,
is purely coincidental.

To the memory of Elizabeth Thompson Steegman

ACKNOWLEDGMENT

To my friends, Agnes Barrett and Mary H. Greene of East Carolina University, my deepest appreciation for all their help.

THE DEVIL'S HALF

PROLOGUE

November 1870

This morning Mr. Raleigh Prescott died—the husband of my friend "Miss Amy." So Raleigh Prescott's death puts an end to a story I have written. How strange it seems that I, decreed by life an outsider, so briefly in the Prescott family, should finally hold in my own handwriting what they don't know of one another and of themselves. And how little they were to know of me—removed by name, age and physical disability from them all—a shy schoolmaster, untried, uncertain, thrust into their alien world.

When the news came of Mr. Prescott's death I was waiting to close Judge Benjamin Whitaker's law office. It is one in a row on Beauchamp Street in Warren—a short block running the length of Courthouse Square and separated from it by a muddy road of hitching posts, a creaking string of wagons and the daylong hoarse sucking of the town pump under the hand of somebody you don't look at any more. The law offices are identical two-room affairs, with their blown glass shimmery windows (through which I had been able to watch people without their knowing it as they passed) and their porches out front almost level with the ground. The offices face an old brick courthouse, the color of which is always changing: from a tomato stain in wet weather to a pink shadowing through the elms in summer with quick splashes of sun. The white spilling and flashing of pigeons from the bell tower seem to make of the high old windows a row of depthless mirrors answering only to the sky.

Judge Whitaker's office is a dim smoke-blackened room with shelves of calf-bound books up to the damp ceiling.

But it has been a refuge for me ever since I left the Prescott plantation two years ago and began "reading law" while helping Judge Whitaker as clerk.

But my help has amounted to more than I'd ever dreamed when I stepped across the threshold of that office. It couldn't have occurred to me then how quickly the honored lettering of Judge Whitaker's name on the window would fade in my mind and that I would picture instead *Judge Geoffrey Jones*. How many times I've spelled it out with an extra flourish to the letters just to see how it looked. Once or twice when nobody was around I almost put that instead of his name on a legal document.

But lately Judge Whitaker has been in the office so seldom that hard-headed businessmen like Mr. Amos Cartwright and Mr. Lemuel T. Jones have begun to stick their heads in the door and call out "Good-morning, Judge," always bringing a little glow of surprise to my cheeks. But I often wonder if they aren't thinking at the same time about my origin and saying to themselves, "You can never tell." I know that origin is what most of them have left now to think about—a yardstick for family stands like a flagpole in the middle of town. I've had to pass it every day.

Judge Whitaker was too old to lose his sons in the war. With his white hair over his blue eyes and long sheeplike face, once so benign, so serene, he now listens to the vexations people have with a frowning weariness as if words added to the weight his shoulders already bore.

I know he took me in because he realized so late that I'd walked from birth with a crippled foot. His so late sorrow exposed me to him.

I hadn't gone to the war. But the war hadn't dishonored me. It had, in fact, evoked a sympathy I'd never had, making some realize that my separation had been real for *all* of my thirty-odd years, that it wasn't just beginning with the war.

For Judge Whitaker, after the death of his sons, sight of

me reminded him that my burden was one that people
could see. Helping me at his age was a late penance I didn't
feel he should have had to make.

It frightens me that I have been able so quickly even in
imagination to replace such a name as his with an unproved
one like mine. It seems that after youth the flow of time is
the only steady murmur we hear.

This reflection is what the news did for me this afternoon.

The coal fire in the smoky grate had almost gone out. I
usually shake the embers down and cover them with ashes
to keep from having to start the fire fresh in the morning. I
can't count on Willie Buck to get there before me. If he's
been drinking the night before, he doesn't show up until
noon, saying rheumatism had put the devil himself in his
bed.

When I looked up from the fire Mr. Colin Ashby, whom
I hadn't seen for weeks, was standing in the door. He looked
about so vaguely that I felt that, this time, only habit had
brought him here. But then he sat down heavily. There was
a surprising unkemptness about him. How long had it been
since I'd seen him last? His black brows over restless eyes
seemed shaggier, the lines of his commanding face sharper,
as if he'd lost weight. Now he seemed dazed as though by
some particularly personal affront. The large mole on his
cheekbone appeared to have been just put there.

To see Mr. Ashby cornered was like seeing the courthouse
flag taken down.

"Geoffrey"—only he and Judge Whitaker and Miss Amy
called me that—he said finally, almost reluctantly as though
revealing some unknown privacy in himself I had until then
been denied. "Raleigh Prescott died this morning." Mr.
Ashby's hat was going round and round in his hand.

"Mr. Prescott! Did he—? Himself?"

The words sprang out. The blood rose to my face. I
couldn't help it. I felt a stranger had spoken for me. In a
flash of panic I wanted to drop from Mr. Ashby's sight.

But with a racing heart in my ears, I saw he wasn't even aware of my shame. My guilty start had frightened none but me.

He'd spoken words I'd known I'd hear. Now that I had heard them, all I was sure of was a pulsing heart, a fresh sense of guilt.

How often during my stay on the plantation had these words been secretly hoped for! Somehow it was as though I myself had created, designed by a shameless prodding of fate, this far-off day.

Now that the day had come the measure of my shame itself was Mr. Ashby's own honorable concern.

"I'm not equal to it, Geoffrey, not to going there." He was talking into the fire. "Amy's father was a gentle man. And all the while I knew that I knew more than he'd ever dreamed."

I heard him distantly.

"You held them together."

Is that what he really believed?

I felt a wave of disbelief. Mr. Ashby knew no more than that about me. What a raw force for survival people concealed in their breasts!

"Maybe I could have done more than I did for Raleigh—but I don't know. But it's no good now, even thinking."

He was rubbing his chin with firm fingers.

"I don't believe I've ever seen people so unprepared for the world. But their people didn't prepare them. Where does this thing *stop?*"

He spoke this, not expecting an answer. Not from me. I was an audience again, not belonging. He spoke with annoyance, in a burst of impatience for people so helplessly fixed upon defeated ways.

"But you held them together, Geoffrey. You—"

He stopped, looked directly at me.

Now I knew. Behind the search of that tired face he was wondering about the hollowness in me: my unambitious, uncomprehending parents, my solitary childhood, my years in a world of my own fancy—what had it done? He'd never seen me as a whole person before. Had I disappointed him? Had so many let him down?

"Geoffrey," he spoke as if a warning insight had prompted him. "You've made obligations. Amy's need made you somebody. I'm speaking frankly. Now they can't help you."

Abruptly he wanted to abandon the subject. "Self-interest will wear the world out."

Mr. Ashby got up from his chair.

"Amy asked for you, Geoffrey. I wasn't looking for Judge Whitaker. Amy asked for you. You go on out to the plantation. *Tonight*. One of Harvey Russell's men will drive you. Tell him I want you out there."

He had his hand on the doorknob, put on his hat, then turned. His face was pained.

"Could Raleigh have done it himself?"

I could feel the warmth of my cheeks. I swallowed. My tongue was dry. I shook my head. I didn't know.

Mr. Ashby looked at me a long time, then he was saying, "Raleigh and Amy weren't meant for each other, Geoffrey. It was her father, his mother. *They* did it. Sealed the next generation with their *need*. Will Pendleton and old Mrs. Prescott! Bequeathed to the world *their* need. Will's innocence, old Mrs. Prescott's pain! What an awful price Amy and Raleigh paid."

In a moment Mr. Ashby's tired figure was framed in the shimmery window, a silhouette about to dissolve in the darkening afternoon. At times I've discovered people like this in surprising perspective, realizing I'd never seen them before. But it has always seemed too late. No amount of calling has ever brought them back. How solitary their lives had been!

Mr. Ashby, I knew, had never recovered from the early loss of his wife, a lady of beauty whom his youth had served. Instead, he'd been surrounded for years by a household of doting dependent kin—an ageless invalid aunt, two unworldly, unmarried sisters who worshiped his steps. He'd spent a lifetime telling others what to do, not because he'd wanted to, but because of some sheltering largeness in him which had always drawn people and which, I then saw, had been his blessing and his curse.

It was he who had sent me as schoolmaster to the Prescott plantation. He'd had a right to lecture me about my obligation, for he'd first found me, unsupported and unencouraged, with only a secret vision sustaining me, and thrust me into a closed circle that hadn't been aware of my existence on earth. I'd always been so proud of my first name, as of some distinguished ancestor. But it meant nothing at all to my parents. My mama said she'd seen *Geoffrey* somewhere in print. And my papa would say, "Boy, your name is 'Jones,' just like mine. 'Spite your handicap, you going to have to work for a living same as everybody else."

But Mr. Ashby found out there were valuable things I could do. He started me off in the world. I remember asking how far the Prescott plantation was from Warren and he'd answered, "Seven miles." For me it could have been a thousand.

The elms around the courthouse were leafless, showing great stretches of emptiness between bare limbs. The old building rose up separately from uncrowding trees. A flurry of pigeons drew my eyes again to the high windows which with palely fading color had already received the afternoon sun. Then, as Mr. Ashby walked away, I realized all at once how much of my own life had already been lived.

So much had happened since my first uncertain journey to the plantation in the fall of '68. It is hard for me to realize how far I have come.

According to Mr. Ashby's word, it was for me that Miss Amy had sent.

BOOK ONE

November 1868

CHAPTER ONE

It was November the third when I left Warren to begin my stay at the Prescott plantation. I'd been sent word the day before that one of the Negroes, who had to come to town, would pick me up at the old Warren depot around noon. I remember that this startled me. I wasn't sure whether a wagon was all the Prescotts had left to transport me or whether it was an indication of the importance with which they regarded me. In my imagination I'd never seen anybody making an entry to the plantation on a wagon.

But on that gray November morning with my suitcase at my feet and a copy of Caesar's *Gallic Wars* in my lap, I sat, a little disheartened, in the cheerless waiting room for an hour.

It was cold. The whole sky was gray. It made daytime seem such a short affair between long delayed sunrise and quickly approaching afternoon.

The floors in the room had the dusty astringent smell of blackened oil. A round stove, with spatters of crusted tobacco stain, stood in a sand box between two long benches worn satin smooth, which a generation of waiting passengers had initialed and carved. Joints of stove pipe floated from looped wires under the smoked ceiling. Mr. Prudy's frosted ticket window behind black grating was down. He had gone home.

I remember how surprised he was, seeing me sitting there in the empty room with my suitcase, asking where in the world I wanted a ticket to, as if I were the last person he expected to see. When I told him (you have to be looking at Mr. Prudy's pale eyes and narrowed face to realize that he has been living his life, day by day, all the time that you have, that his own days have had a separate flow from your own), he stopped at the door and revealed an identity I'd never given him. For me he could have stepped out of a forgotten past. His face brightened. "Remember her from years ago," he said, "riding with her father. A beautiful girl, dark hair and eyes. 'Mr. Will,' everybody called her father. A tall man, very thin, with long white hair about his ears. Always dressed in black, a little black string tie. Looked like a senator." Mr. Prudy shook his head with conviction. "They were *days*. Don't see folks like that any more. No sir. Don't make 'em. Everybody took off their hats, seeing Mr. Will and his daughter. Lord! Lord! Times have changed." Then, as if he'd just realized where I was going, he looked at me curiously, "Good Lord, seems like she just dropped out of the world! Whatever happened to her?"

In a minute, with a faraway look on his face, Mr. Prudy was gone, carrying a memory, like a forgotten treasure, I didn't know he had.

Mr. Prudy left not a living soul in the gloomy old room but me. The dust-filmed windows that looked out on three sides let in a dark shadowless air. They made of the landscape outside a permanent afternoon.

Long low warehouses stretched indefinitely along the rails, their doors closed upon cavernous dark and chill.

Leading from the station, a wide, muddy street where wagon and buggy tracks crisscrossed like separate currents in a stream made the store fronts on each side seem hardly within hailing distance apart. A few Negroes you had to look for to see as people leaned in a kind of fitful wakefulness against closed doors. Swinging signs above them timed the gusts of moving air. These Negroes, forever waiting, seemed to be left over from the day before. In its stillness the town from the window was like an old photograph which a moving wagon would not have disturbed.

In the waiting room the fire against one red side of the

stove kept up its uninterrupted, almost soundless burning.
It was hard to believe that it was so few years ago that
throngs of nameless weary men had crowded these floors,
when the countryside began sending on river barges from
remote plantations, on wagons from small farms, its cotton,
peanuts, corn, wheat and hogs. Chains of wooden boxcars,
old and splintered and patched over, had waited for weeks
for loading. From the ballooning funnel stacks of wood-
burning engines, drifting smoke had kept the station under
permanent acrid cloud. As far as you could see along the
railsides had stretched the molding, darkening rows of
barrels, crates, bales of cotton, for which there were no
shelters.

All day long, Negro laborers, with whips popping and
faces smeared with red clay, had strained and slipped alongside mule teams hauling baled cotton from home-made river
barges below.

And everywhere there'd been the day- and night-long
pressure of nameless train-weary men, all ages and ageless,
under the accident of fate which had brought them to this
point of departure for their separate ways.

They'd looked out from endless windows of trains. They'd
stood in long lines at the sidings. Holding out reddened
hands and wet feet, they'd crowded about the sizzling stove.
They'd thickened the air itself with the smell of their exhaustion, their dirtied slept-in clothes.

In the deserted waiting room, the long scarred benches
were cold, the yellowed flaking proclamations, handbills,
nailed one upon another in smoke and dust stained dissolution—horses, mules, cotton, men—before which groups of silent faces had stood, were now unnoticed, unread.

CHAPTER TWO

But in a moment he was there. I saw a strange, heavily
wrapped Negro cupping his hand over his eyes, peering
through the filmy glass. He and the two mules and wagon
behind him had come up so soundlessly that they seemed to
have been made of the misty air itself.

When I stood up from the bench, the Negro, seeing a
single figure in the dismal room, jerked his head.

Then opening the door barely enough to insert his face,
he asked uncertainly, "Is *you* the one? Miss Amy said somebody be waiting here—schoolteacher."

When I told him I was the one, he still looked at me uncertainly, not knowing perhaps what a schoolteacher was
supposed to look like. Then hesitantly, as though acting
against his better judgment, he stepped across the threshold of the white waiting room.

"She told me lift your bag, whatever it was you had to
tote."

He seemed to be looking for more than I had. Then, picking up my suitcase, he said, "My name is Pettigrew. Born
and raised on the place. Live in the backyard whar I always
been. Miss Amy say tell you welcome and hope you well."
All this he spoke mechanically, without interest or emphasis.

To none of it could I reply, but I was already following
the strange Negro out of the room and leaving the fire to
the benches, long emptied and indecipherably scarred.

Two heavy gray mules stomped and jerked, blowing
smoky breath in the cold. On the seat beside the driver a
horse-hair buggy blanket had been placed.

For barely a second Pettigrew hesitated about helping me

into the wagon. Then, dismissing his hesitation, he said, "Heap of things worse than that," and pushed me into the seat.

"If you ain't never rid in no wagon"—he looked carefully into my face now—"I don't reckon you had no call to—set on part, kiver up with the rest. Out in the open, wind come racing toward you just like it done picked you out, special. Your coat flimsy."

I watched Pettigrew deliberately buttoning his own coat to his chin, pulling his perfectly round hat down to the level of his eyes. His skin was coal black. Big ungloved hands were as wide, as work-hardened, as shovels. There was an unhurried competence about him.

I had sensed already that he was accustomed to authority. Had long association with the Prescotts given him a certainty of eye for people he was expected to help? Unapologetic eyes looked again at me—stiff and uncertain on the wagon seat.

I knew quickly that he missed nothing: my person, my coat, my one suitcase. But I had the feeling, too, that he accepted me, that he would not be unkind. If the Prescotts had their reasons for wanting me, I was to be a small, negligible part of his day.

"Tuck that blanket under your knees," he said, and mounted slowly and heavily to the seat by my side. The seat creaked and sank under him. The gray mules, weighted, stepped back, then stood as motionless as timeless as weathered stone.

For the next few minutes, as the wagon wheels ground out of the stationyard to the river bridge, Pettigrew didn't bother to speak. I was less than he'd come to fetch.

Just my nearness to the Negro, like the unexpected pull of an untracked current, was enough to alert me. I suppose it was an odd sense of inclusion I'd never felt before.

From a red clay bank, soggy and deep-furrowed with years of wheelruts, the high trestle bridge, like stilts on stilts, arched out into space. It looked fragile and shaky against the sky. The rise in the middle almost cut off the view of the other side. Glimpsed so suddenly, the darkly moving depth below was a shock. In summer, far down, boughs of willows from the banks dipped over and penciled the water itself. Now the lusterless slide between bare banks lay exposed, diminished and unresponding under an indifferent sky. Dozens of little boats, tied up until spring, pointing downstream, tugged as jerkily at invisible ropes as fish on a line.

"Trouble is," Pettigrew said, more to himself than to me, "don't make no nail that can hold down these dried-up planks. Skeer a mule to death with the clattering." A faint nostalgia came over him as softly as a stray pigeon to a barn. "Miss Amy say when she got married twenty, thirty years ago, didn't come over her she *was* married till this shaky bridge woke her up, nothing ahead but flat, lonesome country. Pines, pines, pines—she a town girl. Looked round at Mr. Raleigh in the surrey beside her like she warn't sure who he was. One of the boards cracked, wheel sunk a little and stuck. Cried out to Mr. Raleigh she won't *never* go'n get back home. Almost didn't, way things turned out. She a pretty young woman, them days. Said: 'Poor Papa, poor Papa,' right on top of this bridge."

Under the feet of mules, the clattering was enough to startle man and beast. One loose end of a plank would spring up at the clop of a hoof. A current of cold air swept past us. It was as though, high above the river, we'd crossed the wind's secret track.

"Easy," Pettigrew spoke to the mules. He stooped forward, narrowing my seat, held the reins just so. It was his solid balanced weight, his knees firmly placed apart, that kept us on the rattling descent.

From the highest point of the bridge, flat land beyond, in flight before our eyes, ran on and on. The land was featureless under unshadowing sky. Low, distant pines made the dissolving edge of the world.

When we clattered down to the other bank, twin threads of a road were waiting to lead us across trackless space.

The sucking *clop-clop* of the mules' feet in spongy earth made the only sound.

"Been thinking about Miss Amy all the way cross that bridge. Some ways, she ain't ever crossed it at all. Ain't had a chance."

Far in the distance I saw the ghostly beckoning of an old shell of a house. It made so little claim against the landscape in its oyster gray thinness that it seemed to be dissolving in drizzle. Windows were lifeless. It was hard to believe that they'd ever cast back the warmth of summer sun. Wet brick of a smokeless chimney reached up into a single leafless oak. In the yard around it, where chickens, hounds, and half-naked children had made a whirl of life, wind and rainy night had erased all tracks.

Like the traces of extinct people, here about us were the fragments of a lived-out time.

Pettigrew said, "This was *his*, one time. Mean the old lady's. Old Mrs. Prescott. *All* this, even the *folks*. But they gone. Baltimore, Washington, somewhere. Got on the Warren train. Tickets nare one of 'em could read. But holding tight to somebody's name written down. Lord God, take care of 'em."

Pettigrew kept his eyes straight ahead. The brim of his hat low over his face, turned up collar over his chin, he was wrapped in his own recollections. I saw in his black, inscrutable face that I wasn't there.

How little I knew!

What preparation I'd had for the Prescott family was what I remembered of Ella Fitzpatrick's concern for Miss Amy years ago and what Mr. Ashby had supplied me only a day or two before, not grudgingly, but wearily, wanting to provide me with something to go on, but not wanting

to prejudice me. I'd felt in talking to him that he'd de-
spaired of trying to explain, had even wondered in looking
at me, such a distant outsider, whether I could even understand.

"Oldest boy, Blunt," Mr. Ashby had said, "was killed in
the war," adding, not for my benefit, but as if fresh insight
had added to *his* understanding, "Amy worshiped him.
Blunt was all hers."

What I'd tried to ask was why that proud family—I'd
known the name all my life. It had been like a gift of history,
elusive but there, which had somehow lent a sense of old
and accomplished deed to our land—I'd tried to ask how
among *them* there could be any need for me.

And he'd answered that *she* wanted me, that she wanted
the three children—Flora, Louisa, and Otway—to have more
preparation in Latin for some academy away from home.
War and the years since had denied them what she'd had.
As Mr. Ashby told me this, I knew he was remembering with
the anguish of perspective what Miss Amy's beginnings had
been.

What was missing in all he chose to furnish me was any
reference to Raleigh Prescott himself. I sensed that Mr.
Ashby resented the fact that I'd have to know. In my presence Raleigh Prescott's name had always lurked just short
of what people had to say. But it wasn't approval or disap-
proval that they'd seemed to want to conceal, but their own
inability to know themselves.

Pettigrew let the reins go slack.

So many fields we passed had been abandoned, walked
away from, left knee-high in weeds and cockleburs. It was
impossible to tell when they'd been planted last or which
way the row crops had run. Drain ditches finding their way
out of overgrown fields, like snakes after light, were half-
filled with stagnant water and choked with brush.

Only now and then did we pass a little patch of reclaimed

field, of desolation returned to, where the year's crop of corn had been harvested.

But everywhere I saw stretches of cut-over pine, now showing blistered stumps, almost covered over with vine. Birds flew straight through.

Long threads of smoke every now and then reached out from some lonesome cabin and headed for the woods. In the emptiness they made something to ride toward and something to leave behind.

Pettigrew's face was wet from the drizzle. It was hardly more than a thickening of mistiness. I couldn't have said where it had begun. From the brim of his flat hat over his eyes shining moisture dripped to his outstretched arms.

What I wanted to ask him about Raleigh Prescott I felt would be met with an unhurried turn of his head, another appraisal of me, almost without interest, and his doubt about my right to know.

But, then, he did look round and in a voice wholly non-committal, said, "What you aim to do out here?"

I told him I was a teacher; I was to prepare the two daughters and the son in Latin for some school.

"Lord, have mercy," he said. "Miss Amy! Older she gets, the more she dwells on what her papa done! Do you know how old them two daughters and that son is?" he asked me.

When I began that I knew they weren't young, he cut me off. "Naw, they ain't young—old enough to be courting and know they own minds. One of 'em fixing to git married." Abruptly he turned to me, "You know them Carys in Warren?"

It was the last name in town that I expected to hear.

"That's who Miss Flora go'n marry. Worry Miss Amy to death. What you aim to teach?"

"Latin."

"Anything like voodoo? If you aim to rectify Miss Flora, you better give her a powerful dose."

I felt he'd admitted me to the privacy of his wonder accidentally.

"Mr. Prescott knows I'm coming? He wants me there?"

Pettigrew just kept looking ahead into the drizzle. "Mr. Raleigh got his mind full. One more thing ain't go'n change nothing, better or worse."

Then, after a minute or two, he turned to me in afterthought, "What you say that was? Latin? Well, we done tried everything else. Can't hurt. Strange thing, this world. Miss Amy *should* a-had the good Lord on *her* side."

But I knew he wasn't talking to me.

"Who knows how it would a-been if that boy Blunt had lived?"

CHAPTER THREE

In the distance, I saw a single figure on horseback. His appearance startled me. There hadn't been a living soul on the landscape between us and Warren.

A field of cotton, only half picked, and now abandoned to rain and short dark days, lay round us like a dirtied thinning patch of last year's snow.

The man on horseback was skirting the far side of the field. Every now and then he would stop, look into the distance for a minute, straight and unmoving, then ride on. From his height on the flat expanse—his figure itself was in relief against winter sky—he had a view of the whole landscape, including us: a low slow-moving wagon with our covered heads and the pointed mules' ears barely showing above the cotton stalks.

"Mr. Tanner Haynes," Pettigrew spoke out, a lift in his voice. "Weather don't bother him. Don't nothing. He take that tan horse, name Hawk, night or day, and ride all *over* this countryside. Every widow-lady, young gals too, trying to track him! Look at him setting! *Made* to a horse!"

The solitary figure had spotted us. He wheeled his horse at the corner of the field. "Heap of folks thank the Lord for sparing him, few as come back, seed corn. Weighs mightily on him, too. Better than any of us, he knows who didn't come home. Like it was part of hisself he left."

I asked where he lived.

"Lives on his place, through them woods yonder. Old Haynes place," he spoke crossly. I should have known. "Come back from the fighting to look after his pa. Old man ailing. Half the time got a mist over his mind."

Tanner Haynes reached the corner ahead of us. What impressed me about him was the weary authority in his bearing and face, but against this desolate background, an authority that had been earned in another place, at another time. Here there were no soldiers in the field. Was this desolation itself a graver challenge? (But I was to see at a later time that these autumn fields, for other reasons, were the only home for Tanner Haynes.)

Under a gray western hat with its brim stained and heavy in the drizzle, black brows were straight over black eyes. His handsome face was as lean and firm as if it had been chiseled. But there was a hardness about his eyes that jolted you. He saw through and beyond, and not even wanting to, measured you against remembered things. Not arrogance, but a weariness of too much seeing. The army, his father, whatever, had put to rout his youth.

Pettigrew was looking at him curiously. "Mr. Tanner, where you and Hawk been?"

Tanner inspected us in the wagon. Cold had reddened his cheekbones.

It came to Pettigrew as an afterthought: "This here Mr. Jones. Miss Amy took it in her head they need a teacher."

Tanner Haynes was looking thoughtfully at me huddled under the blanket, rain on my hat, on the tip of my nose—a melancholy sight. So had he looked at a thousand recruits.

Whatever he saw he kept to himself. "It isn't far now," he said finally, as to somebody overtired, discouraged.

Hawk jerked his head back and forth, splattering water. The horse's underside and legs were mud-caked. All at once it struck me: what had Tanner Haynes been seeking so long in weather like this?

"Pettigrew, did you see Mr. Prescott this morning?"

"Naw-suh!"

"When did you see him?"

Pettigrew hesitated. "Yistiddy. Come to the mule lot 'bout sundown. How-come?"

"He—hasn't come home."

Once more Haynes turned to me—that same unapologetic appraisal: "Maybe you *can* help." Not caring whether I heard, whether I understood.

Pettigrew scraped his chin with his fist. His black face was wet, suddenly offended.

"I better *git*."

Tanner said, "Pettigrew," then added, "you needn't tell Miss Amy I'm out here."

We left the man on horseback to watch after us, and to start after a moment upon some yet unexplored way.

The mules felt the reins tighten in Pettigrew's hands. They lurched to a hard pull. Gray heads, streaked and rain-darkened, stretched forward into the drizzle as into a dissolving veil. Pettigrew planted his feet firmly apart, pulled his soaked hat lower over his eyes.

The encounter with Tanner Haynes had completely put me off.

I asked Pettigrew, "Did Mr. Prescott know I was coming?"

He looked around at me slowly, as though answering a child. "You ain't what bothers him. Mr. Raleigh knew I won't go'n be here today. Thought up a way to get me to town."

I realized that was all I'd get.

But then he did add as an afterthought, "Do what you can to help Miss Amy, them girls. Wish I could lend you my recollection—on both sides."

In my hands under the buggy blanket I was clutching Caesar's *Gallic Wars*.

"Look at them mules nearing home!"

Spray was flying now from the harness, from the pointed ears. The wagon wheels sliced through softening ruts, threw splashes of muddy water into the weeds on the roadside.

CHAPTER FOUR

For about a quarter of a mile the road followed a split-rail fence around sloping pasture land. There wasn't a cow or mule in the distance. Water holes, choked in reeds and lily pads, lay as lifelessly as sinking rocks. The zigzagging rails, sapless and weathered, were as colorless as the earth itself; they were, in fact, sagging to the earth, old dried ribs.

Within sight of the plantation Pettigrew had become silent.

A cluster of rusty green cedars with flaking twisted trunks had showered an uncrossed carpet of needles on the road. The wagon almost came to a scraping stop for the sharp turn. The gate was open, its free end sunk in weeds.

Whatever private alarm Pettigrew was muttering at the entrance, I couldn't tell.

Cedar trees evenly spaced along both sides of the lane fell in place, two by two, like sentries standing up. Dry needles, crushed to pungency in the tracks, padded the mules' feet.

Between the trees I could see a pink row of brick cabins. Each had a high-pitched roof, a wide door, a single square window, shoulder-high. Chimneys, too, were alike in crumbling decay. Burnt-out brick lay in heaps around their bases. Most of the doors were gone, some hanging at sharp angles over unvisited steps. The cabins had sunk low in summer growth. Whatever shadowless stirring there was about the doorsteps was that of lizards looking out. A bony red cow was staked out at a distance, her tail silently going. She didn't turn her head.

Straight ahead at the top of the rise I saw the house. Something I'd heard and forgotten came to me: an early

Prescott had once lived in the West Indies. A ground level brick basement balanced latticed green doors and shutters. More than head high, the gallery running the length of the house and sides, provided roof for this brick-laid floor, for the benches and plants in heavy stone jars. In front, curving wrought-iron railings lifted a graceful flight of steps to the gallery with its spaced windows. Flights of steps, fragile buttresses, arched from the ends of the porch.

Old oak trees, thin naked limbs, crooked and black, made the thinnest beginning of a roof against the sky.

At the end of the lane, the road split like the two forks of an old tree dying out. Far to the back, I could see sprawling clusters of smaller buildings, barns, kitchens, sheds, a dozen odd sizes, with pointed A roofs, here and there a weathervane. An uncertain tatter of white smoke rose from some pot.

Beyond lay the fields as wide as the sky. Roads leading from every distance made the house the center of a web. Low on the outer rim, a streak of cold yellow had broken under a lifting cloud.

Then I saw the Negro woman running toward us, arm held high, urgent hand waving. A brown and white dog, its tail straight up like a flag, was bounding behind her, closing the distance.

"Whoh, mules! Whoh!"

The abrupt braking of the wagon by an old quince bush caused three or four red and white chickens, cackling and squawking, to shoot out from the dirt.

Pettigrew jumped. "Damn! Five years ago wouldn't a-been no chickens loose this part the yard. Next thing, cow be eating front-door lilacs."

He looked down at the brown hand gripping the wagon wheel, at the panting dog, signaling with its tail. The chickens, turning away, started scratching again.

Pettigrew spoke directly to me. "Ain't never seen so much

hurry for somebody to speak so little content. Sis Hannah Jane," he said as if the name itself would be self-explanatory.

Sis Hannah said, "Who he?"

"He—somebody. Don't burden your mind. I didn't happen to get no snuff. No penny red-striped candy. Ain't had time."

"Ain't no snuff, no penny red-striped candy, I after. You know where Mr. Raleigh at? You ain't seen him?"

"How I go'n see him, me in Warren all day?"

Sis Hannah's lean face was dark and stretched with worry. Her eyes, frightened, looked uncertainly about as if the bare yard had become unfamiliar.

"He come by my place this morning. Something he ain't never done. Come on my porch and *sot*. So tired, he *sot*. I asked him don't he feel good. He said, 'Naw,' say he tired all over. Eyes was wet. Hand shook."

Pettigrew said, "Wait a minute. Who-o-h, mule!" He threw his leg over the side of the wagon, lowered himself, one foot on the spoke of the wheel, cautiously, old-man like, to the ground.

Sis Hannah had said something he hadn't expected.

Two little Negroes, still barefooted, wide-eyed, had come up unnoticed, had just appeared. Right away they caught on to Sis Hannah's skirt. One started twisting a fistful of apron until he raised it a foot from the ground.

"Hold still, Jeremiah." Not even lowering her eyes to see which was which. "Pettigrew, *hear* what I say! Listen me through! I asked Mr. Raleigh did he want some water. Told me bring him some.

"Sot there so long holding that dipper—didn't take no notice it dripping between his feet—felt like I wanted to tech him see was he wake.

"Listen what I say. I been holding in all day. 'Sis Hannah,' he says, 'you *was* born on this place?' 'You ain't heard no diffunt?' I says. 'Don't change mammies on me, old as I is. I done got adjusted.' But I could tell he warn't listening.

"Something's *wrong*, Pettigrew. His *mind* wandering way back. Erecting folks that's dead and buried. That's a *bad* sign. Tell the Lord and the devil their bizness? Folks already divided between 'em? Sis Hannah ain't."

Then she said, "Who was a white woman name something like Katie Williams?"

Pettigrew winced.

"Whar you hear that name?" he shot back at her. "Don't you name her no more!"

"Hisself named her!"

"Mr. Raleigh ain't named no such thing to you!"

"Is."

"Is you tapping a jug broad open day?"

"Ast me did I remember her right out a clear sky?"

Pettigrew looked at her carefully.

"What he done then?"

"Say something 'bout he mama and Miss Amy. Say God help 'em."

"All right, all right, Sis Hannah! Where'd he go?"

"Say he gwine hunt. Face was red, eyes was wet."

"He hunting *all* time. It don't signify nothing for Mr. Raleigh to hunt."

But Pettigrew's hand trembled. He'd forgotten me. He started off toward the house, then turned abruptly, looked at me as if he'd never seen me before. "I get somebody to tote your suitcase. Turn you over to Miss Amy, the chullen."

"It was prophesying, that's what it was," Sis Hannah was calling out to Pettigrew's back. "Prophesying! My mammy got prophesied on, two weeks later fell down, broke her leg. Ain't never walked another step."

CHAPTER FIVE

With my suitcase at my feet I stood in the doorway looking into the sad, dark eyes of the woman waiting for me—eyes beseeching even a stranger. It was almost as if I'd stepped into a void between two parting figures: the faraway beautiful girl in the freshness of her youth at the side of her father and the graying woman before me now, alone, her eyes large and restless from the anguish of an hour which youth could not have foreseen and would not have believed. It was I, at the moment, who came from bright early days into this late, exhausted time.

As I looked at Miss Amy, pale and tense from watching, her hands folding and unfolding under white knuckles, I somehow felt that it was my vision of her youth that she feared she saw in my face. Her brown hair, gray above the temples, had been freshly dressed for a stranger. Eyes, pleading, looked at me across I knew not what space. There was about her a disconcerting fragility. She did not belong to my everyday Warren world. Could isolation here on the plantation have removed her so completely from her youth?

But in only a moment as she held my hand in her thin chilled fingers, I got from the soft urgency of her voice a sense of being needed, or having come at the right time.

"You *can* stay? You *will* stay?" she kept repeating, adding what my presence there would mean to Flora, Louisa, and Otway, and how I was to fill a need for them all. "I want so much for you to be satisfied here."

Whether she knew that she was clutching my hand, I couldn't say.

Oddly, from the moment I stepped across that threshold,

from the surprising, almost disproportionate attentions, I had the feeling of being engulfed, and was only later aware of the presence of the Negro woman looking at me. She had been in the room all the time.

Miss Amy murmured, "Clio." And Clio's inspection of me was silent and complete. She was standing several feet away, but I could tell she'd become Miss Amy's anxious attendant and bodyguard. I was the intruder.

Clio would have attracted attention anywhere. Standing near Miss Amy, she was the most outlandish-looking creature imaginable.

She was black and scrawny. Her straight hair was disheveled. With her toes pointed out, her feet apart, and approval foreign to her face, she was alert to what I had to conceal. A handed-down man's coat hung loosely about her thin waist. I knew the minute I saw her that to be in step with Clio was to be going her way. She would have to be taken on her own terms, like a cocklebur, as a fact of life.

Having taken me in, not to her satisfaction, she was muttering to Miss Amy, "Maybe he worth a try."

Then with thoughtful concern she looked at Miss Amy as she would have at a child. "You was counting mightily on what *he* was go'n do. Lawd God, Miss Amy, don't nobody want to tell you nothing! Otway, Miss Louisa, me neither!" She hesitated. "Miss Flora ain't got no room in her head for book-learning. That girl done packed a suitcase and gone visiting in Warren."

"She didn't *tell* me!" Miss Amy was looking at Clio in disbelief.

"No'm," Clio said. "Way things was, she didn't know how."

"That child *loved* her father!"

Miss Amy's lips trembled. "Oh, Clio, have I *neglected* her so?"

"Let me put this man's suitcase whar he belongs. *He* go'n have to eat and sleep, whether we does or not."

I remember I hadn't been aware of the warmth of the fire
in the room where they met me until I followed Clio into
the interior of the house. We walked into a clinging chill. An
ankle-deep draft on the floor was finding its own way to an
unseen open door.

Passing through the high-ceilinged main hall, I could
tell what a pleasant place in summer the cross breezes must
have made. But now even the two portraits of bewigged,
red-coated figures on the wall seemed out-of-countenance
and withdrawn.

Clio had stopped in front of me. In a back passage she
was pushing a door open with my suitcase.

"Kin *still* smell smoke!" she told herself. "Till this day I
ain't tole Miss Amy. Won't no use to burden her with
that!"

Clio looked about the room. "Smells shut-up, like what was
aired out has done crept back."

The one window in the room, dusty and rain-spotted,
looked across the backyard. A group of Negroes had
gathered at the barn-lot gate. It was a framed pantomime.
An arm shot out in one direction, all heads turned. Another motioned violently down an empty road. Pettigrew
was the tallest in the crowd. They all were beseeching him.
The little scene was as soundless as an old engraving.

In the silent room around me there were two chairs, a
single bed, an ample table under a hanging bookshelf. The
novels of Walter Scott, a volume of Shakespeare, a copy
of Cicero's *Orations* seemed to be stuck permanently together.

"Read them books if you want to. Ain't nobody wore
'em out. Ain't nobody *teched* 'em since Mr. Jasper Hornsby
taught school here. He didn't read 'em, neither. Just *held*
'em. I seen him setting in here, face flushed, nodding, hiding
a jug of grape wine somewhere, calling hisself thinking. I
was skeered he was going to set the whole house a-fire. Almost did! Hisself included! Caught myself smelling smoke

behind every closed door. Buried out yonder, just like folks, in the Prescott graveyard."

Clio looked thoughtfully about the bare room. "Done something to Miss Amy! Him dying! She come in here after we buried him. Tears was in her eyes, seeing the empty room. All she say was, 'What else could I a-done for him?'

"I say to her, 'No more'n you done. How-come lately you got to tote the world?'

"Say, 'We don't ever know, ever know, till too late.'"

Then Clio turned round and looked at me warningly. "He didn't *fool* nobody, Mr. Hornsby. Chullen, nobody else. Lest it was Miss Amy. Anybody fool her. Ain't never seen nobody *needing* so bad to find something good in somebody."

Clio was going to make certain I was impressed. She looked at me directly. "What he done here wouldn't pay for the hot biscuits he et, much less the ham and chicken."

I felt she expected to see the neck of a bottle sticking out of my pocket. But I could think of nothing to give her assurance.

Then she relented a little. "Don't know nothing 'bout your books. Seems like shetting the barn door when the mules is out. But they's something you *kin* do. Miss Amy, she lonesome. Sometime, seem like she trying to get *used* to just herself and worried about starting so late. Brought up hoping everybody good. She lonesome.

"Way *you* is, she go'n try to holp you. You holp her, hard as she trying."

When I told her that was my intention, she looked at me carefully. "You'se right between 'em all: ain't young, ain't old. Way things going, they needs you.

"You know them Carys in town? Fer Gawd's sake, don't make 'em out no wuss to Miss Amy than they is."

CHAPTER SIX

When Clio left, my hand was on the back of Mr. Hornsby's desk chair. In a single spot, the carpet was threaded thin. A table lamp, shaded green, was empty of fuel. Once-white walls, now a smoky gray, smelled faintly of long-staled tobacco. Above the table the gray plaster held like a small window the dust-thickened edges of a square where a picture had been. The only sound in the room was the occasional tired brushing of an imprisoned wasp against the green window shade, which sparkled with web-like threadings of light etched by the sun.

Evidently Mr. Hornsby's narrow bed had been unslept in since the door had been closed behind him. Where he'd come from, when he'd come, I didn't know. But standing in his place, waiting for some recognition from the abandoned household, made his presence as real to me as were the people I'd faced.

It was here that I felt that I'd stepped into the track of time's secret passing. Mr. Hornsby had come here a stranger, had stayed to be buried in their land. I could see as vividly as if they had never been moved from the closet floor the green wine bottles he'd emptied at night. The room itself seemed crowded with solitary hours.

Everything had been cleared from his table. It was surprising to find the drawer still filled with pencil stubs, a crusted ink bottle, flakes of tobacco, a scattering of dust-stained letters and a litter of greasy copy-book papers. I lifted two or three of the sheets from the top. A faint childish hand, in pencil, had spelled out under the name OTWAY the conjugation of the verb: *amo. Amo, amas, amat, amamus, amatis, amant.* Then followed: *Puella* (Louisa) *agricolam* (Tanner) *amat. Puella* (Flora) *amat puerum* (Alex) *amat.* Beneath the line appeared in a firmer hand, apparently a reflection of the schoolmaster himself: *De gustibus non est disputandum.* He'd probably added this a little absently, staring out of the window—at what remembered moment of his own youth?

Then I saw, crushed to the back of the drawer, almost out of sight, a yellowed letter. I flattened it with my hand.

Dear Sister:

You make inquiries in your last about the state of my health. Don't feel the concern which you express. The family has been most considerate in looking to my wants, and I must say that I find the duties unusually light. I regard myself as a companion as much as an instructor. In fact, what I am supposed to be preparing the three young Prescotts for has never been specified. Miss Amy vaguely suggests that the schooling her father got is what she wants for her children, but now she shows anxiety about what *that* was, as if it had escaped her.

I find that Mrs. Prescott—every inch a lady—is still a trifle startled when it comes to facing what we take for granted: thievery in the pantry, weaknesses of the flesh among the Negroes. Disappointment *hurts* her so, I find myself dreading to let her down. It is a strain not to do so. I've never had opportunity to associate with anybody quite like her. My education, too, is being broadened. Evidently there was great distinction in her family. It shows in her voice, in every line of her face. The image of her father seems, just lately, to be haunting her more and more. Somehow I feel she regards my presence as a means of restoring in her children some semblance of what she thinks she's lost. I wish, alas, that I had the boundless faith in Latin that she has. She remembers that her father was a Latin and Greek scholar. For some reason, Latin is supposed to work miracles. But, unfortunately, my own progress in the world doesn't bear this out.

My students are Flora, Louisa and Otway. Miss Flora —the eldest—is, at best, an indifferent scholar. She tells me that she can in no way see how it equips anybody for marriage. I myself share her opinion. But Miss Louisa and young Otway are dutiful and solicitous about their mother. I think they accept the fact, as Miss Amy does, that the best preparation for life is *breeding*: which apparently means the acquisition of useless knowledge.

Concerning Mr. Prescott, I must say that I *like* him. He stays home very little, and I ask no questions. Long ago, evidently, he left the care of house and children up to Miss Amy. But I am disturbed that daylong separations are the compromise they've worked out. I attribute it all to his anxieties about holding a plantation like this together. Too many people, black and white, *needing* what this place cannot provide. The poor man tries to shield as much as he can from his family. I feel that I'm something he *owes* his wife and children. I don't know *why—*

Here the letter broke off, unfinished, forgotten. If "Dear Sister" never got the information intended for her, I must say that Mr. Hornsby served me well. I could not help the philosophical reflection that his letter was finally delivered. I hadn't the heart to return the crumpled paper to the far corner of the neglected drawer, but folded it instead and carried it for several days in the inside pocket of my coat.

CHAPTER SEVEN

A few minutes later I sat across from Miss Amy in front
of the smoked gray marble of the fireplace. How many years
of long-forgotten fires had whitened to ashes and crumbled
there before Miss Amy came? The room smelled like a faraway dry-leaf fire on a cold afternoon—a smell that claimed
the room for an earlier time. Miss Amy, too, sitting forward
in her chair, her hands in her lap, was a stranger here. At
her feet were the time-softened yellows and reds of the
worn carpet, around her the cracked leather of furniture
brought in on wagons by an earlier generation of Prescotts
while she was still a girl in Warren. At her back on a flat
plantation desk, stood an assembly of browning photo-
graphs—not even an intrusion now—goatees, side whiskers,
high white collars, sharing anonymity, no longer earning
the delay of a pause, a glance, the pain of a memory. Now
the fire sent out a slow pulsing of yellow light at the feet of
another who at the moment seemed ready to leave.

Through the window the sky, lifting from surrounding
fields and woods, drew the horizon back and back, leaving
an uncertain mistiness in its place.

A ghost of a moon was beginning to shine like an uncovered silver coin.

Miss Amy glanced at the door Clio had closed upon
us. Her beautiful eyes caught me with an intensity for
which I was not prepared.

"Geoffrey—that is what Mr. Ashby said I must call you—
there is something I must ask. What has he *told* you?"

Her eyes held me.

When I tried to indicate that I knew nothing, she insisted, "He must have talked to you. He had to give you some idea of what you were coming to."

Then with her hands suddenly still and white on the arms of her chair, she said, "I know that you think it strange that you haven't seen Mr. Prescott."

All at once her voice was tense with insistence. "But he hasn't been *well*. He's been anything but *well*. He hasn't been himself. He *hasn't*—not since the war."

Then she looked directly at me for confirmation: "You've seen terrible changes in Warren since the war?"

A nod of my head was all she needed.

"Changes, changes! Everywhere," she repeated.

"I wonder how Mr. Prescott has been able to hold up as well as he has. I keep telling myself—over and over—women know *nothing* of what men have gone through."

She folded her hands and unfolded them.

"But *this*—this afternoon has never happened before."

Turning to the fire, she seemed to forget I was there.

Again and again she murmured to herself: "I do not understand. I do not understand."

This meeting was so unlike what I'd expected that I had difficulty in believing that I was physically present.

As I watched the frail agitated woman gripped within this so-recent urgency, I remembered a conversation between Mr. Ashby and Judge Whitaker I'd heard years ago in Warren—long before I'd ever dreamed that Judge Whitaker would ever take me into his office or that Mr. Ashby would send me to this plantation. I could see the two men sitting on a green bench in Courthouse Square one mild afternoon, their hats on the bench beside them. I sat at their feet on the grass waiting for Mr. Ashby to send me on an errand. He frequently did this, I think, to see that I had a coin or two in my pocket.

They were talking about raising money for repairing St. Bartholomew's Church there in Warren, a little brick church with its square Norman tower and its dark oak ceiling beams arched against white plaster.

Judge Whitaker was saying that when it came to giving to churches you never knew which way people would surprise you. "But one family, Colin, ought to give half they've got."

Mr. Ashby turned to look at his old friend curiously.

"The Prescotts. They got Amy. Mrs. Prescott got her. Remember that wedding? Never saw anything like it."

Mr. Ashby just sat in reverie, shaking his head.

"Mr. Will Pendleton sitting up there all by himself. Always in black coat, a black string tie. Fine white head. Old man had lost everything he had. But, you know, he filled a pew. One of the best men the Lord ever made. Wherever he was, there was space around him. More than anybody I knew, it was on his sensitive nerves that the story of the South played. How often with pain, we'll never know. What's happened to people now, Colin?"

Mr. Ashby was looking into his own distance and didn't reply.

I sensed even then that these were two lonely men.

"All the Prescott kin on the other side, two or three rows, Mrs. Prescott holding them together. I could tell she'd scored by just looking at her straight back. Five thousand acres of land for trading. For Mr. Will's—innocence? Unworldliness?

"What she wanted more'n all the world, old Mrs. Prescott. With Kirby for a husband and that oldest boy of hers. Raleigh *was* her last hope. But it even surprised Mrs. Prescott, what money could do."

"Ben," Mr. Ashby broke in, "Mr. Will Pendleton wasn't making a trade. Never made one in his life. Raleigh *was* a good match. Where *better* could old man Will leave his daughter? Adored Amy, knew she'd be taken care of the rest of her life. Things he'd never given her himself. And they *were* Prescotts. Mr. Will believed in horses, believed blood would tell. Maybe Amy *loved* Raleigh, I don't know. But I do know it was what she thought her destitute father wanted her to do. It had *his* blessing. You can count on that! Young folks don't know the *price* of anything. Don't ask."

Judge Whitaker said, "Maybe so, maybe so. Anyway, old Dr. Jonathan Hall mumbled a blessing over them and sent them on their way."

Mr. Ashby stood up. "Blessed *anything!* What he's going to have to account for in heaven, I'm glad is not on my head."

How little I realized that I myself would ever be sitting in this room. Any privacy of Judge Whitaker's and Mr. Ashby's I hadn't dreamed would ever be mine.

I looked at Miss Amy in disbelief. The thread of her remote life had been so close all the time.

I sat forward impulsively and asked what I could do.

My question seemed to steady her a little. She looked at me a long time. Once again I recognized the inclusion of my whole person in somebody's awareness.

"Mr. Ashby said some very commendable things about you," she returned. "He thinks very highly of your insight, your understanding." After a moment she added, "They *are* rare in this world." Still looking at me closely, "What you can do for me is, as a man of a changed world, to help my children in ways in which I must have been so— neglectful."

In amazement I returned the word, "Neglectful?"

"Does that sound strange?"

Then she went on, "How often have I heard my father say that one is geared only to one time. I didn't even know what he was talking about."

A piece of burnt-out wood fell through the hearth, sent up a shower of sparks. Miss Amy jerked her hand from the arm of the chair. Finally she spoke into the fire. "I want Otway and Louisa to have a chance in a new world beyond this plantation, beyond Warren. Raleigh and I have *lived* our lives; I don't believe I could bear to see *them* repeat."

Then she added quietly, as though not wanting to attract attention to the question itself, "Have you ever heard of a family named Cary in Warren?" Not looking at me.

When I hesitated, she turned. "You must *tell* me things. *Nobody* tells me things."

I said something about good people.

"How?"

I'd never heard of any trouble.

"Trouble?"

I saw it wasn't what she meant.

"My *own* daughter Flora. What haven't I done for her?" She surprised me in a moment by looking directly at me again. "Have you had an unhappy life?"

I think the surprising thing was that she really wanted to know. But she saved me from trying to answer. "Nobody can answer that."

I understood by now that the anguish which had edged her words could only have come from some dread, deeper than I knew, of what the next hours were to bring. I knew that she did not know where her husband was.

At this point Clio burst into the room. Her eyes were wide.

"Miss Amy, Miss Louisa and Otway is coming back!" She threw the words at Miss Amy as if she herself had been personally affronted. "I seen 'em down the road in the buggy. This-yonder way!"

This tireless messenger's coat was buttoned to her chin. She'd brought the cold back with her from no telling how far down the road.

Miss Amy stood up.

"Clio, is he—is he—?"

"No'm, he ain't, he ain't."

Then the colored woman turned on her heels as sharply as she'd entered and slammed the door.

Miss Amy was looking at me pleadingly. "Did you see *anybody, anybody,* when you drove out?"

I told her that we'd met a man on horseback. Pettigrew had called him Mr. Tanner Haynes.

"With Louisa?" The words were out. Excitement flushed her face.

I shook my head.

She came over and gripped my arm. *"Please, please,* help me get my children away."

What I saw in her eyes was fear.

CHAPTER EIGHT

I don't believe I could have arrived at the Prescott plantation on any other day of the year which would have thrust me so swiftly into the privacy of the family.

Suddenly, filling the doorway, stood a tall boy, wrists stretching from sleeves, long legs from ankle-high trousers, damp blond hair over a long sensitive good face. He was breathing hard. All outdoors came with him into the room. "Mama, where did Papa say he was going? He told you something! You *saw* him last!"

Otway was about fifteen, neither man nor boy. Excitement had given to his figure a jerky tautness, to his skin an outdoor glow. He ran a long nervous hand through wet hair.

"Been down every cow path, through every briar patch. Mama, don't you remember what he said?"

It was his painfully reaching boyhood that seemed to be accusing her.

"Your father is hunting, *hunting*, Otway!"

A little frown of anguish came to the boy's face. "Oh, Mama, *this* time, please look at *facts*."

"Facts?" she murmured vaguely.

"About Papa!"

She looked at him, startled.

His youth, so abruptly strained, baffled, checked her. There was nothing to say.

"I mean, I mean—he *hasn't* come home."

"Your father said nothing, son. Nothing!"

I knew it was Louisa who had come into the room. Clio was following behind her. "You catch your death! Hold your skirt to the fire! You, too, Otway. You *wet*."

Louisa stopped.

Only then Miss Amy remembered. Without looking at me, she told them I'd just come.

Louisa, with Otway behind her, took my hand. I knew that the two were inseparable, that each spoke for the other. In their eyes I saw the unabashed pleading which desperate innocence is capable of. I felt I'd stepped at the instant into a place where, before my time, an elder had always stood.

"I don't know how much Mama has told you," Louisa said. "Papa went hunting this morning. He hasn't come back."

Then Otway, hoarsely, almost whispering, "Mama won't admit it, won't admit *anything!*" His long hands were red from cold.

Louisa's brown eyes reminded me of her mother's. Was it the girl in Warren I saw? The delicacy of her face was disturbing. She was her mother's daughter. How transient this moment of brown hair, soft skin and lovely dark eyes! The girl carried no memory of her mother's youth.

All at once I wanted to give them some kind of assurance. It was frightening to realize, sensing their undestroyed hopefulness, that there wasn't anything I could do for their youth, their bewilderment.

"We *have* to go back," Louisa said. "Please go."

Miss Amy was still standing by herself, seemingly so far from her children, her hair groomed for the formality of meeting me, for the formality of an older duty they knew not of.

Then in a voice that must have required great effort for her, she said, "I'm sure that your father will be back shortly. Any number of things could have detained him."

Otway and Louisa, startled, looked at their mother uncertainly. It was almost as if they feared that she *believed* what she said.

BOOK TWO

BOOK TWO

CHAPTER NINE

Since late afternoon gray clouds had parted, deserting a
high cold sky. The change was as complete as if we'd seen
a weary season depart. Low stars now shone like bursting
crystals. But light from the moon climbing higher over the
fields paled the stars on and on. The moon was beginning
to pick up scattered housetops around the plantation, to
give the substance of light and shadow to sheds, fence lines
and trees. Whatever moved now beckoned with a tag of
light to where it was.

Ahead I could see the buggy with Otway and Louisa
moving fast. Wheels were rolling rims of silver between the
fields.

In our creaking wagon, out of an older time, I was sitting
between Pettigrew and a tall silent Negro. The buggy, dividing the dark, left our trail.

The two Negroes on the wagon seat had lodged me, a
captive, between their somber intentness. It seemed that
this task was especially their own. I was no more a part of
their concern than if I had been another blanket added to
the pile Miss Amy had placed in the back of the wagon.
The sureness of their knowledge excluded me.

Theirs was an ageless at-homeness with the road, the pine
scent, the shadow-haunted night. How transient seemed
Miss Amy's and the children's time. My own presence here
was brief at their side.

The straight, silent Negro on the seat with me and Pettigrew—taller than either of us—had a half-hour ago knocked
at the door where I sat with Miss Amy near the burning
lamp, bringing behind him into the yellow light falling from

the doorway a string of peering, wide-eyed faces pulled out of the dark. But his followers stood at a little distance behind him, respecting his message with a circle of space. At first, the only sound was the excited bark of a dog the procession had waked up. It was drawing a muffled, "Hish, go'n, hound dog, adding fleas to trouble."

I could tell by his hesitation that the Negro looking up at Miss Amy had never seen her with such wonder before. What he'd brought with him had given her a pulsing heart, mysterious years of her own. Otway and Louisa stepped outside.

Clio was muttering to herself, "Cold as it is."

"Where is he, Clio? Where is he?" Miss Amy was reaching for Clio's arm as if Clio hid what she knew.

"You stand out of the cold."

"Wakefield," Otway burst out. "Tanner Haynes send you?"

The recognition drew him and Louisa down the steps.

Louisa repeated, "Did Mr. Tanner send you?"

Her question turned all the waiting faces from the messenger, exposed her for a second—her eyes tired from her search—as the center of the circle. Otway looked at her as if she'd taken a step backward from him, cutting an unkind space across which he couldn't reach.

Keen dark eyes shone from Wakefield's copper face. There was an Indian leanness about him. The crossing threads of the lives of the people watching him seemed to have complicated beyond expectation what he'd come to say. It was a frown of weary displeasure at the openness of their needs.

"Him and me found him," he said, his eyes leveled at no one of them—each to take from it what he must. "Wounded in the leg—hunting."

Then Wakefield was looking at us distantly, having no more to give.

Finally he said, "Accident."

But I felt even then that he hated to share Raleigh Prescott with those who couldn't understand.

"Where is my father?" Otway said, an edge of resentment in his voice.

Wakefield didn't even hurry to answer him. "Mr. Haynes' house."

"Why didn't you bring him to his own home? His house?"

"Riding *wounded* ain't easy over a bad road."

Miss Amy was at my side. "You must go with them. You *must* go. I haven't—haven't—prepared them. Not for this!" Her hand clutched my arm.

On the wagon seat between Pettigrew and Tanner's messenger, I knew I'd joined a different, a wearier, search. The bright buggy ahead had left us behind.

Pettigrew spoke first, out of earshot of any listeners.

"Where was he, Wakefield?"

Wakefield seemed to be aware of my presence for the first time. He looked at me casually.

"Go on, say! *He*"—leaning a big thumb toward me without even turning his head—"ain't nothing but a teacher."

Wakefield spoke straight out in front of him. "Edge of the pasture, back where Mr. Tanner had them peas."

Making more of a statement than a question, without raising his voice, Pettigrew said, "He go'n live?"

"He go'n live."

There was a long silence.

Then, still speaking straight out ahead, Wakefield said, "What he wanted was for *us* to find him. Not his folks."

One of the mules stumbled. His head jerked down and up. A spray of water, ice-cold, stung our knees.

Pettigrew abruptly shifted his weight, his feet gripped the floor board.

"You didn't have no call to say that. No call at all."

Without turning his head, Wakefield said evenly, "Mr. Raleigh knew what he was doing, where he was going and why."

The copper-colored Negro, lean and firm, contained and remote, even at my side could have been alone in the wagon. The moonlight lay separately upon his shoulders.

I barely turned to look at his profile—clean, resolute— at his dark eyes, distant and noncommittal. There was something disturbing about his solitariness.

In a subdued voice, indifferent to whether or not we believed, or accepted, a reasoning that was exclusively and urgently his own, he said, "Mr. Raleigh tried to kill himself. Let them find out how they can." He tossed his head back, a movement that included all the acres behind. "Believe what they want to, believe what they need to believe.

"Tried to make it look like a accident. Went to a heap of study to make it look like a accident. Thought that might help them some back home. Got himself all tangled up in grapevines and honeysuckle—a place a rabbit couldn't get through.

"Mr. Raleigh too good a hunter, wouldn't a-made no such mistake. Sure as sunrise, knew who would see, who wouldn't. Knew it won't go'n fool me, won't go'n fool Mr. Tanner—Mr. Tanner the last person in the world. He done seen too many people faking dying, faking living, too."

Pettigrew did not bother to look at Wakefield. Without raising his voice he said, "You ain't told them the truth."

"Half. Ain't no use to push pain no further in the world. Everybody done had enough.

"Been better had Mr. Raleigh stood out in the open, done it clean. When they see him, what little doubt they can hold onto ain't go'n give no comfort at all.

"Been Mr. Raleigh's cross all his life. Dividing himself. Trying to do right by everybody. Failing everybody. Failing everybody who had a claim. Never knowing were it better to give all in one place.

"When me and Mr. Tanner heard that shot, saw that little black boy come running, eyes bulging, both of us was down there before the woods had drowned the sound, before the leaves had stopped quivering a mile away. Were standing up at the house, hadn't gone in out of the cold, just like the shot was already on the way to us from somewhere we didn't know.

"I ain't never seen Mr. Tanner so, like he was cornered. Sitting up there on Hawk, muddy, tired, not wanting to give up. Ain't many things he ain't equal to. He thought he knew Mr. Raleigh. Mr. Raleigh had out-thought him. Had got down there close, closer'n he was supposed to be.

"That shot came, Hawk's front legs was five feet off the ground, head already turned, just like he knew. Half a second, all I could see was back feet throwing mud.

"Mr. Tanner was there, kneeling, long before I got there. And I had *moved*, torn my pants, not even knowing it. Passed everybody left on the place. They'd stepped out of nowhere, standing on the roadside, women and children, looking toward the woods.

"Hawk was standing there, edge of the tangle, reins dangling, looking in like he was trying to see was him and Mr. Tanner separated and when."

The wagon lurched. The moon overhead was racing into flying white clouds as if it had business far over the sky.

Then we entered the tunnel of pines. Darkness dropped around us. The rolling buggy up ahead was too far to see.

"Mr. Tanner had dropped on his knees in that mess of tangle, like Mr. Raleigh was sleep on his side, was go'n wake him up.

"But what come over me was a strange feeling; I just stood back, looked at a man on his side. Could a-been a tramp, drunk, fallen out, gun lying just beyond his reach. A stranger in the briars—without a name. Seems like didn't anything I saw there connect with anybody I knew. Calling him Mr. Raleigh—I knew his old hat, his hunting jacket, his boots (lived in them boots, always moving)—didn't mean nothing at all.

"That's how-come I couldn't tell Miss Amy more'n I did

in that waiting, lighted-up doorway. Knew we weren't talking about the same man. Her man and the papa of them children won't the man I knew. But I saw her like I hadn't ever done: she'd made out for a long time with half Mr. Raleigh's flesh and blood—out of the half his flesh and blood he tried to give her. And I knew she knew there was another half, that she'd spent a life in pain trying to hide it from herself and her children.

"And I knew there wasn't any use telling her about the man I knew—about us boys before Miss Amy ever came.

"When Mr. Tanner said, 'Step here, Wakefield, we go'n have to make a stretcher,' it was just like making me realize that Mr. Raleigh had come home, that the part I knew had let us find him. Seemed like he'd divided himself once and for all. This was the part he wanted claimed, wanted buried and remembered. Put a seal and a signature on something for once that he can't unwrite, that's go'n announce him long as he lives. Looking in the face of the Almighty, he chose. Living, he hadn't been able to.

"Not between people: Miss Amy and the other one, but *times* he chose, peaceful times, before the world saddled him, got him cornered with one claim, another claim, so that there won't no answer to anything. Won't nothing he could do that was right. Nothing that wouldn't hurt somebody.

"Me and him in those early days were charging headlong with young blood. But didn't neither one of us know where to. I been the only steady thing for him throughout these years. Tonight on this earth I'm thankful for that."

Neither Pettigrew nor I had spoken. Wakefield hadn't even turned.

After a long silence Pettigrew, not raising his voice, said, "Wakefield, how close is you kin?"

Wakefield didn't flinch. As calmly as if giving the weather, he said, "His papa, Mr. Kirby, is my papa. He my brother. My mama married Scott Wakefield on the Haynes place when I was born. That's where I was raised, where I always been."

"Mr. Raleigh's mama, old Mrs. Prescott, know that?"

"Old lady knew everything. She was harder, smarter, than Miss Amy, I don't know which. She knew how to fight.

"Fixed Mr. Raleigh's marriage to Miss Amy. Played every trick. Tried to get him settled and safe and took care of before it was too late, before young blood trapped him or got him trapped by somebody that wouldn't let him go. Of the two boys that scared her to death by just looking like their pa, Mr. Raleigh had the softest heart, was the one she could count on to worry for not doing right.

"I wish Mr. Raleigh had the sense me and Mr. Tanner got. Sense or hard, I don't know which. I looked at Mr. Tanner riding off to go get the doctor for Mr. Raleigh. The only one left amongst us still running things—only one keeps folks at arm's length like he remembers how many he's hurt."

"He know about you?"

"Been knowing about me ever since he could walk. Pettigrew, you know I pretty near brought him up, more'n his own daddy done."

Pettigrew said, as if he understood after all the years, "You ain't never took you no wife."

"Which way was I go'n turn?" Wakefield said. "Black or white?"

CHAPTER TEN

Nobody in the wagon spoke for a long time.

Pettigrew with his all-Negro face, black, undivided, turned slowly to look at Wakefield who was staring straight ahead, perhaps not even seeing the moonlight on the top of the buggy bearing Otway and Louisa, not even remembering that they were riding toward that part of their father which they held, that part of the stricken man which Miss Amy was waiting for as she sat, unspeaking, at this very moment, in front of the fire, still dressed for the duty of meeting me for the sake of her children.

For Wakefield, the long stretch of his own years, reaching back between two worlds to a sunny unseparated youth with Raleigh Prescott, seemed now on this cold night in a rattling wagon, with a stranger at his side, so freshly, so rawly, exposed.

When we left the opening and closing dark road in the woods and came out into moonlight, the broad flat earth opened up before us again. The distance between us and the buggy had lengthened so that I was startled by a sense of the separate urgency that drove them on.

Finally Pettigrew said, "How-come he done it *now*, Wakefield?" He was asking of the night itself—the cold night with a brilliant moon upon its silent, ancient course.

Unhurried, answering for himself, Wakefield said, "Folks get tired of this world." Still sitting a little forward, the moonlight still separate on his shoulders, he added, "Get tired of lonesomeness. Wear out their bodies and their hearts."

Finally Pettigrew spoke. (It surprised me to see that he

was wearing steel-rimmed glasses. When he'd put them on I didn't know.) "Things ain't no worser than they been being."

The glasses made him look older, restored his different claim to Raleigh Prescott's life. "I stay here close as you. Watched every day lead to the next. Ain't been no wussening on his face. Nothing 'cept wear and tear—same as everybody else since the war."

But Pettigrew's words were choked in self-doubt. His spectacles made him look like an old and dignified and dressed-up monkey, resentful of the world. For the first time I felt that the news had shaken him, exposed him to an unaccounted-for night, to unseen things about others, perhaps about himself.

He leaned forward a little, gripped the reins, steadying himself. "Watch where you going, mules, before you fall down and break your leg. Road like this, you got to look out for every waiting hole."

This time Wakefield turned to look at him.

Pettigrew said, "You ain't made no answer to what I said." His hands trembled a little.

"What one answer you want me to make? There ain't no *one* thing for something like this. Roof on that barn over here collapse, broke through the other day. I go'n say it give up on the fourth day November, at three o'clock, long as I been seeing it threaten under every wind storm?"

"But at three o'clock," Pettigrew persisted, "not no hour before, no hour after, she broke, fell through and scared every mouse in the barn, let in light enough to make every trembling cobweb shine. *Sumpin* done it at three o'clock. How I know? Three o'clock, be either one more leaf fell, or one more stiff mule kick in the crib. They's sumpin you ain't *said*."

"When you last go over to Squire's Landing?"

"Ain't nothing over to Squire's Landing I wants. Ain't

never been. Tree-stump liquor, a dozen runty hogs, and sorrier folks."

"Worse than that," Wakefield said. "Sooner or later every bad penny in the world shows up."

Pettigrew shot a quick searching look at Wakefield. His glasses slipped upon his nose.

The moon behind a moving cloud dropped a long shadow like a quick floating island across the moonlit expanse.

Wakefield said, "This man here to stay?"

Pettigrew looked at me as if he'd forgotten I was there.

"Seems like don't anybody know how long anybody go'n stay."

But I knew that by their agreement the subject for the moment would be dropped.

The buggy was so far ahead now that it was like a light on a wave racing to spend itself. Abruptly it disappeared. It had turned into a lane of trees leading to a luminous shell of a house far across the field. Under the moon, the house loomed like a ghost ship on a flat sea.

"God knows, Mr. Tanner got something on his hands," Wakefield said.

"Everybody do," Pettigrew spoke to himself.

"Look over yonder at what's waiting in that house right now! His own pa. Half here, and half back there where nobody can remember but him. Now Mr. Raleigh stretched out up there in the front bedroom. Ain't going to be able to move him, neither, even if he outlasts the night."

"What you say, everybody better off he done it over here. If there *is* anybody left, Mr. Tanner used to *facing things*." Pettigrew's sharpened conviction had grown out of the night itself. "Knows what to expect of folks, what not. Take Miss Amy. Bottom of her trouble, putting off admitting that the world ain't the way she thought it ought to be."

When I asked whether Mr. Tanner Haynes didn't have a wife to help him, Pettigrew and Wakefield divided me with their stares.

Wakefield said, "You fresh out here. Everything new to you. Some places there ain't no understanding lest you was born there yourself. This place one of them. Right time, I'm going to tell you about that man. Mr. Raleigh, too."

After a moment he added, "Naw, Mr. Tanner ain't married. But that don't tell you nothing at all."

Then we turned into the lane of trees. The darkened road under dappled moonlight seemed to soften sound itself. It silenced Pettigrew and Wakefield. I realized what a stranger I was at their side. It was like riding through the broken light just inside the edge of a forest and, unseen, looking out on the world.

CHAPTER ELEVEN

We heard the Negro woman's voice before we could see her.

"Lonnie Gee, where you at? Leaving me by myself front of this moonstruck house! Skeered to go in, skeered to go out."

The Negro woman was a frantic shadow caught in flight.

"Hish! Somebody else coming! Should a-left this breaking-up place whilst I had a chance like them others done! You made me stay out here."

"Beulah, he ain't—?"

Sight of her frenzy stopped the Negro man approaching.

"Go see for yourself! I ain't having no part of it! Them churren of his'n is enough in one room. Tole you I been hearing a hooten owl every night!"

"Hish hooten owls! Mr. Tanner tole you to set with his pa till he came back!"

At the sound of our wagon and Pettigrew's "Who-oh, mules, who-oh," the two figures turned.

Lamps in the front windows of the bare frame house made two pools of yellow light in the whitened yard. Louisa's and Otway's buggy, almost indistinguishable from its shadow, had been abandoned midway by the walk. I hadn't at first noticed the little crowd of Negroes waiting near the corner of the house. They were as silent, as unmoving, as the cluster of leafless crape myrtles behind them.

There before them was a stricken house. What had that very day been unlooked-at and walked past, was now under the wide net of the moon's glow as unfamiliar to the Negroes as if it had just risen on the spot before their eyes.

We ourselves, stepping from the wagon, casting our separate, bending shadows, were watched as though we were being delivered by the strange night itself.

Recognizing Pettigrew and Wakefield, Beulah, momentarily stilled, said, "Thank God, *folks* is coming." She started toward them. "*You* his man, Pettigrew. *You* go see."

Wakefield turned to me. "They got a fire going. Come inside."

The two men went ahead, the leaders of their tribes, past the eyes of the waiting, staring Negroes, standing there unspeaking, wrapped in head-rags, coats with turned-up collars, hands thrust in pockets, arms crossed under overalls.

Beulah, at the bottom of the steps, looked at me uncertainly, "You be a *doctor?*"

When I shook my head, she said, "I know. You some kin far down the line. This-here news go'n bring 'em all in."

I stood uncertainly in front of the house, not knowing where I belonged.

Toward the back a circle of black figures holding hands out over a trash fire, caught my attention. Long shadows, like trembling spokes of a wheel, wavered round the leaping flame. As I went toward them, solitary faces turned, I heard subdued, almost formal, mutterings of "Ebening. Ebening." Silently a place opened up for me.

Until I held my hands over the smoke I hadn't realized how cold the ride had been.

Somebody murmured, "You come a long way?"

I looked about at the pinched cold faces, almost indistinguishable in the shifting firelight, brought together to this spot from distant cabins, from wives watching in doorways, from supper plates under dim kerosene lamps. One of the Negroes wiped his nose with a blackened handkerchief in a work-hardened hand. These men, their eyes anxious and dark, their clothes sweat-stained and heavy with field dust, had lived out the years of their lives on this land, knowing little of the earth beyond their own pines. Their hurt faces were speechless, bewildered.

Only this morning they'd believed that Raleigh Prescott would live forever.

Now he'd denied them the familiarity of their day's labor, the comfort of the beds they were to return to.

A thin little man with thoughtful eyes shook his head, "Mr. Raleigh was a good man. Weren't no reason for this." But his words, as though spoken aloud unintentionally, seemed to startle him. Nobody answered. He looked about at the closed, private faces of his neighbors. What was it *they* knew, what had *they* kept back—about Mr. Raleigh, about their own secret, everyday lives? "He was talking to me yisdiddy," he said defensively, then slowly added, looking into space, "Good God."

It was then that I realized that, already, whatever Mr. Raleigh had done, for whatever reason, could not be undone. Unknown to him, unknown to Miss Amy waiting at home, it had already reached out and out, like a wave spreading to a faraway breaking edge.

As I started back to the house I could not help but think of the death of my own father: how, when I was a child, he had stayed so much from home, leaving early and returning late from the lumber mill to our house, which was close enough to the livery stable on Halifax Street for the acrid smell of dust and dry straw, the sound of mule kicks, to hang permanently over our block. I remembered that the longest my father ever stayed within the sound of my mother's voice during daylight hours was on Saturday afternoon when he took his weekly bath, dressed himself in Sunday clothes and marched away to his world.

What surprised me most, when word was brought to us about him, was the number of friends he had. It had been the broken reflection of him I'd had from my mother's vexations, her aches and pains, her broodings, that had provided me with what I believed. Not to see him during the week, to hear him coming in without a light exactly at ten o'clock on Saturday and Sunday nights, to hear my mother's sharp exasperation and my father's determined silence.

But when they came to our porch—the people I least expected to see—that beautiful spring day—when life was just beginning—people so foreign to me in the streets of Warren, showing real concern on their faces and asking what they could do, it was impossible for me to realize it was my father who had brought them. I stood at the graveside the next afternoon in guilty stupefied silence, feeling it was a stranger we buried. I noticed the soft little spots of yellow in the grass where crocuses and daffodils were beginning to thrust out of the ground.

CHAPTER TWELVE

Lonnie Gee, his hat in his hand, his back to me, was bending over the fireplace, stretching the washed-out blue of his clean overalls, turning the showering crackling logs with a poker.

"Didn't he tell you to keep this fire going, Beulah? Cold as it is, and folks coming in the dark. Strangers."

"Since when is telling *you* the same as telling me? Both of us ain't in your clean pants."

Beulah looked in from the open kitchen door. An iron kettle on the wood range was hissing steam. "My hands full. Looking out every window, washing dishes, toting wood. This here is a heavy night. You start thinking for somebody else, you bound to leave something out."

"Ain't said for you to think. Said *do*."

Beulah, framed in the doorway, put her hands on her hips. "Keep on, I'm go'n write somebody a letter, come carry me to town."

"And got to go long behind it to read 'em what it said."

"My own brother done got him a job. Takes writing and reading."

"What he do? Sharpen the man's pencil?"

Undisturbed, Lonnie Gee placed two fresh logs on the fire, brushed his hands together and turned to go.

"Talk lak that with a stranger behind you." Then she added doubtfully, "Could be some kind of kin. Down the line."

Startled, Lonnie Gee jerked his head toward me.

"Wisht it a-been Mr. Tanner looking straight through you. Dr. Pitt right behind him. Then you'd a-see."

"Kin or who, *kindness* done brought him. Come in, mister, warm by the fire." He took off his hat, showing a bald head.

I realized that Lonnie Gee hadn't noticed, out of all the faces in the yard, that I'd come with Wakefield and Pettigrew.

"Ain't no use for me to tell you nothing more'n what brought you. Keep my mouth shet. Your'n, too, Beulah. They go'n *say* what they wants. But warm yourself till they come."

"He say give 'em some coffee, Lonnie Gee, till he come back. Wid no cracked cups."

"Coffee your bidness."

I sat in an old red leather chair which Lonnie Gee pushed toward me.

"What done *happened* ain't your bidness, neither, wid his own churren under the roof. Pettigrew and Wakefield thrown in."

Lonnie Gee was a lean yellow Negro, who'd never grown to his big hands and ears. Beulah wore a full white apron tied tightly around her middle. A red head-rag stretched her well scrubbed face.

Starting for the kitchen door, Lonnie Gee turned suddenly, examined me all over. "You *new?*"

When I nodded, he looked puzzled.

"Soon somebody be here explain to you 'bout Mr. Raleigh. Mr. Tanner do the explaining for hisself." But then he added thoughtfully, as if his uncertainty about me demanded a little more, "Mr. Raleigh ain't so bad off. Time come, maybe he seen he was messing wid the Lord's decree. Whoever you might be, whether it helps or hurts, what he done didn't come from no hate. Knowing him all my life. Ain't his nature to have that set a mind. All he done was hurt hisself. And everybody round him. Making hisself a stranger to 'em all. When the good Lord is ready is plenty time for me. Then some."

"You git a misery, toothache," Beulah said from the kitchen, "you the first man to roll your eyes and pray. Come back this here kitchen whar you belong."

Lonnie Gee gave a brush at the hearth and turned to go. "Least you is go'n keep *warm*."

There was something about the room in which I then found myself alone for which the cold approach to the house hadn't prepared me. It was difficult to believe that I was in that luminous shell we'd seen across the flat fields. Sitting there, I was struck, as I had been in front of the fire with Miss Amy, with a sense of the depth of irrecoverable time. White walls were lined with a bluish green of chair rails and baseboards. A leather sofa faced the fire from the middle of the floor, where an old red carpet caught the pulsing light of the fire. Upon the dark paneling over the mantel hung a portrait of a red-coated Revolutionary War officer, in a flaking frame. Except for a single chair and a round table against the rear wall, there was little else in the room. A gun rack, a powder horn hanging from pegs, and wide polished floor boards.

An image of that solitary figure on horseback searching the empty fields came to me. In the concealed knowledge of his strong face, in the old lived-out elegance of the room in which I sat, in the silent waiting faces outside, and in my awareness of the stricken presences in the house, I felt a sense of the pressing past. I stood at the exhausted shoreline of waves cast long ago.

It was Wakefield who first returned to the room, looked about uncertainly, and, holding his hat in his hand as if he didn't know what to do with it, found a little three-legged footstool which he placed at the end of the hearth. Dropping his hat on the floor at his side, he sat, a tall lone figure, coat still buttoned, and held out strong, oddly graceful hands to the fire. As I watched him on the stool, turned from me, hands outstretched, elbows on parted knees, I realized the chairs in the room were empty.

Presently he spoke from a renewed somberness that had followed him from the other room.

"What am I go'n say to them standing in there now, looking at him, his leg and hip injured and in pain? His own son and daughter and Pettigrew?" Absently he was rubbing his hands. "Mr. Raleigh done spoke himself. Done spoke to them, Miss Amy, them folks outside. To me, too. Spoke in a way he ain't never done in his life. Come over me in there a minute ago, looking at him. I didn't know things was pressing him so hard. Way I feel right now, I wish for his sake he'd done it right. Didn't even have any luck when he looked at things, face to face. Was *owed* that. Mr. Raleigh hid something didn't any of us know, less it was Miss Amy. Maybe I ain't seen her side. Living all these years in my own."

Otway and Louisa had come into the room. How long they'd been behind me I didn't know. I stood up for Louisa to have my chair.

Neither of them spoke. Their eyes were moist.

Louisa's dress still showed the dampness from the brush of their frightened search. Otway's shoes and exposed ankles were wet.

Fatigue had aged them during the hour. Their eyes were tired, distant: what remained for them had no interest, no life. Bewilderment sat cruelly upon their untouched faces of youth.

Together they came toward the fire.

Wakefield stood up, stepped back from his stool and his hat on the floor. He was looking at Otway and Louisa with such absorption that even their eyes were drawn to him. In the long moment of exchange I knew they'd forgotten I was in the room. Was this a so-late recognition of their blood, of the oneness of their humanity? I realized I wasn't to know. Not what they knew, not what they wondered.

Then I heard Louisa say, "My poor father."

"Wakefield," Otway spoke, in consternation and appeal, "my papa has been hunting all his life. You can't *find* a better hunter than my papa is."

Wakefield nodded his head.

"Did you and Tanner—find him?"

Again he nodded.

"He got his feet tangled up in the *briars?*" he was asking in disbelief. Then he added, "Tangled enough to throw him *down?* That must have been a terrible place. Papa doesn't hunt like *that*."

Wakefield was looking at him steadily. Otway's perplexity at the moment was like another presence in the room.

"I know you've been hunting with my papa sometimes."

Wakefield, almost in the shadow behind the stool, barely murmured, "I been."

Then Otway said, "You've been round my papa some. *You* know."

Now Louisa was looking at her younger brother. Even to me it seemed that the space of the room had widened between them.

Wakefield was watching her.

"You can't reason it, Otway. It isn't something you can reason." Her eyes were still wet. "They've told us, they've told us how it was. It *happened*. Papa could have been the best hunter in the world."

Otway turned to Louisa from his abrupt distance. "Louisa, I know better than you."

"You don't. You don't," she said.

"Miss Louisa"—Wakefield had stepped forth from the hearth—"you been out longer'n you know."

He pushed the chair I'd been in close to the hearth. Louisa sat as submissively as a child. She'd never unbuttoned the short coat she'd worn in.

"Wakefield," she said after a moment, "you've been living here at Mr. Tanner's a long time."

"Yes'm."

"When we take my father home, whenever that is, you must come to see him. My father is going to need—friends."

"Yes'm."

"There isn't any better hunter in this whole country than my papa," Otway kept telling himself.

"It could happen to anybody, boy," Wakefield said. "The best hunter in the world would trip in them vines, get thrown flat on his face. A terrible tangle in there. Honeysuckle, grapevine, everything else."

"I know. I know," Otway said.

Without turning her face from the fire, Louisa spoke so quietly, so evenly, that I was scarcely aware that she'd addressed me. "You *are* going to stay with us now, aren't you?"

Before I realized, I'd answered, "Yes, ma'am." It had seemed Miss Amy's voice I'd heard.

"Mama's going to need you. We're *all* going to need you. I hate to go home."

After a pause, "You tell Mama how it was, Otway. Tell her *exactly* how it was. Tell her what Wakefield said about the bad tangle of honeysuckle and grapevine where even the best hunter could trip and get thrown on his face."

"Wakefield," Otway burst out, "can't we take Papa home?"

Wakefield shook his head.

"Let him be, boy. We move him in time. He'll get took care of good over here. Mr. Tanner used to gun wounds. He a good nurse. One of the best in the world." Then Wakefield added after a minute, "Do he need me, I'll help."

Beulah and Lonnie Gee were looking in from the kitchen. She held a tray of coffee cups and a silver pot.

Beulah said, "Miss Louisa, Mr. Tanner said make sho' you got some hot coffee 'fore he come back. Said, see you got warm."

Beulah stepped forward. "Wakefield, step back to the kitchen. Git you some coffee, too."

Louisa started. Wakefield's and her eyes met.

I saw that her eyes were still wet.

CHAPTER THIRTEEN

Beulah, in the middle of the floor, turning about to find a place to put the tray of cups, stopped short. "Hish, ain't that *him?* Mr. Ben back there? Hoping least *he* was sleep." She listened for a moment. "Go back there, Lonnie Gee. Tell him where Mr. Tanner is at."

But at the same time the solid thick figure of Pettigrew was standing in the room. Without his hat, the mahogany dome of his forehead shone in the lamplight. He still wore his steel-rimmed spectacles. With a split tail coat and a Bible, he could have been finishing a blessing over our heads. But there was an unnatural droop to his lower lip as if his wits had deserted him.

"Where Wakefield?" he muttered.

All of us turned.

He seemed not aware of the rest of us in the room.

"Wakefield," he repeated.

Wakefield had already turned toward him, was for the second stilled by the huskiness in Pettigrew's voice.

"Step here," Pettigrew said.

Louisa stood up. A flash of fear caught her face. Her fingers were gripping the back of her chair.

Otway started toward the room.

Pettigrew, unmoving, blocking the way to the door, said, "Yawl set still. Step here, Wakefield. I wants a word."

Wakefield, unspeaking, his hat on the floor behind him, went toward him. His intelligent eyes, his copper skin made Pettigrew's face seem as black, as indecipherable as night.

The two entered the lighted room together and closed the door.

The rest of us were left standing, looking after them.

For the first time I was conscious of the clock in the room. It was hard for me to believe that its steady tick had been there all the time. Even the crackling of the logs was loud on the hearth.

Louisa was standing at my side. She was clutching my arm.

She was murmuring, as though to herself: "You'll *have* to stay with us. For *Mama's* sake. You'll *have* to stay."

"Good Lord," Otway said, "I wish Tanner would come back. Gosh-amighty, how long has he been?" He was still staring at the closed door.

"Ain't nobody go'n drink this coffee?" Beulah's voice came as though from the far side of the house. "Ain't *nobody* go'n drink air drop?"

I heard her turning about, her feet on the bare floor, leaving the room, still talking to herself. "Mr. Tanner drink it. Knows the world's going on. Sun go'n rise and sot tomorrow night."

Then Louisa spoke out to the room: "Did he have to go *all* the way to town?"

I felt I was the only one who'd heard Beulah's voice.

I looked at Louisa, surprised that she was so near me. How little I knew of the girl so close at my side. Her soft dark hair, her mother's olive skin, her face unnaturally lined now, as if she had during the hour moved ahead in time. She seemed to be Miss Amy's other voice—the other voice of the vague image I had of the pretty girl, sitting in the buggy with her father in town. As I looked at Louisa, I remembered the words on the crumpled practice sheet in the drawer in the earlier schoolmaster's room—my room: *Puella* (Louisa) *agricolam* (Tanner) *amat*. Had he— that reticent commanding figure—already awakened in her youth a sense of what life was to be? What was it that her mother hadn't prepared her for?

"No'm, he ain't going all the way." Beulah, with her head in the door, was answering a question I'd forgotten had been asked. "Do, be sunrise fore he git back. Gone to Edgefield—old Dr. Pitt."

"I'm going in that room," Otway spoke out and started toward the door.

But the door opened in his face.

Wakefield came out, then stood, not looking at any one of us, as if he'd forgotten where he was. With long firm fingers he began to stroke his chin.

Then what he said surprised me. "Mr. Jones, step outside with me a minute. Looks like I need a word with you."

Otway and Louisa turned to look at me. I could have been a new presence in the room.

As soon as I took it in that he wanted *me,* I followed Wakefield to the forgotten cold outside.

He was waiting for me at the bottom of the steps. "You a white man," he spoke flatly, unemotionally, "best for me to talk to you. Right now there ain't nobody else."

He started toward the back, looking neither to the right nor left, paying no attention to the staring, still-waiting faces, stepped through the smoke of the trash fire, picked up a path I hadn't known was there and stopped in front of a two-room whitewashed cabin with tremendous fig bushes at the door. Moonlight filtered down through the wrought-iron tracery of a big umbrella tree, dropping a net-like shadow on a shining roof. The netting seemed to reach toward the figure ahead of me and pull it to the house.

Like those on old smokehouses, the door was made of upright hand-hewn boards, with a looped chain and heavy lock. With a firm snap of the hand, Wakefield shook a key from a dozen others on a ring.

Until now he hadn't looked back.

"My place," he said.

I followed him into a dark warm room. There was a small red glow on the side of a black tin stove from which a pipe led into a closed fireplace. Little pulses of light round the stove lay on the floor. The failing glow on the tin looked like an egg sunken in a nest. Under Wakefield's hand a kerosene lamp on the table brightened up, an opening sun flower, reaching out and out to a white double bed in the corner, a goose-neck rocking chair near the stove, and a long table holding guns, a handful of books. Against a whitewashed wall a ladder reached to a trap-door to the loft, where in earlier days children had slept. Wide floor boards smelled as if they'd been scrubbed with lye, astringent and clean. Over the mantel the long free pendulum of a clock carried the strip of a shadow back and forth. There wasn't a picture, not the face of a human being, in the room.

Wakefield pointed to his rocking chair.

Without explanation, he took two letters from an inside pocket. He held them uncertainly, looked to establish me once more, then placed the letters on the mantel shelf.

"Yesterday," he said more to himself than to me, "I didn't know you were in the world."

As I watched his burdened tense figure under this far moon-shattered roof, yesterday did seem a lifetime ago.

"Now you the one I got to talk to. Something done happened. Them letters." He was looking at me carefully. Then he added slowly, in disbelief at the burden of his own words. "There *ain't* anybody else. That boy too young."

Shaking his head, he took a seat on the other side of the stove. "Way things are, it ain't for me to handle this by myself."

Pointing to the mantel, he said, "Them letters was in Mr. Raleigh's coat pocket, 'bout to fall out. Pettigrew found 'em. Been rubbed dirty against his hunting coat. Date on 'em says he been carrying them rubbing, burning against his skin for a week. Was hid in his coat pocket, hunting;

hid in his coat pocket, eating before Miss Amy and the churren. Was hid before every last one of us, including me.

"Out of all the year's months, good and bad weather, if the good Lord let both 'em come at the same time, He put a heavy load on one day."

Wakefield stood up. He looked tired, older than I'd thought him to be. His lean tall frame was stooped.

I realized I'd never seen Mr. Raleigh. A wonder flashed through my mind: what the two shared in build, color, voice? I had to repeat to myself: this man was his blood kin.

Wakefield went over to a table in semidarkness, pulled out a transparent bluish jug and a short glass. "I keeps it for him. I can tell when he needs it. He'll come down here. Mr. Tanner, I'm talking 'bout. Lately, Mr. Raleigh, too."

He drank off a finger or two of whiskey straight. Without apology he said, "You keer for it, there it is."

Even before I realized what the scratching was, Wakefield had opened the door. A gray bird dog with brown spots and long brown ears came into the room, rubbed against Wakefield's legs, then lay down in the circle of warmth on the floor.

Wakefield took his seat near the dog. With legs apart, elbows on knees, he dropped his cupped hand down absently to the dog's head.

Then I realized that Wakefield had been looking directly at me, studying my abrupt presence with the Prescotts, my presence in this room itself.

"You going to have to tell me which way to go."

"Those letters?"

Not looking at me now, not even hearing my question, he said, "All this time, holding back from me. Not even telling me what it was."

These words were a weight, sinking slowly, lower and

lower, into his awareness, into the deep well of his privacy with his half brother.

Then I heard him as though from across an unreachable gulf, "Poor Raleigh," dropping *Mister* for the first time.

"Lay up there like that, he ain't got no land, ain't got nothing left. All he got is a house. Lawyer write that the banks say there *ain't* no more money, lest he want to mortgage that."

I wasn't sure at the moment that Wakefield's eyes weren't wet.

"I knew he been borrowing, borrowing, borrowing. I knew something was draining him away. Could see it in his face." Then he added as if the words were an injury to his flesh, "He oughter said something to me. When he got to this it won't no use to stop."

He was staring so at the flickering light on the floor, he could have forgotten I was there.

"This-here war done took everything."

Seldom have I seen awareness so visibly drain a face. What was coming to him seemed to be almost physically removing the man from me, to that closed world of his affection and memory where there could be no following. Wakefield's eyes were fixed. I noticed that his bird dog was looking up.

"Poor old lady Prescott is going to turn over in her grave. You spend your life fixing things in this world. You die and they git unfixed.

"Raleigh won't ever a good manager. A thousand times I wanted to tell him what to do. Couldn't never be what his mama tried to make him. But didn't want to let anybody down. Not his mama, not Miss Amy, not his children. With Katie Williams he was himself."

The name surprised me, but I said nothing. Looking at him, I knew that the wide net of his memory would have to float at will.

"The old lady was a proud, lonesome woman. She knew

that Raleigh was all she had. Her own husband, Raleigh's daddy, was my papa. She knew that.

"That's how-come she went so far trying to save Raleigh from himself. Raleigh even looked like his daddy. That scared the old lady to death. What she counted on was she knew Raleigh would be whatever folks wanted him to be. He'd *try*. Trouble was he had to *be* too many. Had to *be* too much. What he came to learn was his heart wouldn't follow him back and forth. The old lady thought Miss Amy was the one that was going to make him what she wanted him to be.

"That's how-come the old lady stepped in. Stepped in 'way too late. Didn't know she was taking him from himself, from the only thing Raleigh was ever sure he was. From what I knew he was all the time.

"But it won't fair to Miss Amy. The old lady had done had lonesomeness enough for herself. She knew that one day Miss Amy was going to grow up. Couldn't anybody stay innocent enough not to know when something *wasn't* there. It won't fair in the old lady to let Miss Amy repeat.

"Told Raleigh if he married the first one, Katie Williams, she was going to cut him off without a acre of land. He was going to ruin his ancestors, break her heart, ruin himself. Raleigh couldn't stand up against that. Too soft-hearted. Won't that sure of himself.

"The old lady even went to her—Katie Williams—was going to buy her off. Took advantage. Knew there was something in her she could appeal to. Telling her how life was going to work later on.

"God rest the old lady's soul. Life *has* done worked."

Wakefield got up, as if he'd just recollected where he was. He went over to his table and tossed off another drink.

"Wish to God Raleigh was standing here. Last three, four years, this been the only thing for him that helped."

Wakefield still wasn't including me. I wondered if being a stranger was how I served.

I broke a long silence. I asked him if Katie Williams was dead.

He turned sharply toward me, almost startled. I wanted to remind him he'd asked me to follow him there.

What he said was, "Old lady Prescott has done had her way."

Slowly he walked over to the mantel, picked up one of the letters and handed it to me.

"There ain't no date on it. Looks like he been carrying it a long time."

CHAPTER FOURTEEN

The letter which he handed me was sweat-stained and dirty. The date was illegible, but I could see that it came from Petersburg.

Wakefield said, "Read it."

The kerosene lamp was barely bright enough to reveal the thinly penciled lines:

Dear Mr. & Mrs. Prescott,

It is with a curious sadness that I write somebody I don't know about the death of my Aunt Katie Williams. She died here at my home last Monday night after, I regret to say, a long illness. She was buried in Braxton Parish Cemetery here in Petersburg in the square owned by my husband's people.

Aunt Katie came to live with us about two years ago, after my mother's death.

In her last months she talked so much of her early days in Moratuck County and her old friends there that I felt I had to let somebody know. What a shock it was to realize I didn't know if there were any ties left. I have never had opportunity to get down to Moratuck County, but I feel that I'd recognize every blessed mile. Is my Aunt Katie's home still standing near Squire's Church? Is anybody left? War has made so many changes perhaps it was better for her to hold what she remembered. You may recall she came to Petersburg shortly before the War to join my mother, and after Mother's death came to us. Mother left Moratuck so early that I learned little from her. But Aunt Katie never left there in spirit. She was such a

refined retiring person that I know there must have
been ancestors of whom I'd be proud. I'd like to be
able to let my own children know they have something to live up to. Pray heaven, we don't let the war
completely *bury* the past.

Dear Mr. and Mrs. Prescott, your names *are* dear
because she so often referred to the Prescott family. In
my mind, I can *see* Aunt Katie's place—a long avenue
of trees, carriages and courting couples. But I mustn't
let my imagination run wild. But the present *seems* so
bare, so dreary. I judge you were all *closest* neighbors
and *dearest* friends.

War has stricken everybody. I have no idea that this
will *ever* find you.

But I could not bear the thought of not sending
word to the place of Aunt Katie's birth. I hope there
are people left to tell.

I ask your pardon for the privilege a stranger has
taken in addressing you. If there is ever opportunity,
would it be too much to ask to let me have a picture
of her old place, some word, to pass on to my children?

Faithfully yours,

(Mrs.) Jeannette Wingate Hall

I read the letter a second time.

Wakefield took it from my hand.

He opened the door of the stove and dropped the unfolded sheet on the red coals. Its edges curled up. It
browned from the center out, then burst into flames. In
a minute the whitened ashes disappeared in the coals.

I couldn't help thinking at the moment that Jeannette
Hall would never know how on a cold night on the Haynes
plantation her letter, in the hands of a stranger, was finally
read.

For a long time Wakefield just looked into the fire.
"Woman wrote that letter didn't know much. Didn't know

nothing at all. All she knew was how to send it home. She done *that*."

It seemed at the moment there was nothing more to be said.

Then I asked him how long it had been since Mr. Prescott had seen her, if he had kept on seeing her through the years.

By the way he looked at me I was reminded that I was as much of an outsider as Jeannette Wingate Hall.

But he said, "You going to hear one way or another— now. After today there ain't no telling what you going to hear. Least I know the truth—Raleigh been in love with her all his life—God bless him. There won't a hand on the Prescott farm, on the Haynes farm, for all I know in all Moratuck County, that *didn't* know."

Wakefield looked straight at me. "Colored folks *read* white folks. Did you know that? Colored folks are night-time rovers. They *see* in the dark. They ain't *like* other folks."

I caught a strange note of bitterness in his voice. I couldn't tell whether he was mocking me or not. His Negro blood, for a reason I didn't know, seemed to have weighted him suddenly.

"They hears what ain't spoken, looking at a man's face. For more years than I can count, they carried Raleigh's trouble, knowing everything, not showing nothing at all. White folks think colored folks is empty water jugs that ain't been filled yet. It scares white folks when they find out they have been. I know."

I was awed by the turn Wakefield's memory had taken. I felt that I was with a stranger in the room.

"Don't seem more'n yesterday—first time it came over me who *I* was.

"I hadn't ever known anybody but Raleigh to play with. Us being white and dark wasn't as much between us as a stumped toe. Me and him stayed on the river, hunting and fishing. Did everything together, and right before our papa's eyes. For all them years, being what I was won't no plight. I was near 'bout grown before it ever followed me to sleep.

"Them days, Raleigh had looks. Blond head, tanned in the sun, straight as a buck. A smile and white teeth. That's what worried old lady Prescott, knew the way women folks did him, was scared to turn him loose, like she knew better than he did that with the life he had in him, nobody could tell what was going to happen or where. She saw my papa in his face. And she was *right*. But the last thing in the world Raleigh could see was how the loving he was wanting then could mess the whole world up. Hadn't crossed his mind then that loving was for keeps.

"Didn't cross my mind till that day me and him was leaving in the buggy—eighteen, nineteen years old. Raleigh had done got slicked up. Shirt and tie. I knowed he was going to see Katie Williams then. She and him been looking at each other two, three years—ever since he met her at Squire's Church. Her papa's farm wasn't far from there— twenty-five acres or so.

"And I was going along like he couldn't go without me. He never had.

"Mrs. Prescott was standing at the top of the steps—that same porch over yonder right now—looking. Something struck me. She looked bigger than I'd ever seen her. She was a heavy woman, hair piled on her head, all time like she was going or coming from church.

"But I was so full of knowing *nothing*, and not caring, and happy to be where I belonged, I called up to the old lady, 'Me and Raleigh going to take a trip.'

"It was like shooting a gun and not hearing the sound. But in a second the words were out, over the yard, over the buggy, through my skin and down to my gizzard inside. 'Boy, that is *Mister* Raleigh. Do you understand *that?* Where is your home?'

"Like she'd hit me with a rock. My knees were weak. My ears were 'bout to bust. I couldn't turn my head. I couldn't look at Raleigh's face.

"We just sat there until I turned to see where the words had come from. What I saw through the mist I'd never *seen* before.

"She was trembling, her face was hotter than mine. I knew that all her stored-up pain had hit her, that my papa was the cross she'd had to bear. All at once, I felt sorrier for her than I did for me.

"And what struck me like a lightning flash for the first time in my life, was that people live in pain, that every man is by himself, and will always be.

"When I looked at Raleigh I saw a white man. I knew he saw a Negro at his side. He couldn't say a word, but his lips trembled and tears came to his eyes. I don't reckon I ever loved anybody much but him, and I knew the time had come to lose him that day.

"It won't any longer just a little growin-up girl he was playing with. What he was carrying now was separateness and *need*. It was in his face, in the grip of his hand on the reins.

"Didn't either one say a word. I *couldn't*. I threw my leg out of the buggy and stepped to the ground. Raleigh didn't turn back. The wheels began to roll. Mrs. Prescott was gone."

Wakefield had his chin on a cupped hand. He was watching the fire through the stove door he'd forgotten to close.

I looked around at his room, and saw again the wide white bed, the ladder leading to the loft where in earlier days children had slept.

It was a long time before either of us spoke. But I knew that the surge of bitterness had passed through him and that what he saw was a whole life.

Presently, without any warning, he began again. But his voice was so quiet, so reflective, that I felt that all the while I'd been serving a purpose for him. It came over me all at once, watching him sitting there, what a lonely man he was.

"It was a whole year before I saw Mrs. Prescott again. I stayed over here on my side, where my mama was. Raleigh had to come get me if he wanted to hunt or fish.

"But I had to go over there one day to get something out of their barn. I ran into Mr. Prescott, my daddy. He was a handsome sort of man, too. Looked like Raleigh twenty-five years older. Said, 'Wakefield, where you been all this time?' I reckon I just grinned. Then he reached down in his pocket and pulled out five big dollar bills—the biggest I ever saw in my life. Said, 'Go find Raleigh. Git him to take you to town in the buggy and git you some good new shoes. Walking round here like that.' My daddy didn't do much thinking. He just had feelings for what he saw.

"Then I heard Mrs. Prescott on the porch again, 'Kirby, isn't that Wakefield? Tell him to come here a minute. I want to talk to him.'

"It was hot that day. I walked across the bare space in the sun, looking down at my worn-out shoes, at my trousers heavy with peanut field dust and knees worn clean through. I didn't even mind going up there. I'd gotten over being anything but a colored man. Being *one* thing had made it heap easier on me.

"Mrs. Prescott had taken her seat in a rocking chair on the brick in the shade of the porch. She was waving a big palm-leaf fan. Her round pink fingers held a little lace handkerchief that she passed over her forehead where the edges of her hair were wet. She didn't even bother to watch me until I got up close.

"I knew there was something else on her mind. Hit me all at once. Since the day it happened, she hadn't been thinking about me.

"Said, 'Sit over there on the bench, Wakefield.'

"*She* called me, so I was going to let her talk.

"Then she did surprise me. 'You mustn't be foolish, Wakefield. You're grown. The world isn't the way any of us want it. But it's what was handed us to live with. We have to grow up, all of us. We have to face what is. Both Negro and white.

"'Now I know that you have always been *close* to Raleigh, that he *listens* to you. I need your help. There's something far more important than whatever has worried you.'

"I couldn't tell whether it was heat or dread or hurt that had flushed her face. But she stopped fanning and looked at me.

"There was fear in her eyes. 'Is my son going to *marry* that girl?'

"I told her I didn't know.

"She didn't take her eyes off me.

"'You are *hiding* something from me. You *do* know. Raleigh *talks* to you. Has he even taken himself from *you*?'

"Seemed funny that in a year's time that *that* could worry her. For a second it made her speechless. Her eyes held me fixed. 'My God, it has gone farther than I knew.'

"She dropped both hands to her lap. Looked out at I didn't know what. Then I heard her. 'It will break my heart.' Her lip trembled. I looked away. Came over me then: he was what she had left.

"She was standing up.

"'Wakefield, you must help me. I am *appealing* to you. There's *something* you can do.'

"I remember I said, 'What?'

"It startled her, brought her back to herself, to the woman who owned this land, who wasn't going to let youthful looks, softness of heart, weakness of heart, ruin her world again.

"She dropped her fan. I don't think she knew it.

"'Of course *they* want to marry Raleigh. Why not, in heaven's name? His land, his name, his looks. Some little *upstart*. Some little *nobody* with a pretty face!

"'And Raleigh susceptible to all of them—to the one he talks to last. Of *course* they know how to trap him. They know where his *weakness* is.

"'But the world is *not* a toy, it's *not* for trifling, it's *not* for youth to ruin!

"'I'll not have it! I'll not sit by. Raleigh is as guileless as a child. Knows less than you do. But learning has to *hurt*.

"'I have been. You have been. So will he.

"'Doesn't anybody in this world but me know that there's such a thing as duty, obligation? I'm tired of self-indulgence. I'm tired of the—selfishness of youth!'

"I didn't know how much the lonely old lady had been hurt by my papa till I heard her that day.

"Then I heard her say evenly, almost unemotionally, looking out across the grove and fields, 'What heats the blood at twenty is a *curse* in later years.'

"Her eyes were wet now, and she put her handkerchief to her face.

"'But I'll *stop* it. I'll cut him off without a penny. Without an acre of land. I'll appeal to *her*. I'll tell *her* that life is real. Letting a little nobody down the road ruin the rest of my life. I'll not have *her* mistress of this land.'

"I reckon that it was looking at her that I realized for the first time in my life that wherever there is love in the world there's hurt.

"Long as she lived, me and the old lady understood each other. We went on like two rabbits that had done been shot at together on a hunt years ago."

CHAPTER FIFTEEN

Wakefield stepped out of the door, letting in a knife-blade of cold night air. In a minute he was back with two or three pieces of wood. I watched the fire leap to quick life under the green sizzling pine.

When he took his seat, I asked him what he had done.

"Nothing," he said after a moment. "There wasn't nothing *to* do. Katie Williams was already carrying his child."

Wakefield had picked up a poker from under the stove. Absently he began to tap it on the floor.

"Them were the worst times Raleigh ever had. Clung to me then closer'n a brother. Wasn't nowhere else for him to turn. Raleigh lost his color, all the light in his eyes. Like a boy that couldn't grow up, couldn't believe that what he saw ahead was life. It's easier to get sobered up to the world a little gradual, not overnight.

"But one thing for him, he'd a-paid his price. Raleigh would have married her. He *wanted* to marry her. What we hear after all these years is just a echo, without no throbbing blood. But him and Katie Williams was in love. You got to remember that. What made it all the stranger was that it was *her* that turned. It was *Katie Williams* that done it. Showing herself a *somebody* that hadn't none of them been prepared for, that she won't *supposed* to be.

"It did something to old Mrs. Prescott that made *her* take stock. There's funny twists in this world. The old lady thought she knew 'em all. She won't ready for this one, not ready for somebody's self-denial.

"It upset the plan of creation when she found out the woman had something that she won't supposed to have.

There ain't no doubt in my mind that the old lady came to wonder if she *was* right."

"Did Mrs. Prescott go to see Katie Williams?" I asked him.

Wakefield looked at me directly. "Yassir, she went."

Then he added, "She went and she came back a different woman. Same as if I'd been standing there, I know what she said, looking down at that pale-faced, wide-eyed girl, who was trembling inside her clothes like Judgment Day had come.

"Started off saying what she was going to *do* to Raleigh, 'bout cutting him off from every acre of land. 'Bout Raleigh being all she had in the world, and that all would be lost.

"I can hear every word. Tole her their lives were miles apart. Couldn't no happiness on earth be built like that. Raleigh was just a boy, thought love was just for the asking and the taking. That a boy like that didn't know his mind. Bore down heavy on that: he *didn't* know his mind. Heart was on his sleeve. Be sure, years were going to change him. Years changed *everybody*.

"What the old lady wasn't prepared for was the sadness in the girl's eyes—the sadness that told her that most of what she said the girl had already wondered about, had already glimpsed way-off.

"I don't know how far Mrs. Prescott went. I don't know how far she *had* to go. She might of gone on and told her what the girl and the countryside had grown up with—about herself.

"What Katie Williams told her, what shook the old lady into a feeling for her that she didn't know she'd ever have—Raleigh told me this a dozen times—was that all she'd asked for in the world was a little happiness and she didn't know where that was. Her own daddy hadn't had it. Her mama had done left him years ago.

"Course Mrs. Prescott didn't know the girl had sense enough, feeling enough, to see couldn't no love—no peace—

be taken by force. Raleigh wasn't worth—wasn't *anybody* worth—everything. There ain't nothing in the world that ain't got too high a price. She was older than Raleigh, not in years, but in what she knew about the world, in what she was afraid of about his youth, about Mrs. Prescott, about life itself. Nothing she'd ever seen in life had told her that this *would* work."

Wakefield was still staring into the fire. "I've thought about it a thousand times—one of the strange things. What saved Mrs. Prescott, what saved Raleigh—if you call it saving—was that something in Katie Williams they hadn't counted on. What *saved* Raleigh was what he was in love with. What he was in love with was what lost her for him. And I reckon that *that* is hard to take."

How close that distant story was to Wakefield! Long years, a long war had passed! So *this* was what Miss Amy as a young woman, bringing her innocence to the plantation, had stepped into.

It seemed at the moment that Wakefield was through. He was standing up. The quickened fire through the open door of the stove threw its shadows across the floor.

"It wasn't long before she left here—long before the child ever came. Stayed with her papa's sister out in the country near Bridgeforth, thirty miles away. Left one night, not telling anybody. Was a week before Raleigh knew. Took him longer'n that to find out where she was, and that was a pure accident. Found a colored couple that drove her, not having any idea what they were driving away.

"Then it wasn't so many months later that the child was adopted. Was a long time before Raleigh found out (Lord knows, they say he spent all his time on the road) that a middle-aged couple took the child, lived somewhere at the end of a long train ride. Whoever, they was lucky to git him, that child. From what they've told, I've thought about it, even old Mrs. Prescott would of been proud: what that boy done in the war."

"Did Mr. Raleigh know where he was?"

"Didn't rest till he found out. But that took a long time, took a heap of traveling round. And from that day on, he was sending money for years and years to the couple raising him. Boy ought not to of lacked for nothing, way Raleigh divided what was here—churren here not knowing he *was* dividing. It took Miss Amy to know that.

"But a letter came from that couple—Raleigh's churren were all getting up—saying not to send any more money, any more letters, that the years long ago had buried the past. Saying the boy knew no name but theirs.

"But when Raleigh wasn't tracking him, he was tracking her, till long after he was married to Miss Amy he knew where Katie Williams was on the map. Knew when she left her aunt's in the country near Bridgeforth. When she went to Richmond, that she was working and living in a place where all the folks thought a heap of her. Was even courting a man that she kept putting off. Knew when she came back to Petersburg to live with a sister whose husband had died—the mama of the woman who wrote the letter that has ended up in my stove."

I asked him whether during all these years of tracking, he ever saw her face to face.

He looked at me as if to say, "How little you know."

"Saw her off and on for years. But it wasn't *her* doing. It was *all* him. Saw her long after *she'd* put him behind her. Things had turned so, *she* could be sorry for him.

"If I live to be a thousand, I won't ever forget the last time he *did* see her. By that time he'd been married seven or eight years. Went up to Richmond with him on the train. *Always* wanted me to go. It made things look right. We took a hired buggy out to the place where she was staying on Franklin Street. Houses built right on the sidewalk. Step up two or three steps and ring the bell. I was sitting in the buggy, could hear every word. Raleigh was so jumpy riding out there, he was spilling cigar ashes over a clean white linen suit.

"Little white-headed lady came to the door, open just a little, told him to wait on the stoop. Raleigh remembered he had a cigar, threw it on the walk, straightened his coat and tie, stepped down a step.

"Then the first thing I knew *she* was standing there, all the way out on the porch, the door behind her closed. She looked older, but she was still a pretty woman, a little gray at the temples of her brown hair. Her brown eyes were quiet and smiling like we were friends she saw every day.

"'Raleigh Prescott,' she said. (Been two years since he'd seen her. And she was holding out her hand.)

"Then she said, 'Isn't that Wakefield? This far from home?' Just like she was glad to see *me*.

"Raleigh turned round to me, forgot I was there. 'Drive the buggy around a few blocks. See the sights and come back.'

"'No, no, Raleigh.' She was shaking her head. 'He must stay here. He's a visitor just like you.'

"I couldn't see his face, but in a second I heard him. Me setting there wouldn't, couldn't, stop what had to be said.

"'Katie, Katie, what is it you want? What is it you need?'

"'Need?' she said like she didn't understand him.

"Then a little smile came back. I had the feeling that she was looking at somebody younger than she was, that she was feeling kind of sorry for him.

"'Why, nothing, Raleigh.'

"But all at once it looked like there was fright in her eyes. 'I don't need anything, Raleigh. Nothing at all. Please. Please. Go home, Raleigh. Wakefield, take him home. Raleigh, can't you see? There's nothing. Nothing. I'm happy here. Home is all behind me. I've put it behind.'

"Then, kind of pulling herself together, she looked at

him real soft. 'Time has passed, Raleigh, can't you see? Don't make it hard for me again! They are waiting for you. All of them. Black and white. They are waiting for you. Your *own* children, Raleigh. Your own.'"

Wakefield walked over to a back window, looked out at fields bright under the moon. I knew he was through. But then he said with weariness in his voice, as if his quickened memory, like a series of waves, had cast him on a rise of land from which he could see, "Raleigh never wanted to hurt anybody. Ended up hurting everybody and himself. I done changed my mind 'bout what he did. It was a accident. He ain't ever closed a door or burnt a bridge behind him. His two women has been too forgiving, kept him from seeing himself. Everybody has loved Raleigh."

CHAPTER SIXTEEN

"It wasn't a year after Katie Williams left her daddy's farm that first time," Wakefield told me, "that old Mrs. Prescott was scheming. Them days, there *was* a separation between Raleigh and her. But *she* was smart, knew when to push, when not. Don't follow up no victory too quick. Was counting on young blood, changing seasons, and *his nature* to be on her side. But *his nature* she underfigured. Before she died, she saw that! Him divided. Him not sure of anything. She saw it long after he was married to Miss Amy, saw it long before Miss Amy did—knew on her death bed that part of him wasn't there. The old lady had to pay full price for everything all her life. Her victory came as high as getting beat. Always had. All it took was seeing Amy and Raleigh together them first years to make her wonder if any one thing in the world is all the way right.

"But she started off scheming. Told me one day, 'Make Raleigh go on a fishing trip with you down the Moratuck River. Why haven't you two been out hunting quail?'

"I could see the old lady thinking. 'He needs to see *young* people, Wakefield. Young people of *his* sort. He needs a change. That's the trouble with these distant plantations. We forget what the rest of the world is like. The world is full of charming, wonderful young people. There's no need for loneliness, *his* age.'

"It was the thinking that day that started her.

"Called in every yard-boy, cleaning-woman, and cook on the place. Turned that house and yard upside down. Washing windows, polishing floors, cutting grass, raking leaves. Got out big trays of silver, had it shining. White tablecloths

hanging outside floating in the breeze. Little barefooted
black boys she didn't even know by name was running their
legs off. And cutting flowers out of that pretty old garden
that there ain't any more of but weeds. Every crisscrossing
walk used to be graveled. Every blade of grass pulled.
Them petunias, tall white daisies talking to one another,
nasturtiums, marigold, sweet William—every color that
growed.

"And the day they started coming—buggies and surreys
filled with clean young faces and suitcases, one or two on
horseback—had a half dozen black folks dressed up in
starched white coats, standing round grinning, not knowing what to do, but glad not to be chopping, not to be
feeding mules, for a day or two.

"And old Mrs. Prescott standing at the top of the steps,
dressed up in something she got out of mothballs, her hair
done up fine, and powder on her face, a little shining gold
watch pinned to her waist, making out like the papa and
mama of every last one of 'em was the best friends she'd
ever had.

"But the one I took most notice of—(I was holding
horses for the unloading. Raleigh had come over here early
to get me. Said me and him was going to drink some
liquor that day)—the one I took most notice of was the
one Mrs. Prescott came down to the bottom of the steps
to meet, holding to the rail with one hand and holding
up her skirt a little with the other. Heavy, she always had
to be careful how she walked.

"'My dear Amy Pendleton,' she called out, 'how generous your father is to share you with us.'

"Even in the midst of all them whirling, excited young
folks, the girl *did* stand out. Long brown hair that was
done up pretty on her head. A big waving straw hat with
flowers on the brim. Dark eyes and skin that was darker
than most, like she'd come from some place not around
here. White gloves and a all-white dress. But there won't

nothing pushing or claiming about her face. Strange, even if she looked like she owned the world, she was asking them all to accept her, let her be one of them. Face was glowing. Didn't know how to beg them to come to her and to forget the old gentleman, her shadow, the world didn't know how to touch. Envied the young folks around her, in as many colors as a flower garden, jumpy as kids out of school, their voices high enough to make the grazing sheep turn round and the white guineas in the yard stop chasing bugs and each other and start *ca—racking* right where they were.

"Raleigh was still standing off behind me, like he was helping. During the day me and him took two, three drinks of liquor in the barn.

"He nudged my side. 'Hope Mama enjoys her party. Hope her high class friends don't forget their ancestry and get drunk!'

"But then a look came over his face, saw something he wasn't prepared, wasn't *ready* for that early, like time had moved too fast. His face even looked hurt. 'Who is *she?*'

"Could tell he didn't see nothing else.

"'Ask your mama,' I told him. 'What you looking at has been picked by hand. Your mama did the picking.'

"Frowning like the news he heard was worrying him, he was running his hand over his blond head, straightening up his tie. In a minute or two he was walking off.

"'There's old man Raleigh!' some of the boys started calling out to him. 'What you been doing, farmer? Hiding in the hay?' Raleigh turned red as a beet. 'Bout give his own self away.

"Lord God," Wakefield said, "that seems like yesterday."

His brown-gray dog lifted his head, got up and walked over to the door, his nose at the crack, his head still.

"Hears something," Wakefield said. "Off. Me and you, they'd be right on us."

At the moment I didn't know when this chance I had—

Wakefield so lost in the past, so needing to talk—would come again, whether it would ever come again.

I asked him whether after his marriage to Amy Pendleton, Raleigh had done *all* the "tracking" of Katie Williams, as he said, in trying to follow her from place to place. Had Katie Williams never tried to reach him?

"Once," he told me. "In all those years—one time. Nothing less than what it was would have made her do it then. About the boy—theirs.

"Little nigger boy came over here riding a mule bareback—late one afternoon. 'Where Mr. Wakefield at?' The black ones called me that. Mr. Raleigh Prescott had to see me. Had to see me right then. Knew it was something. Didn't have to tell me take off dirty clothes, put on clean ones for town. Got there, saw the buggy already hitched up, boy holding the horse. Black woman, big white apron on, was dozing under a tree in the yard. Miss Amy's children—'cept the baby—was playing round her, running circles round her chair.

"And there was Raleigh—town suit on—waiting, watching for sight of me. All he said was, 'Get in.'

"'Tell Colin Ashby I said to come out soon. Tell him I haven't dropped out of the world.' It was Miss Amy, straight, a little pale, calling after us. How time had fled! Right then had a picture of old Mrs. Prescott dressed up for Raleigh's party, going down to greet the young lady from Warren at the foot of the steps. 'Wakefield, take care of my husband! Bring him back!' Knowing, then, that he *had* to come back! Knowing there won't nowhere for her to go. If her voice didn't quiver it was for her boy Blunt standing there beside her: she was clutching his hand.

"We were out of the cedar lane, on the country road, before Raleigh said, 'It's her.' He was driving. He was nervous, hands trembled holding the reins. 'Eight years, she hasn't done this.'

"Had to pull out of him what it was. Letter had come

that day saying she was going to be in Warren depot eight o'clock that night. Was an hour lay-over for the next train. She had to see him. Bring Wakefield. Raleigh said, 'She hasn't ever done this. Not all these years. It's always been me.'

"Wasn't any use talking. Raleigh didn't know. All he could do was wonder. Don't think *all* of his past had ever rushed at him so at once.

"All I could figure it was something about the trouble that *had* started, had taken so long to start that I didn't think it ever would. But I had looked for it from the first. Katie Williams' daddy and some of her kin.

"He was a church-going, kind-hearted old man. Loved his daughter Katie better than life. Whatever *she* told him, he did. But when she finally went to Richmond, he about pined away from lonesomeness. Sold out his farm, went to stay with his sister, her folks—near Squire's Landing. Sure, they were glad to take him. Had a little money, was getting too old to know or care how things went. But it took them *all*—his younger sister and her children—a long time to see what else he had besides cash from a few acres. Old Mr. Williams was the grandfather of Raleigh Prescott's son— Raleigh already married, children of his own.

"First letter came without any name telling Raleigh he done ruined *one* life, was now neglecting her child. Raleigh didn't *know*. Katie wouldn't have said. But he sent money like they told him and burned the letter up. Then, later, came word her pa was *needing*, was old and spent out.

"In every letter he ever got—spread out over the years— they didn't come out with a actual threat, just enough to let him see they could get worse. Had sense enough to know that the way they was doing was *working*. Enough to keep his conscience divided, not too much to back him up, force him out. Wanted it long drawn out.

"Only once did they make it hard. Would he be interested to know that *his* son might some day want some land?

"Katie Williams up in Richmond must finally got wind. The letters stopped.

"All I could think about riding to Warren in the buggy that afternoon to meet Katie Williams was that something had happened that *she* couldn't stop.

"Could see the depot from the high trestle bridge over the Moratuck River. Her train was in. Thick smoke from that old funnel smokestack was swallowing up a half dozen buggies and wagons. Between trains like this, the yard was always full, folks traveling, some not. Swinging lamps had just been turned on in the waiting room.

"Most of the way in to Warren Raleigh hadn't said a dozen words. But sight of the depot made every muscle grow tight. I heard him talking to himself. 'Katie hasn't ever done this.'

"Raleigh turned to me briefly. 'Wakefield, she said bring you.'

"She was standing by her suitcase, away from the crowd. That's how we spotted her so quick.

"She looked like a city lady then. Didn't look like one day years before she'd left from this spot. Folks noticed her, not knowing who she was. City clothes, a little feathered hat.

"But close, it surprised you to see her brown eyes were frightened, her face pale. She reached for Raleigh's hand, held it for a minute or two. Her lips trembled.

"'I didn't want to call you. It wouldn't have been fair not to let you know.'

"'What, Katie, what?'

"Her eyes glistened a little as she spoke. 'They've sent for me. He has typhoid fever, Raleigh. *He* isn't going to live.'

"It came to me for the first time that I didn't know the boy's name.

"And I heard her saying, 'I couldn't bear not to let you know.' And Raleigh saying, 'I'm going with you. I don't care what you say.'

"But she was shaking her head, 'No, no, no.' Her eyes were wet now. 'It was part of my promise to myself that I wouldn't let you go.'

"Without saying a word, he picked up her suitcase, took her by the arm, and led her away. This time he was getting away from me.

"I went back to the buggy, watched the two standing there away from everybody, beyond the light from the depot yard. What they were talking, even if they were talking, I couldn't tell. But his arm was around her. A few minutes later, when the train was behind her and the conductor was picking up her suitcase, before the yellow lights, like a row of jack o'lanterns from the train windows, came between them, he kissed her on the cheek.

"Raleigh asked me to drive home that night. And for the rest of the way he didn't say a word."

Now the dog was leaping against the door, his front claws scratching the wood.

Wakefield barely noticed him.

"Did the boy die, Wakefield?"

"No," he answered. "Got over typhoid fever, lived to be killed in the war. A whole company wiped out. Which would have been easier for her, I can't say. The first or second time. From what Raleigh found out, the boy died in the war—as brave as anybody going. The second time Katie Williams had more to lose."

CHAPTER SEVENTEEN

The dog barking at the outside made Wakefield look to the door.

We kept silent for a minute.

"Ho-o-o in there!"

"Why don't he come to the door, knock like folks ought to do? Think he was quieting a mule in a barn."

"Ho-o-o in there!"

"Hush, dog. Get back."

Wakefield pulled the door open, framing Pettigrew's solid figure in a square of yellow light. His spectacles shone accusingly.

"Got to learn 'bout knocking 'n everything else," Wakefield muttered to himself. "Colored folks."

The dog turned around, went back to the stove.

Pettigrew didn't bother to take off his hat. He looked at me carefully, now interested in my presence in a way he hadn't been.

Wakefield didn't give him a chance. "Dr. Pitt done come?"

Pettigrew nodded his head. Not looking at us, "Say not to move him, let him stay whar he's at."

"Where he *wanted* to be, first place. He *came* over here," Wakefield said.

"Say want to keep him still, two, three weeks. What he tore up worse was his knee." Pettigrew seemed to be reporting this resentfully. Relief about the gravity of Mr. Prescott's injury had been quickly replaced by a kind of second-thought anger—at this room.

"Me and Mr. Tanner able to take care of him," Wakefield said.

"Ast me, you *done* took care of him."

Wakefield looked up sharply. "What you hiding behind your face?"

Pettigrew looked at me again, but then overrode whatever hesitation he'd felt.

"How much liquor you and him been drinking?"

Pettigrew's question was so unexpected that even Wakefield was caught. Wakefield said nothing, kept his eyes on Pettigrew's face.

"Other folks got claims on Mr. Raleigh long before you folks over here. Got a wife, churren at home. Something I been noticing, been on my mind."

The bluish glass jug on Wakefield's table shone dully in the lamplight.

Finally Wakefield said, "How-come you say that?"

"I know Mr. Raleigh been drinking liquor over here. Or you been bringing it to him. A long time. Miss Amy knows it been coming from somewhere. Been the old lady, his mama, stead of Miss Amy, she'd a-known who."

"Mr. Raleigh is a grown man, free to go at will."

"Even old Dr. Pitt hit on it, first thing. Give him a pill, put him to sleep. Turn round to me right off, like I done it. Say, 'B'lieve my friend Raleigh been drinking a little liquor.' Said, 'It takes one old thief to catch another one,' and nudged me in the side. 'How much he been drinking lately, Pettigrew?' Looking at me over his specks. Had to ask *me* that."

"Too many folks been tending to his business. Always has been."

"Doctor *got* to tend to it."

Pettigrew sat down, placed his spectacles in his pocket, dropped his hat on the floor at his side.

"Trouble is, over here yawl ain't got no women folks to rule you. Ain't got none to answer to, night or day. Mr. Tanner a good man. Ain't no better. Man all the way.

But he be better off did he git married, settle down. Women folks scattered round the country, stid of at home."

A flash of anger crossed Wakefield's face. The righteous old Pettigrew, hiding his chair under his heavy figure, had gone too far.

"What Mr. Tanner do ain't none of your business. If you knew what you were talking about, you'd find out that what Mr. Raleigh do *ain't* none."

But Pettigrew was undisturbed. "My business is helping run that place over there. Miss Amy *looks* to me. Been looking to me for a long time. I the one pick up the pieces. That's how-come I'm setting here thinking right now, seeing how much yawl been aiding and abetting him. This place over here been bad for Mr. Raleigh. This place has took him from home. I hates he got to stay."

Pettigrew turned suddenly to Wakefield. "You tell *him*" —nodding toward me—"what's in them letters?"

"I told him what was in them letters. And I told him more than that."

Now Pettigrew was looking straight out ahead. "Wasn't no call to."

"This man has come to live in that house. He got to know what he living in. Else, how he go'n help?"

"Miss Amy getting so she going to have more sense than any of the rest of us, more'n I ever give her credick for. I can see it now. The time don't come when you don't have to *try* to put up a front. If not for yourself, for other folks. That lesson has done come hard for her, but I b'lieve she's done learned it. And her churren is better off."

Wakefield wasn't prepared any more than I for the depth of Pettigrew's concern. He was looking at him now with a quickened wonder about what Pettigrew *did* know.

"Pettigrew," he said finally, "you come over here sitting in my house, telling me about Mr. Raleigh and Miss Amy. What they're thinking and what they ain't. You don't know nothing, nothing, nothing." His voice trailed off to a bare whisper. "Nothing at all."

After a while Pettigrew spoke slowly, reflectively. "You know, Wakefield, I thought about it a heap of times. Sometimes I think that you forgits that you are a colored man."

CHAPTER EIGHTEEN

Back in the house, the slow-moving, unexcited old Dr. Pitt, pulling on his coat, plodded in from Mr. Raleigh's room. In a minute the light behind him went out, and Tanner Haynes followed, closing the door.

Dr. Pitt was a big-boned man, his body thick in his lower half, as if gravity or years had pulled his weight down. He wore gray side-whiskers which had slipped from a bald head. A long, hanging turkey-neck went into the "V" of his wingback collar and string-tie. His white shirt front beneath a black, ill-fitting coat with bulging pockets, was soiled and dusted gray with cigar ashes. But eyes beneath ragged brows were clear blue and sharp. A pair of folded spectacles seemed barely caught in his upper pocket. The knees of his trousers were rounded out, and the leather of his black shoes was cracked. He'd slit the leather for an inch or two for his foot to spread.

I'd heard about Dr. Pitt all my life. He'd buried the children of parents he'd brought into the world. Dr. Pitt had for so long been a law unto himself, that it was said he made no recognition of seasons, wore the same high collar, sagging coat and bulging pockets winter and summer. He reminded me of the old turtle; he'd started long before any of us in the room, had kept going in all seasons and had never hurried a step. We were all latecomers alongside him.

Tanner Haynes said, "Dr. Pitt, sit over here in front of the fire a while and rest."

"Going to, boy. Tearing me over the countryside, seven or eight miles an hour. You ain't go'n turn me round and race me right back. Get me a little spot of something. Brandy will do, if you got a good kind."

Hands on the arms of his chair, he lowered himself carefully. His body went down like a slowly sinking weight. "A-h-h," he said.

I remembered that Dr. Pitt had been an unofficial surgeon in the Army, hadn't worn a uniform, hadn't complied with a rule or regulation, hadn't known a general from a private, and, when confronted, had replied, "The minute you find somebody kin do better than me, let him put up his tent. I'll be in business here, private practice, when the rest of yawl been shot at and run." And he'd run his own show with his side-whiskers and tie on until the end, his shirt covered with ashes and his pockets bulging still, and a thousand troops remembering the times, as though in a moment at home, that they'd been under his skillful hands.

"A-h-h," he said again, his hand moving around in his pocket like a mouse, his long knowing fingers exploring the Lord only knew what. He pulled out a match.

It was a great compliment if Dr. Pitt remembered your name. After he'd practiced for forty years, he said that anybody who came along from that day on would have to answer to what popped in his head. He wanted the earlier names he carried affectionately to remain uncrowded and undisturbed.

"What's the matter out here?" he said in a minute. "Who is married and who ain't?"

He looked around at us all crowding round. Wakefield and Pettigrew were back of me. Otway and Louisa had got up. Beulah and Lonnie Gee were looking in.

"Whe-e-w, Raleigh's waked up the countryside."

He turned his head, looking for Tanner. "Raleigh left you any liquor or did he drink it all up?"

Both Otway and Louisa winced. Their faces, as if they'd been slapped, flushed red. I was sure Dr. Pitt hadn't placed them.

Tanner glanced at Louisa. He was holding a brandy glass directly in front of the old doctor, as he would have done for a blind person. "If this isn't good enough for you, I've got some more."

"Tell you in two minutes. See if it gets to my toes."

He tasted it. "Bound to be your papa's. Now, *he* was a connoisseur. Not bad at all. Catch my breath and I'll go back there in a minute and see what he's looking like. Prepare him a little. Tell him his old friend Theopholus is here. Don't want to walk in on him, stone cold. He'll think it's Judgment Day, and he ain't ready. Me and him were friends for too long."

He tasted his brandy again. "Now tell me who all these folks are. See who I know. Don't expect me to call too many names, but I can tell 'em all something about their folks that they don't know."

In the kitchen door behind us Beulah was whispering, pushing Lonnie Gee forward.

"Dr. Pitt," Lonnie Gee said hesitantly, "Beulah back here say ast you, you mind naming her some medicine to take. Her back been hurting a week."

"Where she at, John? Tell her to step here."

Beulah almost tiptoed as if treading sanctified ground and stood in front of him.

Dr. Pitt leaned forward a little and said, "Turn round." He pressed two long fingers into the flesh above her hip. "Where's it hurt?"

"Whar you teching sometime. But sometimes it moves back and forward and sometimes up and down."

"Un-u-h," he said. "Pretty near all over. You bad off."

He punched once more into her flesh and sank back into his chair. Said, "Turn round" once more and looked into her face. "Tell you what you do. Listen to me good. Get you a quart of blackberry acid, apple cider'll do, find you two black-eye peas, drop 'em in, stir 'em round good, then throw 'em out. Let the juice sit for two days and three nights. Then take you a swallow first thing every morning, last thing every night. Give John a swallow. Help him, too."

Dr. Pitt had lit his cigar and was blowing smoke.

Beulah, wide-eyed, was saying: "First thing every morning, last thing every night. Two black-eye peas and throw 'em out. Yassuh, I sho' will. Listen to what he say, Lonnie Gee. Remember what he say for me."

"Tanner Haynes," Dr. Pitt said out to the room. "Here I am sitting in his house. Your papa named you for your mother's folks. That was right. You got the looks, boy. Your papa didn't have any to spare. But your mama was a beautiful woman. A *beauty* in this world.

"Everybody knows about your fighting. Making a hero out of you. Never took much stock in heroes. But one thing: your daddy had guts."

The smoke floated out in front of him. "Need to get married, son. Out here in this lonesome place. Take my advice. I never did."

Otway and Louisa, confused, looking about from face to face, moved over to Dr. Pitt's chair.

"Tell us about Papa, Dr. Pitt. What are you going to do for him?"

He took his cigar from his mouth, looked them up and down.

"So you are Amy's? Son, how is she getting along? Pretty as she used to be? Ought to be some brains somewhere in this generation. Your gran'daddy was a gentleman if there ever was one. 'Bout the only one I ever knew—Will. A fine man."

Without stopping he went on, "I tell you what I'm going to do for your daddy. I'm go'n let 'im rest. Took some buckshot out of his hide, cleaned him up good, patched him a little and put him to sleep. You getting to be a grown boy now. You keep him out of the woods."

But he hadn't relieved the anxiety in Louisa's face. "Dr. Pitt, please tell me. Is he going to be all right?"

Something in her voice caught his attention. He looked at her carefully. "Amy's, too. Daughter, ain't anybody living *all right*. That's too much to say. But he's going to get along. Going to see the world's the same place, going to see that there ain't anybody it can't do without, that it might of been him."

Suddenly Dr. Pitt pulled up in his chair, looked around the room at every face.

I saw the waiting eyes. Pettigrew's, Wakefield's, for the moment Tanner's, too, waiting, looking at Louisa.

"You young folks," he said. "What's the matter with you? Pay attention to the seasons, the good Lord's night and day. His winter and His summer. His rising and setting moon.

"Too high bred! That's the trouble! Torn between what the world is and what you want it to be. Carrying your innocence around like it's some fine china you scared to break.

"All of you 'cept the hero over here."

He was looking at Louisa and Otway and pointing a long shaking hand toward Tanner. "He's mean and tough. Is go'n last. Look at him! See, it takes one old rascal to catch another in this world."

"But, Dr. Pitt," Otway exclaimed. His voice was hoarse with uncertainty, his eyes imploring. "You mean Daddy did it himself?"

For a long time Dr. Pitt looked at the abject boy waiting in front of him. Slowly he sat back.

"Man alive, boy, let's give everybody the benefit of the doubt. Your daddy was human, too, boy. More so than most."

But I knew for Otway in his high trousers and his sleeves too short for his wrists that the answer to his question made the difference about whether life was worth living or not.

Otway looked suddenly at Louisa. The space of the floor was between them now. The light from the blazing fire seemed to reach out separately toward every person in the room.

BOOK THREE

CHAPTER NINETEEN

Back at the Prescott plantation I was to be deserted for the next two or three days. Otway and Louisa, their eyes subdued, their faces showing the fatigue of grief, drove Miss Amy over every morning in the surrey to the Haynes place and stayed until noon, leaving to me an empty house and yard.

Of all the family, it was Miss Amy who surprised me most. When I met her that morning after our return I saw tired eyes but a purposefulness, which she had summoned from I knew not what depth. In fact, it rather startled me to see her, with a black hat and coat on, as though she had dressed for town, leaving the house that morning, a hatless Clio behind her carrying a straw hamper covered with a white napkin. I think she must have surprised Otway and Louisa, too, waiting in the surrey, for they watched her every step of the way down the brick walk toward them, with a kind of thoughtful deference which, somehow, made them seem older. Otway got out of the buggy quickly and stood formally at the step of the carriage. It was as if he'd seen afresh a measure of her life in the lone woman's resolute step down the walk. I wondered how long he and Louisa had known.

But, then, as they were ready to leave, Miss Amy sent Clio for me.

"I must ask you to help me," Miss Amy said, holding out a slender hand for me to take. There was no agitation in her voice, none in her eyes, only the fatigue of a final resolve. "I must put you in charge. If my daughter Flora comes back, if Colin Ashby comes, tell them what it was."

She hesitated a minute. "My dear Raleigh had an accident. Tell them that I am going to bring him home." I realized she was looking pleadingly into my eyes. "Tell them it was an accident. Please." Then the surrey pulled almost soundlessly away.

A few minutes later, sitting in the chair near the hearth that Miss Amy had occupied the afternoon before, smelling the distant ashiness of the fires of uncounted winters and falls, and seeing outside the stretch of century-old fields, it came to me all at once, what I had really not had time to take in: *that I was where I was,* alone, almost the master, in a house I'd never dreamed I'd enter.

The fragments of Raleigh Prescott's story which Wakefield had uncovered, not for me, but for himself, over the now destroyed letter about the death of Katie Williams, seemed to awaken like small candle flames reaching deeper and deeper into a wood some of the leaf-covered memories of my own childhood. What I'd heard years before from Colin Ashby, Judge Whitaker, from Miss Amy's friend Ella Fitzpatrick, those glimpses of a storybook lady not of the world I knew, began to gleam again in my memory like lost silver coins recovered.

The last twenty-four hours had given sound to old voices and life to old figures. They had been there all the while, strangers then, waiting for me to understand them in my time.

It was during these years when I was errand boy for Mr. Ashby and his sisters. Frequently at night, to keep from going home, I'd sit there near him and his company in their rocking chairs on the deep shadowed porch of their house. Always there were visitors, neighbors, kin. The breezes through the maple trees in the big yard made the porch a cool and pleasant place. And always the conversations were about people, strangers to me, but people who were *their* common inheritance and in whose changing lives they, sometimes with sinking hearts, took the measurements of their own advancing years. For a long time Will Pendleton's daughter was their repeated concern.

What they revived for one another during those summer nights, while July flies were strident in the trees and lightning bugs wove vanishing nets over the yard, and palm leaf fans were occasionally stilled, always sounded very tragic and for me, a sensitive youth, very faraway. I remember that the judgments of the ladies were often urgent, and those of Mr. Ashby, slow. For Ella Fitzpatrick, gaunt and powdered, wide-eyed, and shallow-minded, conclusions had to be perpetually revised. I can hear her nervous alarmed voice, punctuating every other word with her own agitation, as well as if I were still sitting behind her chair.

"But, Colin, *you* never think ill of *any*body. By the time you get through *you*'ve got them *excused!* Don't sit there and tell *me* that this thing hasn't *amazed* you."

"Let *her* talk, Brother," Mr. Ashby's sisters said, their rockers stilled.

"Ella. Ella."

"But you forget *I*'m married. Have seen *plenty*, heaven knows. But *this!* Mr. Will Pendleton's only daughter. *Amy*, I count a *close* friend. Heaven's sakes, you and Lily and Lucrezia know. Telling *you* that.

"But Amy *has, always* has, made me feel so *ordinary*, so *fleshly*, I *suppose* that's the word. Said to me once, 'Why can't *I* have your friends? *Every*body loves you. Is it *Papa* they're afraid of? Think *I'm* him? I haven't got his *sense*, Ella, his *anything!* I haven't! I haven't. I'd change with you!' She was *lonesome*, Amy was. I've thought about it a lot! People *made* her play the little princess.

"Colin, I don't have to tell you and Lily and Lucrezia who *my* people were. But I *married* young. Knew that somebody would *have* to take care of me. But *this* thing has upset *everything*. Made me wonder if *I* know what life's all about. It has *frightened* me, Colin. I'm telling you the *truth.* I'm *dependent* on people. If reliable people fail *me,* I'm *lost."*

Ella's hoarse excited words died off for a minute, as she sat there in the dark contemplating the reversal of all she'd believed to be true.

"If it can happen to *Amy,* I shudder to think about *us.* Lily, I don't mean you and Lucrezia. If you aren't *safe* I'll give up.

"The minute I saw *Amy,* saw her *stricken,* nothing had ever *touched* her before, I went to my Willy T., said, 'Listen, don't you *forget:* I'm *married* to you. Took the oath and plighted my troth'—whatever that is. Looked at me like I *was* crazy. But right then I didn't care *one* whit. Not after I saw Amy *Pendleton."*

"Ella, who told you all this?" Mr. Ashby's troubled voice came from the dark.

"Brother," Lily and Lucrezia spoke reproachfully, "everybody knows it's true. You don't want to hear."

"Now, *Lily,* I didn't *want* to hear. Give me credit for *something.* Amy Pendleton left the plantation and stayed in Warren for *two whole weeks* before she went back. She *sent* for me. Not once, but *twice."*

"Ella, Colin Ashby knows all this as well as we do," his sister said. "Sitting there clammed up. Who do you think Raleigh Prescott would make a bee-line to? Who would Amy listen to but him?"

"Colin, I should have known. You let me *sit* here and *tell* you this and you were in the *middle* of the whole thing?"

Ella Fitzpatrick leaned forward in astonishment.

"Ella, I wasn't in the middle of anything."

"Well, I *was.* That little nigger works for Mr. Will came to my house with a note. Poor Mr. Will, frail as he is, I don't know what he'd do without that little nigger. Written by Amy herself, asking me to come to her father's house. I'd just *seen* Amy and Raleigh in town two *weeks* before. Talked to them. Waiting in front of the livery stable for

Raleigh's horse. Amy dressed *beautifully*. *Never* saw her looking better in my life. *Everybody* saw it. Told her what living in the country had done. Why, you wouldn't believe it. She couldn't keep her eyes *off* Raleigh. *Amy!* People said all kinds of foolish things about eggs and milk and country air, but they *meant* it, every bit. And Raleigh Prescott was as *bad* about her. Remember I said to myself: 'I never thought I'd see Amy Pendleton like *that*.' Hadn't been married to Raleigh but a year. But her face had— *softened*. Prettier'n I ever thought she *could* be. Hit me out of the blue. Amy Pendleton was in *love!* And somebody I'd *never* picked out. I hadn't *dreamed* that some *local* somebody, seven miles away, would be the one to do this to Amy. But he *did*. Of course I'd always thought Raleigh was handsome—all the women did—but he didn't have her— *class*."

"Character," Mr. Ashby said.

"Well, whatever it is she's got. And, *anyway*, I didn't dress or anything. Followed that little nigger right over to Mr. Will's house, her note right in my hand."

"When was this, Ella?" Mr. Ashby asked her seriously.

"Brother, I'll never trust you again where other folks are concerned. You haven't told me and Lily a thing."

"*Well*, I'll *tell* you when it was. I found out later it was two *hours* after she got back to Warren. Three weeks this Sunday. Two unpacked suitcases still in the hall when I got there.

"Remember I had just *seen* her and Raleigh together just two, three weeks before at the livery stable, I told you. *Talked* to them, heaven knows, for thirty minutes, when I remembered saying to myself what a transformed person she was."

Ella Fitzpatrick hesitated for a minute. "Now why in the world had I ever thought that Amy Pendleton *couldn't* be in love? Maybe I thought that all men were like my Willy T. Hadn't had sense enough to see that beneath

Amy's *surface* all these years she'd *needed* somebody, too. *Well*," Ella said, "I found out how human she *was*."

There was a quiet over the porch as if Ella Fitzpatrick's discovery concerned them all.

When she began again, her voice was a little less urgent. It surprised me to hear that her words had a disturbingly reflective tone. I wanted to look at her face.

"Amy was standing in that little parlor on the left of the hall. I'll *never* forget her face. Just two weeks before I'd seen her. She wasn't crying. It wasn't that. It would have been better if she had been. What came to me was the strangest thing. Amy Pendleton was like the rest of us. Amy Pendleton was *flesh* and blood. She was like *me*, of all people. I'd never known it before."

"What did she say, Ella?" Lily asked her quietly. Neither her fan nor her chair moved.

"You know Amy has always had beautiful olive skin, dark hair, dark eyes. Now her eyes were circled, a little swollen. She *had* been crying."

Ella Fitzpatrick added after a moment, "I couldn't say *anything*. In a minute I heard her, 'Ella, I *need* you. I've got to have *help*.' Amy Pendleton saying *that* to *me*. All I could think was Mr. Will had died. Then she said, looking directly into my face, just like she was trying to remember who *I* was, 'You've got to go out to the Prescott plantation and pack my clothes. I'm leaving Raleigh Prescott. I can't sleep under that roof.' *Amy* saying that. Two weeks before the bloom of *love* on her face. Worshiping Raleigh Prescott so that I couldn't even believe who she was.

"I said, 'For God's sake, Amy. For God's sake.' Excuse me, Lily. But I couldn't think of anything else.

"Then she *did* shake me. 'I must tell you, Ella, Raleigh Prescott doesn't belong to me, Ella. I know now that Raleigh Prescott is not mine.'

"Then she looked at me so pleadingly, so *hurt*—tears had come to her eyes. 'Does anybody belong to anybody in this world? Oh, Ella, all I wanted was to be myself. All I wanted was to be in love.'

"It was like seeing a flower stepped on, knowing it would never grow back the same. Hearing her say that, I *trembled* all over. I really *saw* her through a haze. Here was this, I thought, self-sufficient girl standing there in the room by herself. Portraits of all those *aristocratic* people looking down. Room filled with *heirlooms.* You'd have thought *she'd* disgraced them all, that everything *ended* with her right on this spot.

"She stood up, she sat down. Thought to myself if she would just stay *still,* I could *think.*

"'My poor father. My poor father! How can I tell him, Ella? What have I done?'

"What she *wanted* was to be herself! To be in love! *Amy Pendleton!* Sounded like me!

"All I could do was use her words. 'Amy, for God's sake, what *have* you done?'

"I thought the only way I was going to get *anything* out of her was a threat. Said, 'Amy, I'll do anything in the world you ask me. Go *anywhere.* But I won't go out to that *plantation* till you tell me what *for!*'

"Said, 'Please, please, Ella. Just believe I can't stay there any more.'"

Then Ella Fitzpatrick said reflectively, soberly, "Take a face like mine, one expression isn't going to help or *hurt.* But the expression on Amy's face was a—*violation.* It was a *violation* on her face.

"Maybe you don't believe it but Amy Pendleton standing there with her ancestors *looking* at her *frightened* me. Have seen a lot of folks get their deserts. *Deserved* them. But seeing *Amy* was like cutting down the only tree in the yard.

"My hands were hot and wet. I saw the world *changing* in front of my eyes. I never thought *I'd* shudder at what I *didn't* know. Wanted to look back over my shoulder to see what was there.

"The one person who had given her life she'd never known wasn't even *hers* any more. And such a *short* time."

Ella Fitzpatrick sat back in her chair. "I'm telling you things I've never told *anybody*. Never will. I wanted to go home and look in Willy T.'s eyes. I thought that if I didn't find what I was looking for, I couldn't bear to live."

She waited a long time before she added, "I'm afraid to trust anything, anything. I'm *frightened*. Oh, Colin, who *is* safe?"

While Ella Fitzpatrick was looking at Colin Ashby, a heavy silence fell over the porch. It was as if each of them had forgotten the others were there. The breezes stirred the full-leafed maple boughs. The lightning bugs worked ceaselessly at their stitching in the dark.

Finally it was the elder Lucrezia's voice that broke the quiet.

"Brother, is Amy bearing a child?"

Colin Ashby was roused from some reverie of his own. He spoke with annoyance. "I don't know these things, Lucrezia. I don't know."

Lucrezia said, "You do. Why had Raleigh Prescott been haunting our doorstep day and night?"

Then Lily spoke out of the depth of her own concern, to herself, not even expecting an answer, "What will Amy *do*?"

Colin Ashby said, still annoyed, "What *can* she do?"

"I'll tell you what she'll *do*," Lucrezia spoke out. Her fan was going faster, as if in contempt at the conclusion forced upon her. "She'll cover up. She'll cover up for the rest of her life. Pride!" She threw out the word. "She'll live in lonesomeness, that's what she'll do. What everybody does!" Her fan was going furiously.

The elderly unmarried sister was unaware that everybody was looking at her.

"She'll *excuse* Raleigh Prescott. She'll learn to live with what's *left* her. That's what she'll do. What everybody does."

Colin Ashby was looking at his older sister thoughtfully. Was it an old loss of hers that she remembered as she sat there fanning that night?

"I've got to go home," Ella Fitzpatrick spoke suddenly. "Colin Ashby, you've got to walk with me to my door. I know that Willy T. is sound asleep in that house."

Mr. Ashby stood up.

But Lucrezia wasn't through. "Old Mrs. Prescott! Possessive! Possessive! Filling her own need!"

Mr. Ashby's voice was pained. "Sister, Sister. Let me tell you something. Raleigh Prescott loves Amy. Can't you *believe* that?"

"She'll cover up! Cover up! She'll make something out of him that he *never* was. For the world, that's all she can do!"

CHAPTER TWENTY

There was another time I remembered hearing Ella Fitzpatrick's anxious, excited voice. It must have been three or
four years later. But it was still the voice of astonishment
at the changes that time had brought to the faces of everybody she knew. The little company around her in the dark
of Mr. Ashby's porch was unusually quiet. They all that
afternoon had been out to the plantation to the funeral of
Raleigh Prescott's mother. They were tired, subdued. It was
a hot close July night. Not a leaf moved in the maple trees.
The only suggestion of motion in the vast vacuum of heat
was the play of sheet lightning, an infrequent blossoming
of yellow gold, so low in the sky and so distant that it
seemed to be signaling from the edge of the earth.

One of Mr. Ashby's sisters had put a tray with glasses
and a sweating white pitcher of lemonade on a table against
the wall.

On this second occasion old Dr. Jonathan Hall, the St.
Bartholomew rector, was there. But the July heat had forced
no compromise in his clerical dress. He sat there all in black
except for his stiff white collar and big white handkerchief
which every now and then he put to his forehead. He kept
the damp wadded handkerchief on his knee.

Mr. Ashby had taken off his coat for which informality he
kept apologizing to the minister. And Miss Lucrezia kept
whispering, "Brother, put it on."

The discomfort of the uncompromising minister seemed
to make the others nervous with the realization that they
were creatures of flesh.

"Lucrezia, you will have to *excuse* me for saying so, but I have always *promised* myself that I would *never* sit on a porch and *fan*, no matter how hot, until there was nothing *left* to do. You're not much *older* than I am. And *excuse* me for saying so, but it makes *anybody* look older. Feel the way I do, my poor dear mother sat on the porch and literally *fanned* herself to death."

"Tommy-rot, Ella," Lucrezia said, "everybody fans."

"That's what's so *depressing*. Everybody my age.

"Dr. Hall, I know you think I'm as light-headed as a sparrow, but, my nature, some things I can't *help*. But sight of change has an *effect* on me. Promised myself that I would *never* go to another funeral. Everytime, Willy T. says, 'Ella, who is going to yours?' 'Not those I'm *going* to, I can *tell* you,' I always tell him. And I end up *going*. Afraid *not* to."

"No, no, Ella," Dr. Hall told her. "A good heart, a good heart." And he wiped the perspiration from his forehead. "Being what the good Lord made you. Being you." He spoke as he would have to a child. "Just one you, Ella. Just one you."

"Dr. Hall, tell me the truth. Are you *thanking* the Lord or *blaming* him?"

"Ella, for heaven's sake," Lucrezia said.

"There's room for us all, Ella," Dr. Hall said. "There's room for us all."

"I don't know what kind of an answer *that* is. But I'll *take* it. I don't care if the rest of you are sitting uncomfortable. Dr. Hall knows I tell him *everything*. He is my *prop*. Hates to see me coming, I *know*."

"Ella hasn't got any troubles," Dr. Hall told the others. "I'm her safety valve." Then he said, "Lucrezia, give me some of that iced drink you've got there."

"Long as you all have known me, not a one of you believes that I *feel*. But I *do*. Just don't keep it shut up, like every last one of you. Sometimes I have to *catch* Dr. Hall to know what he *thinks*. This afternoon—"

"Ella, *suppose* I showed everything?" Dr. Hall asked her. His eyes were tired.

"I know, Dr. Hall, *you couldn't.* You'd wear everybody out. Have us *worrying* to death. But *this* afternoon I thought I'd lose my *mind* if I didn't get *away* from that plantation. Dr. Hall, you weren't long-*winded.* I don't mean *that.* But standing out there in that hot sun in that little Prescott cemetery, I thought time had *stopped.*"

"Ella," Colin Ashby stopped her, "what in tarnation are you going to say?"

"Pshaw, Colin," Dr. Hall said, "let Ella talk." He leaned forward, a little wearily, stroked his brows with his forefinger and thumb. "I'm listening," he said.

"First place," Ella went on, "the country is *not* for me. I've got to walk out my door and see a *face.* Whole time I was thinking—here is *Amy,* born and raised right here in Warren, people all round her. People bowing and scraping to Mr. Will and to *her,* too. Was *used* to it. All *you* remember how Amy was looked *up* to. Didn't know there was one *evil* in the world."

"Wait a minute, Ella," Lucrezia said. "Amy was no *child.*"

Dr. Hall broke in, his forehead still supported in his fingers. "Amy had," he hesitated for a minute, "an—unexposed mind. Mr. Will did, too. Else he did a good job hiding from the world."

"Well, *whatever,* when I saw her standing there under the hot sun with Raleigh Prescott near the old lady's grave— poor Raleigh, he looked like the world had *ended*—I asked myself: 'How long *has* she been married?' Couldn't believe it had been just four or five short years—I counted on my fingers—since that day that she *sent* for me to *pack.* But there was that first child of hers—Blunt—three or four years old, and an ancient nigger mammy trying to catch him in the yard. *Five years,* I said. Seeing her then, it looked like *ten.*

"First place, she had on older *clothes.* Clothes Amy *Pen-*

dleton had *never* worn. I thought—what has Amy been *doing* out here." Ella Fitzpatrick hesitated for a minute, then added lamely, "Under these *circumstances*."

"*Exactly* what I told you all the *first* time," Lucrezia broke in. "Ella, don't forget *we* were at the funeral. I saw Amy Pendleton myself. Every sign I told you was on her face. She'd learned how to cover up, to show a face to the world over a broken heart." Mr. Ashby's elder sister spoke this belligerently, and started fanning again.

"Well, Lucrezia, I *know* you were at the *funeral*—along with *all* her Warren friends—but you weren't inside my *mind. I grieved* for her. All of you standing back in the *shade,* under those *cedar* trees. Dr. Hall, I know *you* were burning up. I said, 'Poor thing has to wear that thing *all* the time.' I wish you could unloosen your collar a *little.*

"But Amy—she hadn't *lost* her looks, she'd *aged.*"

"Ella," Mr. Ashby said, "anybody *looks* a little solemn standing at somebody's grave. Ella, you look like you are the one getting buried."

"Now, Colin," Dr. Hall said, "don't tease Ella."

"My *only* friend," Ella said. "But I'm *serious* about Amy. She was a—a different person. I could see *that.* Knowing the situation the way she *does,* what does the poor thing *do?* You'd have thought she was Raleigh's older *sister,* way she tried to comfort him. And Raleigh clung to her, too. It's *strange.* All the time Dr. Hall was praying, Raleigh was *gripping* Amy's hand."

"Hear that, Dr. Hall? Ella wasn't even bowed," Colin Ashby said.

"I saw her," Dr. Hall said.

"Dr. Hall knows that I hate to pray. I don't feel like I've got any *business* talking to God like that. It used to drive Mama crazy. *First* place, He wouldn't *listen* to me.

"But what took my mind off poor old Mrs. Prescott—God rest her—"

"*Requiescat in pace,* Ella," Dr. Hall said without interest.

"Is *that* what you were saying out there? Well, what took my mind off her was *Amy*. Amy and Raleigh holding on to each other in that hot sun. '*Trapped*,' said to myself. If you all *were* praying, I was *worrying*. What had Amy been *doing* out there, knowing what she knows and, Lord help us, how much more? I couldn't help wondering if Raleigh ever *saw* that other one, if Amy had to live with *that?* Colin Ashby is sitting over there right now knowing *something*, but I don't expect him to *say*."

A sudden breeze stirred the leaves in the maple trees, releasing a cool breeze over the porch. The sky brightened overhead, and there was a faraway rumble of thunder.

Everybody on the porch turned and looked out.

Ella said, "Thank heaven for that! *Had* to speak to her afterwards, though I had no *idea* what I was going to *say*. Looking straight at me, *she* knew that I knew *everything* —almost. Startled me. Had I made that *up*, asking me to *pack* for her that time? Amy's face was—*calm*. Said, 'Poor Raleigh. It means so much to him that you came.' Raleigh! 'These last months for him have been such a strain.' For *him*, she said."

"Do you know what she said to *me?*" Lucrezia broke in. "'Raleigh needs *our* help!'"

"He *does*," Colin Ashby said very quietly.

Lucrezia and Ella both turned toward him. Dr. Hall was still rubbing his forehead.

"With Amy *knowing* that the man she'd fallen in love with, *married*, wasn't even *hers?* If she hadn't loved him still, she would have *left*."

"Now, Ella," Dr. Hall said softly, "life is not as simple as that. Amy Pendleton will become a mature woman. She will face what she must face."

"Live with *emptiness* inside her the rest of her life?"

"There are *other* things, Ella."

"Heavens knows, I don't know *what*. How terrible!"

"No, no, no. She'll learn how deep, how wide the world is.

She might learn to wonder how much of her father's kindness was possessiveness, weakness, weakening what he loved. She'll learn about herself."

"But, Dr. Hall, that's what I'm *afraid* of. Myself."

"Dear Ella," he said, "I wish I could spare you. I wish I could spare us all."

The breezes now were lifting as if wakened from night sleep. The boughs of the trees began very gently to rise and fall.

Ella Fitzpatrick was silent.

"Did you notice the Negroes out there, Ella?" Dr. Hall asked her patiently. "One by one, they came up to her."

"And *every one* of them *knowing*."

"Why, certainly," he said. "And every one of them trying to tell her that she wasn't by herself in the world."

CHAPTER TWENTY-ONE

At first when I heard the carriage outside I thought that Miss Amy and Louisa and Otway had come back from the Haynes place. The wheels came to a quick stop, a door slammed somewhere in the back of the house, and there was an exchange of voices, unidentifiable, between the steps and driveway. Remembering the long stretch of bad road between the two plantations, I couldn't account for the brevity of their trip. I opened the door.

A hatless blonde girl who looked to be nineteen or twenty was pulling at the elbow of a thin sandy-haired youth of about her age. Two suitcases stood on the walk beside them.

It was Clio's open-mouthed speechless amazement that caught my attention. Pulling on a coat, one arm in, one out, she stopped midway down the walk. A black kitten just behind her, as though pulling a string, began immediately to weave in and out between her feet.

"Bless God! Lightning's done struck the poor house! Him two feet behind you! And suitcases multiplied!"

"Where *is* everybody?" the girl called.

"*Better* ask where they at! Schoolmaster setting here waiting to learn you books, and you pleasuring yourself riding back and forth to town!"

"What is the *matter*, Clio?"

"Matter? God bless me!"

Clio thrust her other arm into the hanging loose sleeve as if she and the coat had a private conflict.

At this (I knew now that she was Flora, Miss Amy's oldest living child) the girl left the two suitcases and the bewildered youth, seeming more to retreat than to advance at the reception he'd received, and came toward Clio.

Flora had the oval face of a cameo, a head of elaborately arranged, closely pressed blonde curls. Her gray woolen dress was trimly cut. High on her waist a jeweled pin sparkled beneath a yellow rose bud. She had pretty, fresh peach skin, but there was a doll-like fixity about her expression except, at the moment, for a slight petulance in her eyes. Her fragile china-like femininity, here on the plantation, seemed oddly out-of-place. It came to me at the moment that I could not remember what her sister Louisa had worn. Louisa's distress and fatigue had in my mind turned her dress to gray.

Looking at Flora was like trying to connect a piece of distant landscape to a close-up view before my eyes.

There before me was Mr. Jasper Hornsby's favorite scholar with whom Mr. Hornsby had been in secret agreement about the value of Latin in the heart's affairs.

The youth, still over the suitcases at the end of the walk, was working endlessly trying to straighten the knot of his tie.

"Do riding over a bad road to Warren and back take all *that* dressing up?"

"The place is deserted? Where *are* they, Clio?"

Alarm now clouded Flora's eyes. She turned quickly.

"Alex, Alex, come here."

The youth reluctantly stepped forward. Clio had become a barrier across his path.

The dismay on the faces of the two drew them together. Whatever had happened at home—the measure of it they saw in Clio's face—now weighted them with guilt.

"Let the man in there tell you where Miss Amy is at."

In a minute I was looking at the two faces: at their forlornness. Alex ran a long hand through the wind-blown hair over pale blue eyes and looked vacantly about the room.

Flora looked at me up and down.

"Are *you*—?" Flora asked.

"Schoolmaster that you run out on," Clio retorted.

"Tell me, *please*, where is Mama?"

"Gone to the Haynes place with Otway and Louisa, seeing about your wounded papa."

"What *is* she talking about?" Flora was appealing to me. When I told her about the hunting accident, she broke in: "Oh, my poor daddy!"

She sat down abruptly. "*Why* did it have to happen *now?*"

"Devil ain't got your clock to work by," Clio said. "He busy day and night."

"My poor daddy! I was counting on *him*." Then the thought struck her. "My daddy is going to live?" She looked from one face to the other.

"He go'n live. But he go'n *stay* there. Stay where he's at."

"*He* was the one I was going to *tell*."

Flora and Alex exchanged bewildered glances.

"What you done that one can hear, one can't?"

"Oh, Alex," Flora got up, put her arms around Alex. "We don't have *any* luck."

Alex was patting her shoulder gently.

"Let your mama catch you hugging."

Alex's hand slowed perceptibly under Clio's eyes.

Then I heard Flora's tearful voice. "It had to happen *now*."

"It's all right, Flora. It's all right." But there was no conviction in Alex's voice.

Clio's eyes were sharpened with certainty. "What yawl done?"

A silence hung over the room.

Flora pulled away from Alex, turned, including me as an object of her defiance, her face flushed with excitement, impulsive resolve. "We got *married*, that's what! Alex and I got *married* in Warren yesterday, and we came out here to tell Mama and Daddy. It was *Daddy* I was going to tell."

Without looking at Alex she reached for his hand, gripped it tight against her side.

"Please God, I reckon! You done grieved Miss Amy again! How-come you got to crowd misery in one day?"

"Misery!" Flora returned. "Is that what everybody out here thinks of *my* marriage? The most important event in *my* life?"

Alex was looking from Flora to Clio uncertainly.

"Daddy *knew* I was going to get married," Flora said defensively. "I told him right here in this room. *He* put his arm around me. Said I had to live my life. My poor daddy!" Tears were trembling in her eyes.

"How-come you didn't tell—Miss Amy?"

"Because, because Mama doesn't—understand! You don't want to—hurt Mama. After Blunt died I didn't want to hurt her any more."

"Hurt less, you'd *told* her."

"Oh, Clio, you know Daddy *understands* me. He *knows* how people are."

"Your mammy knows more'n you think. One day, you see."

Clio was buttoning up her coat. "I'm going to git them suitcases. Whar you aim to *sleep*? You and *him*?"

Alex looked as if he'd just realized that he was included. He moistened his dry lips. His face had drained of blood. "Flora," he said pleadingly, "why don't we go back to town?"

"Alex," she said sternly, "you are my husband. I am your wife. We're going to *stay* here until I find out something! This is my own poor daddy's house."

"What you better do," Clio said at the door, "is study 'bout helping your mammy, stid of yourself."

"Oh," Flora exclaimed after Clio's departing figure, "when is she coming back?"

"Flora," Alex spoke out—he was working at the knot of his tie again, "why do we have to tell her at *all*? Why do we have to be so *quick*?"

Flora looked at Alex for a second. Her moistened blue eyes seemed larger. A streak had been left across the powder on her cheek. "I'm not *ashamed*," she said. "Are *you?*"

"No use worry her with everything all at once. Your daddy—"

"But we've *told* Clio."

"*Talk* to her."

"I can't *talk* to Clio. Nobody out here is on my side." Then the distraught girl turned to me. "They're *all* against me. Always have been. Everybody except my poor daddy."

Her lips trembled. "They think Louisa can't *do* anything wrong. But I'm not *like* her. She's just as *wild* about Tanner Haynes. It doesn't fool *me*. But Mama and Clio!"

My attention encouraged her. She looked at me, an ally, with alerted interest.

"Tanner Haynes is the—*wildest* man. But I'm not going to *tell* some things I know. He *goes* with two or three older women. *Everybody* knows it. But he was a *hero*, and his name is Haynes. That's all that matters. If you're *named* right. All my life I've had things like *that* to contend with." She looked at me pleadingly.

Alex Cary stood helplessly.

"Mama is old enough now to know that family isn't *everything*. Yet she'll let Louisa *dote* on Tanner Haynes. Doesn't say a word. Alex would have been just as much of a hero as Tanner. But he wasn't *old* enough to go. Tanner's too old for Louisa. I *always* thought he understood *me* better'n he did Louisa."

Flora's nervous excitement seemed to have tired her. She sat down. "Oh, Alex," she exclaimed, "please give me *some* support."

Alex came over to her chair and took her hand. Vexation weighed heavily on his face.

Seeing them holding to each other, I was disconcerted to see how abruptly their youthful ardor had been chilled.

Alex now, his hair disheveled, his blue eyes dulled with perplexity, was seriously considering me.

"What do you think we *ought* to do? Tell Mrs. Prescott today or wait? I can wait."

Then Flora's eyes sharpened a little.

"Suppose we *tell* her," she said. "What on earth could Mama *do*? Nothing," she added.

I watched Flora lost in some revealing recollection of her own.

"Maybe Mama *would* understand. Used to talk to us about Daddy so much, saying he *needed* to be himself, you couldn't *keep* anybody all to yourself. Told us people cared in *different* ways. You had to let them go."

CHAPTER TWENTY-TWO

During the hour or so that followed before Clio burst back into the room with the news of Miss Amy's return, Flora and Alex sat in nervous waiting, pacing back and forth to a window to look for the surrey.

From the plantation desk behind the hearth chair, I picked up a photograph of Miss Amy and a handsome youth in uniform. The two were standing against the graceful curve of the wrought-iron railing on the fan of steps in front of the house. With his hands barely resting on the shoulders of his mother, the young man stood a little to the side on the higher step behind, looking down at her profile. His uniform was pressed, trim, yet unexposed to the stretch and stain of any march. A smile had come to the black eyes of his clean-cut youthful face. Evidently just discovered by Miss Amy, the brim of his cap barely looked over the braid of her dark hair. She'd raised a protesting hand at the black-covered tripod, but her full dark eyes, so much like those of her son, were lit with pleasure. How odd it seemed to catch her in this rare second of pride and fullness. This picture couldn't have been taken more than four or five years before, but the contrast with the woman who'd left in the surrey this morning was remarkable. There before me, in her proud eyes, was an incommunicable, a complete fulfillment of her own. I thought of Ella Fitzpatrick's startled meeting with Amy standing over an unpacked suitcase in *her* father's house on that day long ago: Amy's anguished, bewildered cry: all she'd wanted was to be herself!

From behind me I heard Flora's uncertain voice, "That's my brother Blunt you're looking at. Everybody that comes out here says that he *looks* like Tanner Haynes. But he *doesn't*. Blunt was better looking and just as much of a hero. How can you be so much of a hero and come *back?*" she said. Then she added, "Alex looks just as much like Blunt as Tanner does. Alex was just not *raised* in a saddle the way they were."

The town youth took the picture from me and studied it with curiosity.

"Was this him with his picture in the *newspapers?*" he asked, his eyes wide.

"*Doesn't* Alex look a little like Blunt?" Flora appealed to me.

Only the fondest eyes could have seen any likeness between the thin sandy-haired boy and the dark-eyed manly face of the uniformed youth.

"He's *heavier*," Alex Cary said.

"But you just watch Mama hear *any*body say that Blunt looks like anybody. *Nobody* looks like Blunt. Not in this world."

She added in a moment, "She won't *ever* get over it. Me and Louisa and Otway put together couldn't make up the difference for him."

I hadn't noticed until then that the photograph had been one of a pair on the desk: the other was that of the lean, benign, clear-eyed face of Amy's father with his white senatorial locks brushed back behind his ears. The picture now hit me strangely. Was it all *his* need, his loneliness for his wife, that had kept him from seeing his daughter's separate, silent longing?

Alex Cary was looking at the photograph now with complete absorption. He exclaimed to the room—the realization had just struck him—"He was *killed!* Flora," he asked in amazement, "do you *remember* him?"

For Alex Cary, with his unlined face, memory was yet to include the tragic and the lost.

"Of course, I *remember* Blunt. He was my *brother*," she

said impatiently. "I remember when he left after that picture was taken. Mama standing on the steps waving and smiling, brave as you please, just like he was going hunting. And five minutes later she was *shut up* in her room. The buggy just out of sight. Wouldn't let *any* of us in. Not even Papa. Stayed two whole days. All Papa did was pace the floor, call at Mama's door. I *did* take her supper that second night. Mama must have learned from somebody not kin to me to suffer by herself. I can't hide *anything*." She spoke as if she'd been denied part of her inheritance.

Flora's eyes, dry now, were reflective with private wonder. Alex was looking at her soberly, his eyes fixed on the yellow rose bud, the sparkling pin.

"Mama was sitting by the window, where she could look over the fields. Dark circles were under her eyes. Hadn't slept, hadn't changed clothes. Her face was white, frightened, almost like she wasn't even sure who *I* was. I started crying, told her to please come downstairs. Cutting herself off wasn't doing any good. She said, 'Leave me this time! This *one* time! I'm tired, Flora. I'm tired.'"

Then Flora looked at me absently, a little removed by the pull of her memory. "That's the only time I *ever* saw Mama give up. Not like that even when they *told* her about Blunt at the last.

"I couldn't understand her feeling like that when she *hadn't* lost him, he hadn't even *got* to the war. It was more like Mama *knew* something, remembered something. Just sitting there, saying she was tired, tired, tired.

"She was *always* funny about Blunt. He was *hers*. Never felt like he was Daddy's at all."

Flora, sitting there in her gray woolen wedding dress, the rose on her shoulder drooping, her face flushed with the unkind emptiness of the moment, seemed to remember all at once that her father *was* wounded.

"How *bad* is my daddy hurt?" She looked at me. Her lips trembled. "He was the one I was going to *tell*. I thought I had *one* friend. Daddy *always* took up for me. Like he knew we were *kin*."

She sat there in reflective unhappy silence. "Only time I ever saw Mama *mad*. Blunt and I were the oldest. If he wasn't playing with the little niggers, he had to take me. Dared me all the time to do what he did. I followed him across the log over the creek, and I fell in. Looked like a drowned rat. Papa saw us coming back. Didn't say a *word*. Just walked up and *slapped* Blunt hard.

"But Mama saw *him*.

"'Raleigh Prescott,' she called out. I'd *never* heard Mama call him that. 'Don't you touch my child.' *My* child! All of us were so startled, even Blunt, we just *looked* at her. Mama's face, for once, was furious. Hadn't ever seen her like that. She grabbed Blunt by the hand and led him off. Left me and Papa just standing there. And Papa's face was red. Papa almost hung his head. Just *stood* there, looking at *nothing*, not saying a word. Then, presently, he just leaned over and patted my head."

Flora was almost tearful, remembering this. "Oh, Alex," she burst out, "if anything happens to Daddy, I don't know what we'll *do!*"

She stood up, walked over to the window and back.

"We can wait," Alex said.

She appeared not to hear him. She was looking at the wilting rose on her dress. Tears came to her eyes again.

"But Mama *lost* Blunt," she said quietly. "Every time I look at her now I can't help thinking she *knew* she was going to."

She unhooked the pin, slowly pulled the yellow petals from her wedding dress.

CHAPTER TWENTY-THREE

We hadn't heard the surrey in the driveway.

Clio stuck her head in the room. "She back. She back too early!"

Miss Amy's tireless attendant, half in, half out, of her coat, her face gaunt and distracted, was spreading alarm in her wake. It came to me, watching the flash of her eyes in the door, that there was for her no security other than that which the moment gave, other than that she'd learned to read in Miss Amy's face. It was impossible to see Clio sitting in a room by herself.

"Wait, Clio, wait!" Flora called out. "Don't say *anything* to Mama now about—"

"Think I'm going to *add* to what she got?"

Then Flora's eyes widened with fright. "Clio," she burst out. "What did you do with *his* suitcase? If it's in my room, take it *out!*"

Alex Cary stood up. His pale blue eyes flashed. "If you feel so all-powerful strong about it, I'll take it out myself. In fact," he added, "I can get in the buggy and go home, same way I came out here."

"Oh, no, Alex," Flora, completely distraught, turned toward him. "I didn't mean *that!* But for a little while— tomorrow maybe—we've *got* to wait."

"I don't want to be the tail to anybody's kite. Not even yours, Flora! You can have Tanner and Blunt and all the rest of 'em!" He sat down.

"Oh, Alex," she looked at him pleadingly. "You're *all* I've got."

"Sometimes, I can't tell."

"Alex," Flora looked at him with concern, "don't you *know?*"

"Not since I got out here. I'm not sure. Been wondering who the heck *I* was!"

"Are you jealous, already?"

"Didn't marry the whole blasted family, I hope."

"Alex, Alex, *please* stand by me!"

"You Prescotts think you're everybody! But you're not!"

"That doesn't *sound* like you."

"Nobody wants to be left *all* the way out!"

"You know better than that! It just *couldn't* have happened at a *worse* time."

She went over to him, leaned down and kissed his cheek.

Then, mollified, but still sitting, he said, "Just don't forget you're married to *me,* not everybody else. My daddy's *brother* was somebody in that war, too. Tanner Haynes and Blunt weren't the *only* soldiers!"

Miss Amy's questioning about the Carys flashed through my mind. Even to an outsider it was shocking to realize that the son of Abner Cary had married into this house. I was surprised at the little twist of resentment I felt.

Otway was the first to enter the room. The boy's eyes were red from sleeplessness and fatigue.

He barely noticed Flora and Alex before he sat down, dropped his chin into two cupped hands, and began to stare into the fire.

Alex got up from his chair. He and Flora glanced at each other nervously. Otway's visible exhaustion quickly registered on their faces.

Otway still wore the short trousers and jacket which legs and arms had outgrown. Hardening boy's hands showed a tenseness of disbelief.

Finally Flora said timidly, "Aren't you going to speak?"

"There's a lot to say, Flora," he said evenly, flatly. "Want me to *welcome* you home?" The soberness in Otway's voice was ominous. He didn't look back. Shoulders bent toward the fire.

"At least," Flora ventured, still softly, "you can be polite —to—our *company.*"

"*Polite?*" he turned slowly. There were dark circles beneath his eyes. A fuzz of hair caught the firelight on his cheek and chin. "Company?"

He looked at them together in amazement: at Flora's gray woolen dress, Alex's blue coat, stiff collar. Flora's hand flew to the jeweled bar which had held the rose bud.

"Flora," he said, "while you've been to a party—in case you're interested—your daddy has had an accident. Your daddy might lose his leg. He almost lost his *life.*" Then he added, "I think, maybe, you might want to know."

Never before had Flora heard cutting sarcasm from that young voice.

All at once she burst out crying.

Alex Cary stepped over, put his arm round her shoulder.

Between sobs, she was muttering, "That's *cruel,* that's *cruel* to me. I *love* my daddy. I *love* my daddy. I *always* have. More than *any* of you."

Otway stood up. He had frightened himself. A painful frown came to his face.

"Oh, Flora," he said, "we've *all* got to grow up. We've *all—*" he stopped. Tears trembled in his eyes, and he turned away toward the mantel.

Alex's face went white, his hand dropped from Flora's shoulder.

It was then that I knew Miss Amy had returned. She was standing there. Her eyes were on Flora.

"My poor child, have I neglected you so? *You* were his, daughter. I know now. *You* were his."

Silence cut through the room. Everybody turned to look at the woman returned, pale and alone, in the doorway.

She'd taken off her hat, unbuttoned the black coat of her suit at the neck. Graying braids of hair circling her head showed the pressure of the hat she'd removed. But her appealing eyes were tired and lusterless. I thought of the forgotten picture on the plantation desk: of that one far-away moment of fulfillment when Blunt in unstained uniform went away from her side, taking with him what the lonesome woman had to give. Not her father's, not her husband's, but her own.

"My dear child," she said, looking at Flora's distraught, bewildered face. "Hasn't your father *talked* to you, Flora? Did he say *anything*? Daughter, your father *loved* you!"

Standing there, Miss Amy seemed to see us all, to remember the separate closed hearts of each of us in the room.

Without speaking, Flora went over, dropped her head upon her shoulder. Miss Amy took her daughter in her arms.

"Oh, Mama," Flora murmured, "is Daddy all right?"

"All right?" Miss Amy repeated. She clutched her daughter to her. The simple words seemed to have pained her with their youth.

"Your father is ill, Flora. Your father is ill."

"I've got to go see Daddy, I've *got* to go." Flora was sobbing. "I'd die if Daddy thought I didn't care. He *can't* think that! I was *gone*, Mama. I *was* gone. Everybody but me was here!"

Miss Amy was holding her daughter back, looking into her troubled face. Had she known so little about the girl? "Maybe *I* wasn't there, Flora. After this morning, I don't know, I don't know. I wasn't there, and I *could* have been."

"Flora," Otway, his voice hoarse, spoke out, "Flora, Daddy doesn't *want* to see you. He doesn't want to see anybody. Louisa and I didn't see him." He hesitated, then said slowly, quietly, not yet believing his own words, "He wouldn't even see Mama."

Flora dropped her arm from her mother's shoulder. "*You* haven't seen Daddy?" She barely whispered the words.

I hesitated to look at Miss Amy.

Finally her quiet answer, perfectly controlled, came from a privacy that for a moment was like an unfamiliar presence in the room. "*Raleigh*," she said, "is an ill man now. We need more help than we give each other. I *should* have known."

"Mama, Mama," Flora said.

I couldn't take it in at first that Miss Amy's words were meant for me. "Geoffrey, this has been a terrible time for you. But we need you badly. I'm going to rest now, but later on I want to talk to you."

Now she saw the silent, waiting, unknown Alex Cary. For Miss Amy, this lone boy was another so-late glimpse of an ever changing past. Impulsively her hand went out.

"This is Alex—?" she spoke hesitantly.

"Alex *Cary*, Mama! Oh, Mama, you know that Alex is a —friend of mine in Warren!"

The boy took a step forward.

Miss Amy reached out for his hand. "Oh, Flora, *please* forgive me. Forgive me, this time." She spoke beseechingly to her daughter, "I knew so little about people in Warren, so little, so little."

CHAPTER TWENTY-FOUR

When I told Miss Amy to send word whenever she wanted to talk to me, I left her to go to her room and Flora and Alex to separate their yet unpacked suitcases under Clio's eyes. Clio had told the forlorn couple that, sooner or later, the devil took his half. They'd looked at her blankly, as if they'd never seen her wrinkled prophetic old face before.

Only Otway was left in the room. Perhaps he was then beginning to put into words what the real emptiness around him was: his longer and longer separations from Louisa.

It was a fine autumn day outside. After the obscuring wet chill of the day before, which seemed to stretch the world no farther than the sound of your voice, the sky was bright, clear, and faraway. The air itself smelled fresh and green, cleansed of insects and tatters of fall mists. There was a spring-like freshness and sharpness of line upon distant trees and roof-tops. It was as if a dark landscape painting had been cleaned during the night, reviving farther and farther depths of hidden life.

Too, there was a strange silence round the house and yard. Whatever had swept the skies had pulled with it all close-to-earth sounds.

This spring-like day had put the past itself to rout.

On the front walk with the graceful fan of steps behind me, I was surprised at how little I'd seen on the miserable ride out.

Except for a few scattered tags of clinging foliage riding as high as birds' nests, the vaulting limbs of the old oaks had been stripped of leaves, leaving the black ink tracing of a forgotten calligraphy against the blue still sky. Ground underfoot was ankle-deep in gold-draining leaves.

A row of crape myrtles curving with my path had peeled white and bony. Long runners of moss were stitching the sunken brick of the walk into the earth.

Unexpectedly the ground in front of me dropped. Two steps down put me on the level of an old garden. Walks bordered with untrimmed English box were all but lost in the maze. Only a central circle enclosing an ivy-covered bird-bath remained visible. I hesitated to follow out any of the paths for fear of what lurked hidden below.

Beyond the garden and a falling picket fence loomed the cavernous mouth of a barn.

For a minute I stood inside its dark entrance out of sunlight. Then the silent gloom of the lofty roof was netted with pinpoints and trembling arrows of yellow sun. A larger shaft of light lay across a row of silent stalls, bringing to life great whorls and loops of silver spider webs. The thick pungency of the air in the barn was that of dried manure and infinitely powdered rat-ground corn. Once the splintered planks of these stalls had clattered through the night from the restless explosive feet of horses and mules, holding the mice momentarily silent before they started scurrying again.

I followed the road from the barn to the pink row of slave quarters which glimpsed distantly the day before had seemed to be sinking in summers and summers of growth.

The choked thread of a path led me to the first sagging door. As far as I could see stretched a row of eyeless shells. Raleigh Prescott's domain had once been large indeed!

Over the sinking threshold, the fireplace was filled with a lifeless crumble of mortar and brick. Remarkably, an old poker still lay across the hearth. I thrust it into the fallen brick and uncovered a wet layer of black ashes. Rain and sun through empty doors and windows had swollen and bleached the plank flooring. The trap door to the loft was

open, where once a ladder for the children had reached.
Dark stains of spreading mold softened the gray-white plaster walls. Forever inescapable was the damp mustiness of a
room once crowded with Negro life.

When I stepped out the back to the ground, I could see
a dead weedless circle. Here, I knew, a big black pot on
three bricks had steamed and curled with smoke.

It was at that moment that I heard the dry cracking of
brush. It came from some distance in the thicket behind the
house. It startled me, for until now I'd had an almost soundless walk.

I stood still, ankle-deep in weeds.

Suddenly the cracking of dead leaves and twigs under
foot came again. As abruptly it stopped. It occurred to me
that it was the watchful tread of an animal, perhaps that of
the red bony cow I'd seen the day before, or that of a stray
hog or goat.

Then, turning toward the vine-tangled undergrowth, I
saw a quick dip of a late-autumn red bough of a dogwood
tree. A tearing of cloth, a scraping of bark, then a long subdued *Ou-u-ch.*

From the edge of the thicket, I called in. A whimpering
child's voice, abject in surrender, came back: "Hit's me."

"Who?"

"Mama know who I is," the child said.

Finding a way in, I saw, three or four yards away, sitting
flat in a tangle of briars, a little Negro boy, about six years
old. His smooth skin was coal black. The black wool on his
head was as close as a piece of knitting. He'd torn his shirt
front wide open in falling from the tree. Big white eyes
were fixed on me. A fine pin-stripe of blood ran across his
flat chest.

"Mama know who I is," he defended himself.

"You lost?"

"You go'n *git* me?"

For the first time he saw the trickle of blood. His lips trembled.

"Jeremiah, whar you at?" A woman's voice, almost a whisper, came through the thicket.

There in a moment, between parted brush, peered a face I remembered. It was Sis Hannah I'd seen running across the yard the day before, the dog behind her, bringing to Pettigrew the first alarm.

Looking at me cautiously for a minute, she stepped forward. "You what he heered?" Then thrusting her hand toward the child to pull him up without looking at him, she said, "Ain't nobody told you to climb nare tree. Said see who was that *lurking*."

"Mah, *he* go'n *git* me?"

"Hish, boy." She thrust the child behind her. Sis Hannah was dressed for traveling. She was weighted with clothes. She wore a man's hat over a red headrag, a brown threadbare coat buttoned up and bulging over dress, jacket and apron. Thin wrists reached from sleeves that were rounded and packed. Her walnut-dark face was alive with darting distrustful eyes. What she needed was a winter of snow and ice to invade.

"What you aim to do? I ain't got nothing 'longs out here. Nothing that me and Little Man ain't *sot, slept* or *et* on. Let Mr. Raleigh—any of 'em—see for hisself, unload the wagon piece by piece. Wagon and mule borrowed, too—go'n be brought back. You come—see."

The woman was almost frantic in the web of her defense.

"There ain't no law says we can't leave, can't walk off *any* time, day or night. What you aim to do?"

But her agitated claims of rights sounded thin in her own ears. A wonder flashed through her mind: "You ain't some kind of patter-roller, done been sont back?"

When I shook my head, she still wasn't convinced. "Look at them doorsteps behind you! Ever' last one done walked off! *Been* walked off! Taking pot and pan and rocking-cheer.

Plenty that won't theirs. Glass out er windows. Mr. Raleigh hisself said it: 'You got to let 'em go.' Dey laughed in Pettigrew's face."

"Sis Hannah," a man's voice came through the thicket, "who be you talking to?"

She didn't bother to answer, but still watching my face said, "You come—see."

Pulling the child along behind her, she plunged back through the brush, leaving a broken path for me to follow.

A few yards beyond in a narrow clearing I saw the mule's gray ears.

Then there in front of me was a wagon weighted-down with a pile of spilling furniture, looped and tied with plow-lines. Shuck mattresses, broken chairs, up-ended tables, black pots and pans.

Sis Hannah, pointing, said, "Ain't nare thing hidden in that-there wagon 'cept what we done *slept, sot,* or *et* on, got claim to. Onliest reason we tooken this covered-up, played-out road was to keep from worrying Miss Amy to death, riding in broad daylight by her door."

"Mah, he the one go'n *git* us if we don't shet our mouf?"

I hadn't noticed before the second child sitting on the floor of the wagon, almost hidden under the collapsing load of furniture. Big white eyes in a black little face watched every step I made. "Let he *git* Jeremiah," the frightened child said. "Jeremiah *et* the bistits offen de table."

Jeremiah turned a startled face toward his brother.

The lines on the mule were dangling. The driver had gone.

"Whar Little Man?" Sis Hannah asked.

The boy's face in the wagon brightened. "Let *he*," pointing to me, "*git* Little Man. Little Man hiding a pig."

Sis Hannah jerked toward me. "His'n, too! Fed 'im a day old! Pettigrew ain't no friend of Little Man's. Is scared of a scolding." She stopped. "Come out them bushes, Little Man, pulling that pig behind you. *Tole* you he was your'n."

All faces turned toward the trampling in the bushes. In a second we could hear protesting squeals. Little Man had a cord around the pig's neck and was pulling him helter-skelter through the briars.

From a network of honeysuckle Little Man peered out at me.

Sis Hannah turned, looked me up and down, said, "Who you?"

When I told her, she called back over her shoulder, "Ain't nobody sont him looking, Little Man. Step out."

The figure that appeared had a cocked eye, a toothless mouth, and a vacant face. He wasn't over five feet tall, but he had muscled arms and a thick chest. An old hog horn on a heavy string looped from his shoulder.

"Was the hog feeder on the plantation long as there was hogs. Mind done faded a little. Forgits there ain't none. Keeps on looking. Comes home night-fall, all wore out. Keeps that little white pig tied up. Ain't go'n let him go."

I asked Sis Hannah where *they* were going.

"Whar the rest gone! Warren!" she said as if I should have known. "Little Man got *powers*. Don't *nobody* bother him. Folks comes to him from everywhere. Puts his cocked eye on misery—mind or body. Two days time, hit's gone; 'cept hard cases, takes three. Hard cases brings two chickens, two dozen eggs. Git in the wagon, Little Man. Man ain't no patter-roller. Gov'mint done opened the gates, cleared the roads."

Little Man placed the squealing pig in the wagon; then, looking at me uncertainly, climbed to the wagon seat.

"You thinks, this back way, that we creeping off. We ain't. Hit's *him* didn't want to drive off. Past the big house. He *l-o-v-e-s* Miss Amy more'n he do anybody. More'n me. One time they was go'n take him off. Had him in the wagon, Pettigrew telling him to set still. Miss Amy came out, shook her head at all 'em. Say let him down. Say *this* was his home. 'Longed here much as *anybody* 'longed here, 'clud-

ing her. Learned him how to tell weeds from flowers, which
stalk to pull."

She paused a minute, turned to look at Little Man.

"You know, notion strikes him, he go'n jump out that
wagon 'fore we git to Warren, and run all the way home."

Burdened with all the clothes she possessed on her back,
it was hard for Sis Hannah to climb into the wagon.

"Wouldn't e'em *take* him," she said as much to herself as
to me, "but this place has been *prophesied* on. What Mr.
Raleigh done yistiddy was a signal and a sign and a burning bush. Birds feel the cold a hunnerd miles off. Mices
sneak out 'fore a house catches fire. What Mr. Raleigh done
was handwriting on the walls." Her mind that had been
racing for the last twenty-four hours seemed to have slowed
down a little. The great uncertainty of the open gate ahead
was closer than she'd stopped to think. But she added in a
moment, "My mammy didn't *never* git over her broken leg.
Prophesied on."

With Little Man beside her, with the two big-eyed boys
looking out from under the broken furniture, Sis Hannah
picked up the reins. But she hesitated to give them a pull.

Her face clouded over, her dry lips quivered. Looking
straight ahead, she said, "You see Miss Amy, tell her do she
need me *bad*, me and Little Man, we come back."

I heard the wheels turning and watched the slow creaking
wagon down the played-out road.

CHAPTER TWENTY-FIVE

Remembering the urgency in Miss Amy's voice when she told me after her unexpectedly short trip to the Haynes place that she had to talk to me, I started back to the house.

This hidden road which Sis Hannah had followed to escape Miss Amy's eye was no more than two wheel ruts through wagon-scraped weeds. Overhanging growth—sumac, and the ever present shiny green of myrtles—had all but choked out the road. I could see the crushed path Sis Hannah's wagon had left. Flattened weeds making a kind of greenish silver wake were slowly rising back. Along the roadside, branches were stripped fresh of leaves and here and there shredded. Sis Hannah's wagon was taking along with it to Warren many a snagged weed and many a torn leaf.

Rather than retrace my steps through the thicket to the slave quarters, I took this path on back.

The trees on both sides of the road were almost bare, letting yellow sunlight filter through to damp hidden places on the ground untouched by sun since winter. The carpeting below the bare branches under splinters and shafts of sun was brown and gold. Midday picked out every squirrel and bird nest overhead. Only a pine and a holly rising from drying brush, like winter sentinels finally arrived, remained dark green. Sparkling high-hanging mistletoe, independent of vine tangles below, answered from branch to lofty branch.

In only a minute or two I was to find out that the path I followed led into the road we'd passed the night before, going from the Prescott plantation to the Haynes place.

My approach was almost soundless over the dampened leaves.

It was just before my way entered the traveled road that I heard the voices and stopped.

From my protective cover I could see the back of the buggy and Tanner Haynes' horse. He'd stopped at a wide place, a half circle, evidently used for turning. The horse was drinking from a hollowed-out cypress log as long as an Indian canoe, which had blackened with age. Around the basin it was edged with moss and looked over by sprays of fern. From a cold sweating pipe leading from a mound of black slick rocks came a slow dripping of water into the rippling surface.

Tanner and Louisa were sitting apart in the buggy. Louisa was looking straight ahead. The reins were slack. Tanner, bent forward, was absently tapping at a weed with his black whip. Neither of them was paying any attention to the watering horse.

The silence that separated them for the moment was the silence that conversation on the way had led them to. It was the moment of their uncertainty about where the hour and their loneness had brought them.

Louisa's figure was perfectly still as if in numb acceptance of whatever it was she was to hear.

Only Tanner's gentle tapping of the weed betrayed reluctance, searching, delay, surprisingly for me, for I'd seen no hesitation in his direct dark eyes. He'd looked about the day before as if he alone saw through and beyond people, not even believing that he himself was seen.

As they sat apart so lost in this one moment of their lives, it was Louisa's need—hers was a solitary waiting figure—that somehow seemed final and complete. It was the sudden and disturbing wonder of what his need was that moved Tanner's slowly tapping, reflective hand.

I'd never felt silence so throbbing with currents unrevealed.

Had the events of the last twenty-four hours been for them a leap in time? Advanced, for Tanner Haynes, the waiting, deeply responding, undemanding girl into sudden womanhood? Was this what delayed the passage of the buggy taking her home from her stricken father's side?

So, once, Miss Amy had left her father with an innocent knowledge of awakening love, with an innocent knowledge even of her father's love.

The jacket that stretched across Tanner Haynes' firm shoulders was taut with an independent, achieved life. The scattered brief glimpses of that self-contained lone figure came back to me.

He must have been ten or twelve years older than Louisa. Hers was a fragile girlhood at his side. Was it the image of the gallant and lost brother that Tanner brought back to her? It was in the shadow of this man that Flora had measured the youthful Alex Cary. And the others? Tanner Haynes seemed to have eluded them all. His, I knew, had been a man's outdoor world. A disillusionment I was yet to understand had been his childhood school. Feared and followed in the Army, he was disturbed now by an innocence he'd never quite believed, seemingly resentful of any beguilement from a way he'd already found.

The stillness of the day carried voices as the breathless hour before sunset carries them across an open harvested field.

"When I left here," Tanner was speaking slowly, thoughtfully, recovering for himself what way had brought them here, "Blunt and I were carrying you on our shoulders to get you across a creek." In a moment he added, "There are years between us, Louisa. You don't understand." And his whip was going absently over the weeds.

Louisa's quiet voice came steadily, quietly. It was touched with a sadness that a sleepless night had found.

"Nobody believes that I have grown up. Mama doesn't.

Mama fears it for me. I can tell it in her eyes. I think only Flora and Otway know. Not even you."

Tanner turned to look at her. Black searching eyes rested on the fragile figure, seeing resentfully, perhaps for the first time, the woman, the need, remembering the girl with ribbons in her hair fondled by an older brother, "I don't know how to tell you, Louisa." There was a long pause. "I haven't had a sheltered life. You can't believe I'm not your kind."

"I know," she returned steadily, "that my brother Blunt wanted to be like you."

"There were things I could teach him."

"I know that my father went to you and Wakefield—that he left home."

"We let him be what he was."

"Mama didn't let him?"

"He couldn't live up to her."

There was a long silence.

"I never understood your mother," he said. "Not until this morning. Her blood was always too rare for me. I didn't quite believe her, Louisa. I don't quite believe you. How did you and Flora get to be sisters?"

For the first time she turned to look at the man at her side. Finally she said, "Did you and Blunt carry *Flora* on your shoulders?"

He answered with a directness that surprised me, "Flora has always been older than you." Tanner now was looking at Louisa. "Or *was* she?"

She said evenly, "I've never been sure what older was." Then she added after a minute, "And I've never been sure about what you've always wanted to say about my mother's blood being too rare for you. You've said it before. Unless it was in her that you've always recognized yourself."

Tanner's whip was suddenly still over the wheel.

"I've always known it," Louisa added. "You two are lonelier than any people I know. Whatever her rare blood means, it's what you've got. There's a—a purity—I don't know any other word—about you both. You could have been her child."

"Good God, girl, what are you talking about? Your mother and I live at opposite ends of the world."

A frown over his dark eyes, he looked at her as though trying to relate the words to the girl at his side.

After a moment she said, "That's what everybody but me believes."

"Miss Amy and me? Good God, Louisa!"

She went on. "Just as much as Mama ever did, you still carry a childhood memory of what the world, of what people, could have been. What is it—the curse of—I said 'purity?' Of being older, of knowing more? Has nobody ever lived up to what you wanted or expected of them? Now you don't expect anything of anybody. You don't believe anybody. No motive is pure. You've come to terms with everybody's failures. Just to protect yourself."

In a moment Tanner Haynes added so quietly that I could barely hear him, "I saw some brave men in the army."

Louisa added, without even turning her head, "And they were all killed. They and you alone knew what the world was meant to be about. It's what you've got that nobody has ever touched. The rest of us—don't matter. We're just—people. Disappointment is so old in you—that you won't even let *anybody* get close. Not anybody that *cares*. You've picked people that don't *care*. Is that what keeps you going? Knowing you can't *hurt* them?"

"Listen, girl, I'm too old for you. I told you we carried you across the creek on our shoulders."

"It would be easier for us all to let time stop. We wouldn't have to change what we remember. There you and Mama are again. You've named the one difference between you. She has practiced a self-delusion. She's still looking, still trying to believe that things might be what she once thought they should. Bitterness has never destroyed her charity. It hasn't destroyed yours. You tell yourself that's all people can do and take what little there is, and go your lonely way. Sometimes, I don't know who is right, who is older. You two understand each other without saying a word. And you talk about her blood being too rare for you."

After a long pause—the whip was still motionless on the buggy wheel—he said, "How is your mother going to face what happened this morning? What happened at my house?"

Without hesitation, Louisa said, "She's going to explain it to us, the way she's always explained my father to us. Oh, Tanner, I know better."

He said, "It's a way she's found to live."

"And yours not to let anybody mean anything to you any more?"

A long silence came between them.

Finally he burst out, "Good God, Louisa, I've had—" He stopped short of his word. "You know your mother is afraid of me. Doesn't want me to see you."

"Because she knows how much you *can* mean—to any girl—to—me."

She spoke the words so honestly, so naturally, he turned suddenly, put out his hand impulsively as if to touch her hair, her cheek. But in the quiet of the moment which held her waiting, unmoving figure, he drew back his arm abruptly. "I'm going to take you home, Louisa." His cheeks reddened beneath his dark unrelenting eyes. "God strike me if I'm not fair with you."

She echoed his word so faintly that I wasn't sure I'd heard. "Fair?" It seemed such a fragile word to carry such a burden of loneness.

"You need to help your father," he spoke almost sharply, as if he had recovered himself, had restored the distance between them."

"I can only do that by living myself."

"Will your mother resent Wakefield—after this morning?"

Louisa slowly shook her head.

"God, what a lonely man *he's* been."

The wheels of the buggy had begun to turn almost imperceptibly as though from some impulse of their own.

I watched the two separated unmoving silent figures in the buggy until the road turned into the undergrowth.

CHAPTER TWENTY-SIX

I had sat down on a stump near the old waterlogged black-ened trough when I heard the slow steps of the mule through the drying weeds. The tread into the sun's brief winter meeting with the leaf-covered earth was so quiet that it seemed like a discovery time had made of a neglected place. The steps of the mule pulled the silence of the woods behind them to erase their prints. It was not surprising in a moment to see the figure of Wakefield, a lonely rider, on the white mule. I knew that his directionless ride was away from rather than toward a meeting.

He looked at me as if he couldn't remember to what recent hour I belonged. I was just within the net of his memory.

He drew up at the trough, his long legs dangling from the saddleless mule. I remembered that I hadn't seen Wake-field in daylight. He was looking down at me from the spreading edge of the present moment's forward wave. He wore a fresh white starched shirt. The graying of black hair over light brown skin and distant black eyes gave him a sensitive, almost ascetic, face. He struck me as an older, darkened and, somehow—I saw without knowing why—a finally defeated Tanner Haynes. At the moment so many of his years seemed behind him.

Just the night before, under lamplight and under the rest-less flickering of flame from the stove, when he had the letter in his hand, his eyes had held an urgency, an intensity of remembering, almost as if in anguished hope of some return. Now it was the absence of any seeking in his eyes which held me. I was at a loss to know what the few short hours had done. With an unseeing gaze he looked at me.

Expressing no surprise at finding me there, showing neither pleasure nor resentment, he spoke presently out of quiet sadness rather than from any compulsion to know, "Is *she* all right?"

"She?"

"Miss Amy?"

"What was it, Wakefield? This morning?"

"Raleigh didn't want to see her. He told us to send her away."

He didn't even seem willing to pursue it.

I must have spoken with surprise. "Did the letters mean that much to him?"

Wakefield turned and looked down at me thoughtfully.

"It's Miss Amy I'm thinking about. I ain't ever done right by her—not in my mind. Seems like people don't ever get through learning. Folks don't stay the same even in the grave."

Whatever it was that brought the strange heaviness of reflection to his voice was completely lost on me. It didn't seem possible that anything could have happened so quickly to change his view of Katie Williams' lonely years.

"Katie Williams?" I murmured.

He shook his head almost with annoyance at my misjudgment. "No, no," he said. "Miss Amy been on my mind. Way I seen her this morning. First time in my life I saw my brother Raleigh through *her* eyes."

He waited a long time before he went on.

"A strange thing, Miss Amy standing there in that room with everybody around her, holding a basket of food too heavy for her, that she'd forgotten how heavy it was, like it was something she'd gotten used to carrying, so long without knowing it that she couldn't say where the hurt was. She had a black hat and a good dress on that people saw her in when she went to town, the people who remembered her and remembered how things used to be. And she was asking Mr. Tanner how his daddy was, what a winning man he used to be and how his mother had been such a beauty. And all of us—Mr. Tanner, Miss Louisa, me—were looking at the lonesome woman—her fine face, her brave eyes that had once been the face and eyes of such a beautiful girl with all the world before her, now not even asking for help, not even from her own daughter. And it came to me (and I think it came to them—they were watching) this is what the lonesome woman had been doing for years and years: saying the things that had to be said in this world, holding with all her courage to the thin thread of things that kept people from breaking apart from one another, the old from the young, and that kept her from sinking into emptiness, into the pain of seeing the helplessness of the people around her to be more than they were. What it was that had carried her on, what it was that was driving her now—meeting the sad faces looking at her, was maybe nothing more than the memory of older faces watching through time, or maybe it was just the habit of going on, the old habit of meeting expectation in the eyes of the young. Looking at her, I knew for the first time that all her life all she'd wanted, all she'd needed, was to have some one thing left to believe in, something of her own. Something besides memory. That basket of food was a last try."

Wakefield had dismounted from the mule so quietly that I felt I'd lost a minute in time. With his strong brown hand he was absently stroking the mule's flank.

"Pettigrew came out of brother Raleigh's room, closed the door behind him. Just stood there for a minute, not knowing what to do, not knowing what to say.

"'Raleigh?' Miss Amy murmured, a look of pain on her face.

"Pettigrew didn't even want to look at her, just looked down at the floor. For a minute seemed like there won't nobody in the room.

"Then Pettigrew said, 'He don't want to see nobody, Miss Amy. Said he don't feel like seeing nobody at all. It grieves me to be the one to say so to you.'

"Miss Louisa took a step toward her mama. Mr. Tanner was frowning. He was rubbing his chin. All at once there won't nothing between Miss Amy and herself. Her lips trembled a little. Her eyes were wet. All she said was, 'Raleigh, poor Raleigh.'

"You'd a-thought in that second Pettigrew had told her he was dead.

"And he was," Wakefield threw out, turning to look at me directly, as if he suddenly felt it necessary for me to understand.

"My brother Raleigh had killed what she'd made herself carry in her mind. He'd uncovered what all the years she hadn't wanted to see. Everybody in the room saw her trembling hand.

"Mr. Tanner walked over and took the basket of food that she was still holding and had forgotten out of her hands. For a second he just stood there with his hands on the basket, looking at her, like he was the only one in the room who knew it was some valuable thing he had to take. Like he was the only one in the room who could take it. They was looking at each other, two strangers that had met in a crowd and remembered each other from a long time back.

"Then Mr. Tanner was holding the basket. Miss Amy, not bothering to look at the rest of us, maybe not even remembering that we were there, said, 'Maybe it would have been better if I hadn't tried again.'"

Wakefield was sitting on the edge of the trough now, his legs apart, leaning forward on knee-supported arms.

"All through the years," he said in a minute, "I'd been thinking about what my brother Raleigh needed, how his life was divided, how he hadn't been sure for a whole day which way he ought to turn.

"And there she was, stepping out of the past in front of me, her life all of a sudden a heavier burden than his. She'd even lost Blunt—the one thing that reminded her of what life could have been.

"I knew this morning that my brother Raleigh couldn't ever have been what Miss Amy needed, couldn't ever live up to what she was looking for in the world.

"This morning he was just admitting it—once and for all —that she might as well stop looking, that he couldn't ever be anybody but himself. Not wanting to see her was just like saying to her that what she thought he was, wasn't there."

Wakefield got up from his seat on the trough.

"Trouble is that some lonesome folks like her don't get over the need to believe. Can't say to themselves: this is all there is.

"I learned quicker than Miss Amy. Mr. Tanner did, too. But don't let nobody tell you it's better to stop.

"It gave me a lift of spirits yesterday—a lift I didn't even know I could feel, when it struck me all at once that my brother Raleigh had come back to me to do what he done. Seemed almost like he'd come back home.

"I wish my brother Raleigh could have lived up to her. Maybe it's her—her searching, her needing, that makes the difference in the world."

Wakefield got on his mule. He looked around at the flickering sunlight under the bare trees, sunlight like falling yellow leaves.

"I'm going on back to see what I can do for Raleigh."

He looked down at me as if he remembered something I ought to know. "It'll be a while before we're able to move him. One thing you all are going to have to remember —maybe Miss Amy learned it this morning—after this, he's going to be her son."

CHAPTER TWENTY-SEVEN

It was hard for me to tell what had happened when, coming back toward the house, I saw the little crowd standing near Tanner Haynes' buggy at the end of the walk. All were facing Clio, a frail figure, trailing an armful of blankets. The wagon which we'd driven the night before to the Haynes place sat empty, unnoticed, in high grass across the road. It could have been abandoned for a season. A chicken sat imperturbably on the wagon seat. A half dozen white guineas looking out from a row of boxwood stood stock still, *karacking* desperately at this intrusion into their sun-streaked yard. Under the sketchy trees, the fall shadows lay so softly that the earth seemed to be absorbing them.

Flora, Alex Cary behind her, had come halfway down the walk. Under outdoor light, in their wedding clothes, they both were harshly disheveled. Flora's eyes were red, her blonde placed curls disarranged. Alex Cary, his tie loosened, looked as if he'd been traveling for days.

Tanner and Louisa at the step of the buggy, emerged from their separate way, confronted the unexpected, distraught couple.

It was the familiar Clio, secure within the tether of the need of another, now recovering the blankets which hadn't served for their father's return, who reminded them, singly, of how far they had traveled.

Flora had not been home since early yesterday. There, behind her Alex Cary—who was he?—had followed her to this spot of their hurriedly crossing paths, to the physical presence of Tanner Haynes, the strength of whose youth had been for them a part of childhood's wonder and dream.

In the quiet and older patience of his dark eyes, Tanner Haynes carried wherever he went the calm of courage experienced and youth spent.

In this unexpected moment each of them had caught a glimpse of another's lonely way.

Clio stood uncertainly between them. The day had given wavering filmy edges to every person she knew. Their private coming and going had obscured for her the familiar track of her morning's course. Miss Amy had told her to bring the blankets back. Her fire was going in the kitchen for the meal she was to cook. Now she was incapable of censure or warning, of finding a voice that would reach to these strange, growing-up faces. Her black face was pinched with displeasure. Too many paths led from the spot where she stood. She looked vaguely around her, then, jerkily, turned toward the house. A blanket trailing from her loaded arms caught under foot. And, there before them, she stumbled and fell to the walk. The awkwardly flailing body of the dry, light-boned old woman, wrestling in blankets, lay sprawled on the ground.

"Clio," Louisa murmured, telling herself who she was.

The calling aloud of the woman's name was a shattering of the strange moment itself.

They all ran forward, made a hurried circle around her. Louisa and Flora looked down, startled. How far back in memory did this faithful old face go? Pain and fright in the woman's eyes now denied what they remembered. She had been as much a part of their childhood as the sun-softening oaks at their windows. It was as if Clio had deserted them, had been caught in a wild stray current of time and would in a moment be cast nobody knew where. What else, unchanging, had outlasted their youth?

Louisa said again, "Oh, Clio!" and knew in the second that she spoke that someday Clio would die.

She went down on her knees to reach for Clio's arms. But

already Tanner Haynes had his firm hands below her shoulders and was lifting her seemingly weightless body.

"Oh, Clio," Flora burst out, "don't let anything happen to *you*."

Alex Cary, his arms dangling, a step or two behind them, was looking at his wife, uncertain that he knew who she was. The old Negro woman had withdrawn them all from him, cut him away from the childhood of their lives. A stranger, he stood outside.

"Oh, Clio, are you all right?"

Clio burst out in reply, "Mr. Raleigh done got every last one of us off the track! Miss Amy, the chullen, and look at me—flat on the ground, like a used-up June bug somebody go'n brush away."

Without the wrappings of her blanket, her passed-down coat hung so loosely over her thin frame that she looked like a sinking-in empty bag which the wind could find its way through. Her eyes startled, her thin hand rubbing the sagging brown skin of her bruised elbow, she seemed so vulnerable to the day.

She said in a minute, frightened at what she saw, "My head swimming! Straight-up things is falling down!" Her arm went out in an awkward reach.

Louisa tried to grasp her.

"Oh, don't let anything happen to Clio!" Flora burst out. She turned to her husband, just remembering him, "Alex, Alex, *help* her!"

"Me?" he said in surprise. "What you want *me* to do? Don't know what to do!" His pale unlined face was frightened. And Flora was looking at him curiously. Was it yesterday that she'd married him? She felt impulsively for the pin fastened to her waist—for some concrete sign that her marriage was true. It was he, not Tanner Haynes, that she'd married. The youth stood behind them, his eyes uncertain, his tie loosened, his fingers nervously fingering the pressed crease in his trousers.

She looked at him, not remembering how he had reached the spot where he stood. "Alex, can't you *help?*"

"Let me git a holt, Miss Louisa," Clio's voice was a whisper, "to keep from—" Her thin bony fingers gripped Louisa's arm.

"Oh, *why* did this have to happen to Daddy?" Flora cried out.

"Tanner," Louisa said, forcing her arm below Clio's shoulder, "she's as cold as ice."

Tanner Haynes was on his knees. Wordlessly, quickly, with his firm hands, he was straightening the crumpled blanket heap into a pallet on the walk. "Here, Louisa," he said in a minute, "let her lie down." Now behind Clio, he took the weight of the sagging figure from Louisa's arm. Her eyes barely open in her frightened face, Clio sank to his support.

Tanner lowered her gently to the ground. Not indicating he knew the others were there, he placed her almost weightless figure on the pallet he'd made. The skirt of her dress lay heavily on her bony knees. Her eyes closed in her thin face.

Tanner dropped his hat on the grass behind him. The brim had left a line through his black hair, over his dark attentive eyes. He pressed two fingers on the pulse of a limp wrist. Briefly he waited. "Get a wet cloth, Louisa."

Louisa, kneeling on the other side of Clio, appealed to Flora.

"Oh, *Alex,* get a cloth," Flora threw at him.

"A what?" as though she'd spoken to him from across the yard. He pulled a fresh white linen handkerchief from his pocket, looked at it, then quickly thrust it back.

"Take this," Tanner said, not having seen Alex's move. His own handkerchief he thrust toward her without looking at her face. "Wet it, Louisa, over there! There's water in the barrel at your door." His hand went to Clio's forehead. The strength of his agile body worked over a defeated figure, drained of life and protest. Clio's thin chest almost imperceptibly rose and fell.

Flora and Alex parted for Louisa to pass, holding the handkerchief, oddly weighted.

"Man *died* like that right on the sidewalk in Warren the other day," Alex said to nobody but himself and stepped closer to Tanner's elbow, where he could look directly at the prostrate figure. Tanner was folding back his sleeves.

For the first time, Tanner raised his voice to a command edged with impatience, "*Move*, Alex. You and Flora, *move.*"

They both stepped back, wordlessly, uncertainly, looking at each other. Then, as soon as she realized what had happened, Flora said, "After all, she *belongs* to us, Tanner Haynes."

Tanner appeared not to hear. He put the cloth to Clio's forehead, and upon a doubled-over blanket raised her heavy-shoed feet from the ground. The laces were dangling. Clio's hand lay lifelessly where it had fallen. With the tip of his fingers he touched the loose veins in their tired seeking along her arm, the arm of a thousand forgotten tasks lying inert. Tanner Haynes had a faraway look in his eyes.

Louisa still kneeling across from Tanner, said, "Flora, please don't tell Mama. Don't tell Mama any more—"

"Tell her what?" Flora's cheeks flushed.

"About *Clio.*"

"I'm not the *only* one that adds to Mama's trouble." Then she burst out, "I wish my poor daddy was here."

Without looking up at her, Tanner said, "Clio *is* here."

"Why do you two think I'm the one that's going to bother Mama? Why has it *always* got to be me? Just because everybody knows *I* was Daddy's favorite? I happen to know a lot of things I *could* tell."

Neither Tanner nor Louisa looked up at her. Louisa's face was pained. "Oh, Flora," she said in a minute, "can't you think about *somebody* else except yourself just *once* in your life?"

Clio's hand moved a little. Her eyes flickered. A current of life that had almost lost its direction had found its old course in her veins. In a moment she was looking up at them vaguely, having lost who they were. Then wetting her dry lips, she murmured, "What was it Miss Amy told me to do?"

Tanner was studying Clio's tired defeated face. He seemed to have forgotten the others were there. Then entirely to himself, returning to a privacy where the others could never follow, he said, "There isn't much here but skin and bones."

Louisa's lips parted in wonder as she looked at the withdrawn man across from her. Again he was a stranger.

Finally she spoke, seeing for the first time his dark troubled eyes, "Your father has been ill so long."

What she saw frightened her, for in her youth she hadn't expected to see weariness on the strong face of Tanner Haynes.

CHAPTER TWENTY-EIGHT

Bright horsetail clouds, as vivid as a child's water color, were stirring up the sky. The earth itself catching darting shadows was a basin for the motion overhead. Fractured sunlight through the trees around the house—the borrowed golden sunlight of a far-off day—crowded the ground with streaks of light and shade. In pulsing waves they gave depth to the air itself.

I saw Miss Amy alone with her back to me sitting in one of a semicircle of wrought-iron chairs in the yard. She seemed to be waiting at a great distance, as though seen through shimmering water, in the dissolving golden afternoon.

I had a sense of her release from time. Sight of the lone figure—unaware of me—reminded me once more of how solitary she'd been. The hour had freed her from the urgencies of her waiting children and the tyrannies of their youthful needs. In her own enveloping afternoon, Amy Pendleton Prescott sat outside the pulsing of *their* later day.

Seeing that detached figure, I realized she didn't know what had happened so recently, almost within the distance of her voice. Her children had withheld from her the sight of her long-attending Clio prostrate upon the ground, of their support of the worn woman into the house, and of their discovery that some day Clio would die. They had tried to administer to Clio, to restore her, in order to present to their mother, once more, the face that she knew.

Miss Amy was at the moment a figure irrevocably submerged in old tapestry, threaded in light and shade. Fallen yellow leaves were underfoot. Bare trees overhead held in their net-like branches the golden glow of the afternoon.

On a high bare limb of an oak at Miss Amy's back, two squirrels, their tails up, sat in arrested flight. Answering to a summons below, they scurried out to a long tapering end which floated ever so gently as above breathing water. Then in the flash of an arc they leapt to a lower branch where with grappling, scratching paws they clung high above the ground, ground that dropped so far below. After a moment, as softly as two late-hanging leaves taken by the wind, they were gone.

Two blue-jays, in startled flight, *chip-chip-chipping*, shot out from the tree, carving a streak of darker blue against the sky.

Routed, they darted angrily back, their *chipping* trailing them like sun-sparkling chains. A leaf dislodged, floating as hesitantly as a feather, settled at Miss Amy's back.

Miss Amy looked at me, a little startled. "Geoffrey?" I, too, waited indecisively in the warmth and chill of the deceptive autumn light. I had an odd sense of belonging neither to her past nor her present, a sense of the dissolution of time. "Geoffrey?" she said uncertainly. "I'd almost forgotten where I was. Almost forgotten where people belong."

I sat in one of the green wrought-iron chairs, a little removed from her.

Here was I, an outsider, stepping so abruptly into the flowing privacy of her moment. I *was* unknown to her. A wariness that seemed almost instinctive shadowed her face: a caution that she herself wasn't aware of.

Then, impulsively, as if *need* to trust me had overcome her hesitation, she said looking into my eyes, "I hadn't realized how far I'd gotten away from—*talking* to people."

Slowly she pursued, "Colin Ashby told me a great deal about you. He said he'd known you as a little fellow when you ran errands for him. You must know—" and she was looking at me closely, asking me to confirm her own hesitant conviction, "he *still*, after all these years, has great trust in you." She spoke thinly, repeating with difficulty something she'd memorized and was trying to persuade herself the validity of.

But, then, abruptly, "Tell me something about your parents."

I could see in her fine dark eyes that her desire to know *was* real.

"How strange it seems that as a girl in such a little town as Warren I knew so few people. So few in such a little town."

Even now, this was a fresh wonder in her eyes.

My father, I told her, had not been a successful man, that possibly she would have had few occasions to encounter him.

"Successful?" she murmured vaguely. Then, "Is your father—dead?"

I nodded my head.

It occurred to me all at once how cold it was sitting in the shade. I couldn't help wondering why Miss Amy hadn't felt it. There was a pinkish glow about her cheeks, a luster about her eyes. It struck me: she seemed at home here. Was this the natural self that reached all the way back to the secret loneliness of her years with her father?

"Do you remember," she said after a moment, "a little man in Warren named Whittington? Cyrus Whittington?"

The name meant nothing to me.

"Of course not. He was before your time. Years before I was married.

"Mr. Whittington used to pass our house twice every day. A perfectly harmless, demure little man. He was type-setter for the Moratuck *Gazette*. As a young girl, I watched him pass our door for years and years. His passing was as familiar to me as old John Clanton's garbage cart and sway-back horse. Always dressed the same, winter and summer."

She paused. Her memory was so fresh that she seemed

for the moment youthful. "But one afternoon I was sitting on the porch with my father. He was reading his Richmond paper. To this day, I don't know why it happened. But the sidewalk in front of our house seemed empty. A dog may have been barking a block or two away, but there wasn't a soul in sight. It came to me as if that old tree I'd played under as a child—heaven knows! They kept me close—as if that old tree had disappeared during the night. I asked Father when he'd seen Mr. Whittington?

"I can hear the rustle of his paper, the silence. Father was looking at me curiously. By asking him, I'd added years to my age. 'He's gone, Daughter.'

"This was unbelievable. There was nowhere for Mr. Whittington to go. Nowhere except whatever rest the Lord had waiting for him.

"I actually wondered if my father was in his right mind. If Mr. Whittington had died, *somebody* would have told me. Father folded his paper, got up from his chair and walked over to me on the steps.

"'Where, Father? Where?'

"'Mr. Whittington has gone back home.'

"Home! That was Mrs. Jesse Parkerson's boarding house! Father smiled. What a simple little girl I was! I'm sure I looked like a little prig! But would have given *anything* to be turned loose with Ella Fitzpatrick!"

She was speaking to herself now as much as to me: "Do you know nobody ever believed *that?*"

Miss Amy wasn't even looking at me.

"Father sat down behind me very deliberately and told me that Mr. Whittington had gone back to his home in South Carolina, to the little town he left years ago. He spoke as patiently as if he had to explain a hard lesson to a child. Always helped me with arithmetic. I remember it as well as yesterday. Told me that long ago Mr. Whittington was tried in the courts there for murdering his wife, that he was

tried and acquitted. The jury acquitted him. And he'd always believed Mr. Whittington was an innocent man.

"I remember that my father was no longer talking about
my loyal little Mr. Whittington who'd been passing our door
as long as I could remember. He'd invented some far-off
storybook figure who had no place in my frontyard. But
Father went on explaining, trying hopelessly to make of the
two, *one* man. The courts didn't think the evidence conclu-
sive. There was too much reason to think that his wife—an
unhappy, strange woman—had done it herself. But he didn't
want to stay there. Her people lived there. Mr. Whittington
came to Warren as typesetter for the *Gazette*. Warren was
a long way from home."

In Miss Amy's absorbed recollections, the distant words
were still in her ears.

"Then Father told me Mr. Whittington had gone back after all the years. Who knew? Perhaps he was trying to settle
something that the courts hadn't settled in the minds of the
people. Perhaps he couldn't bear to reach old age thinking
that he *couldn't* go. Maybe it was forgotten. Maybe there
was nobody left. But he'd had to see. Father said it was a
strange cross for an innocent man to have to bear. It didn't
seem fair.

"Father was looking out over my head. I felt for the first
time in my life he was including me in his old world.

"'Why? why?' I asked him, 'didn't *anybody* ever tell
me about Mr. Whittington?'

"He looked at me a long time, 'You are all I've got,
Daughter, in this world, all I've got to protect.' Geoffrey, my
father was such a gentle, gentle man. Lately, I've thought so
often he must have been terribly lonely. Maybe I didn't even
understand."

But, then, her hands folded in her lap. Her knuckles
went white. I barely heard her words, "My father *stood* for
something, Geoffrey! He *stood* for something! I *know* he
did."

CHAPTER TWENTY-NINE

Miss Amy looked over at me, remembering I was there. "What a long time ago that seems."

The sun reached the open blue of the sky, leaving behind it a frothy continent of clouds. The embraced landscape round us rose to meet the flooding warmth. Yellow light lay separately upon us, the fallen leaves, the bare trees.

I wondered whether Miss Amy wanted me to stay. Looking at her in the warming sun, I remembered I'd intruded upon her private meeting with the outdoors.

As though she felt my uncertainty, she said, with a surprising smile, "What is it, a sign of—age—when you begin to *see* the world around you? Lately somehow, I don't want to be closed in a house again. All the autumns I've missed."

Then she explained, "I was town-bred. How little I knew about plantation life!" After a moment she added, "I've *always* been a late-learner. Have you ever watched how close to earth the Negroes are—the country Negroes? How they see the balance in things around them? Fight for survival *they* are born knowing."

I told her that I was almost grown before I realized (and I hated to say it) that they died alone and were buried.

"There's a Negro on this place they call Little Man, a dwarfed little figure with just a part of a mind, trusting, as responsive to kindness as a child. I was amazed to discover the touch he has with living things. I don't know how to say. *Acceptance.* Unprotesting. How do *they* know things so early?"

She was asking me, but she went on, "His attachment to me lately has frightened me, in a way. Sensing better than I do what I am. Little Man and Clio. I shudder for her. Do you know I feel she couldn't recover from an emptiness I left?"

She was looking at me so pressingly that I knew the fact was still remarkable to her. "I did something the other day I've never done—I told them all where I want her buried."

The rattle of a wagon broke Miss Amy's reverie. It startled me. Sis Hannah's wagon disappearing down the hidden road flashed through my mind.

"I suppose you've been able to tell," she said, "I haven't said one word I intended."

She waited. "What surprises me: there are so many *other* things."

That glimpse of the sheltered lonely girl on the steps of her father's porch came back to me. I could see Mr. Will Pendleton putting down his paper, coming over to where she sat, glimpsing a separation he wasn't prepared for. Now I saw the gray of her temples, the fine, far-seeking eyes, looking out from loneliness that she'd never dreamed would have to be hers.

Was this just an accident of the years? Of old Mrs. Prescott's desperate need? Of her father's helpless devotion? Or was it a solitariness of spirit, like that of Tanner Haynes, that would have found no home anywhere?

Quietly she said, "I suppose you know that Pettigrew told me there were letters?" She was looking directly at me. "Letters they found in Raleigh's coat?" Each measured sentence came separately. "Pettigrew can read only enough to know what he can't read. He's tried to sift things for me. But he knew the letters *had* to be read. It was only natural for him to go to Wakefield. It was *right* that he should." She hesitated before she added, "Pettigrew did no more than Raleigh had already done—going to Wakefield."

Her words defined an act which I'd hoped she wouldn't be aware of.

She looked at me, startled, as for confirmation of what she'd said.

"What *was* it?" Appealing to me all at once, "What did the letters *say?*"

Her plea was direct. I wasn't sure what she knew.

I was obviously hesitating.

She saw every reluctant line on my face.

"They *were* from Katie Williams?"

A silence fell between us.

"One was *about* her," I said.

Every now and then the wind would pick up a scattering of yellow leaves as if they were on a string and then let them settle brokenly, separately, to the ground.

Then I heard her words, out of a privacy beyond my reach.

"Katie Williams is dead," she said quietly. "That is what Raleigh was carrying these last weeks."

She wasn't looking at me now.

"Poor Raleigh, after all these years."

Again, the wind, making kite-tails of the leaves, flew in and out of the grove.

"Do you mind telling me where she was?"

"In Petersburg with a niece of hers."

"All this time."

Her voice was surprisingly calm. "It amazes me. I'm able to say these things to you. What has happened? It rather frightens me to think about it. All through the years I've had so few to talk to." Miss Amy spoke the words slowly, absorbing their meaning for the first time.

"Now I can say to you that Katie Williams is dead, and all I feel is pity. What a difference it would have made years ago! How lonely Katie Williams must have been! How lonely—it frightens me to say it—most people must be! Just lately, I've seen everybody around me—the Negroes, my children, Tanner Haynes, with a kind of trembling wonder, almost as if they were going to escape before my eyes."

The sunlight now, great slanting shafts of yellow, was

seeking the faraway edge of things, releasing around us the chill of autumn mists from the ground.

In a minute or two she went on, as from no volition of her own. The force of her recollection itself was a momentum of discovery she was powerless to conceal.

"Poor Raleigh," she said, "never freed of divided obligation. As naïve, as incapable as a boy of concealing his early wound. A boy he's always been. I wish there *was* some way I could reassure him."

She was looking absently at me. I wasn't even sure she could call my name.

"Katie Williams is dead," she said again. "I don't know what it is I can do. There isn't any way now to save Raleigh from himself.

"For a time Raleigh brought me such happiness—the happiness I had no way of knowing wouldn't last forever—that my father tried to secure. I'm indebted to Raleigh for what he did bring, for the share of him I had. I wish I could make him believe it now.

"I remember once years ago," she began again, "it could have been the last trip he made to see her—he and Wakefield—to Richmond, Petersburg, wherever it was. Raleigh has never been able to deceive anybody. What he's thinking is written on his face. He always made such elaborate plans to conceal, to spare me. Wakefield, the urgency of business, banks—anything.

"That day I watched him and Wakefield, dressed in their town clothes, driving away in the buggy. I remember that I waved to them. I watched them disappear down the lane. What I felt standing there by myself was what startled me. Those earlier times, after I knew, and I knew *so* soon, had been such anguish. Every separating step those early times had been a twist of my heart."

Miss Amy was speaking with such deliberate calm I had the feeling she wasn't even talking about herself but a person she remembered.

"I was left there with numb emptiness: knowledge that I *could* let him go. The old ache wasn't there. I remember saying to myself, 'In a day, two days, he's coming back to this farm, his children, and to me. From whatever doorway, in whatever town, *she* is going to be left again, looking down at empty steps.'

"For the first time I could feel for her. I knew how solitary she, too, had been."

After a while she added, "I've been saying things to you I'd never dreamed I'd say to anybody. And it doesn't seem to matter. Not at all."

It was the absence of her voice that alerted me. In her need to talk she had come once more to a bridge of words that had to be of her lone making. She waited uncertainly, looking across an untried way she must go.

"This young man with Flora—" she said finally, "do you know *anything* about him, about his *people?* For some reason, I was *compelled* to look at him. I've paid so little attention to Flora's affairs. Maybe it was just *this* morning that did it, I don't know. But, all of a sudden, there *he* was. It was strange. I had no way of placing him, nothing to relate him to. All I felt was—he wasn't my son Blunt, he wasn't Tanner, not any of the ones I remembered who were here before the war. It would help me," she said, "if you could tell me something about him. I'm so out of touch with Warren. Tell me, please."

She had turned to me.

What was there for me to tell her? I knew that Alex Cary's father had worked at the lumber mill there in Warren for years. I knew that his mother was a large woman of plain face and straight hair who rarely left the little fenced-in yard of their house on Halifax Street. I knew that she watered rows and rows of plants in cans and boxes on their narrow porch. And I knew that an older sister was married to a brakeman on the railroad and that every Sunday they, with their children, filled half a pew in the Baptist Church.

And I knew that I'd never seen Alex when he wasn't well dressed. How or when he'd ever met Flora, I didn't know.

"Does it put you in such a position, asking you this?" I finally told her that I knew so little.

"I won't press you," she said after a moment. "There's nothing *to* say."

But I noticed that her hand trembled.

It was their voices on the front steps that made Miss Amy and me turn. Flora, Alex, and Otway. Excitement had given to their voices a sharpness reaching all the way out to us across the yard.

Miss Amy stood up. A white hand sought nervously for the back of her chair.

Then Otway's flushed, unhappy face was leading Flora and Alex toward us.

Their approach put us in silence.

"If you don't tell her, *I* am. Looks like *some* things, Flora, you'd *know*. Some things you don't *hide*."

Otway, tall and strained, had been carrying a burden of his own. How separately he had been carrying it!

Flora's face was flushed with unhappiness, tears. Alex's white, unlined face behind her was silent.

"Mama," Otway said. Blond hair over his forehead, an unshaven fuzz on unwashed cheeks, his eyes tired, he looked directly at his mother and stopped. "*They, they* got something to tell you."

Flora, looking at her mother, was bereft of speech. Her eyes filled with tears.

"Daughter," Miss Amy said, looking at her daughter, at her youth, her uncertainty, recognizing a forgotten anguish.

Her hand went out to touch Flora's shoulder.

"Me and Alex," Flora sobbed, "are *married*."

A silence fell between us all.

"Oh, my daughter," I heard Miss Amy say after a moment, "why *didn't* you tell me? Have I neglected you so much? What have I done that you had nobody to tell?"

BOOK FOUR

CHAPTER THIRTY

It was several days later when, after taking a walk around the plantation, I returned to the house and, surprisingly, found a note signed by Louisa saying that she and her mother and Otway had gone to Warren on business. I was at a loss to know what could have, so unexpectedly, taken the three of them away. I could only surmise that Miss Amy had been obliged to act in her husband's stead at the bank.

The deserted house was so strangely quiet that I was reminded of the stories of rescuers coming upon an abandoned ship at sea and finding uneaten food on plates, open books half-read, cast-off clothes on chairs, perhaps even a warm stove, but not a sign of life.

My own footsteps sounded loud through the drafty hall. The dim red-coated figure on the wall seemed for the first time to take notice of me. The sourceless bang of a shutter from some distant part of the house stopped me at my bedroom door. So many of the rooms I'd never entered. I'd never climbed the stairs to the second floor. Streaks of chill from beneath old, ill-fitting doors cut around my feet, released during this hour of desertion in ghostly pursuit. The house itself, as through sleeping, unwatched hours, was returning to its own secret life.

As I stood at my door, I had the feeling that Mr. Jasper Hornsby, the old schoolmaster, had returned, was waiting inside at the moment to greet me. The room was his.

Since his time, a few stray wasps, endlessly seeking their escape against the green shade, the cold panes, had marked their separate passage of time in the deserted room.

Hesitantly I pushed at the door.

"Who that moving about in this lonesome house?"

My hand dropped from the chilled knob.

"What I heard was *something*. It was moving wid shoes on. It *warn't* in my head!"

I looked back over the empty hall through which I'd come. There was nothing. My own pulse raced the minute.

Then the voice returned, private and faint with doubt and alarm, expecting no answer. "Was that *opening* and *shutting* and *stepping* just in my head?" After a second or two, "I ain't fit no more to be left by myself. Don't no house stay empty. Do somebody step out one door, somebody else go'n step in annuder one. One more day in this-here bed wid-out nobody to talk to, I go'n lose track of who I is."

Clio's voice, from the door partly ajar near the back entrance to the hall, was high, quick, nervous.

"My age, folks don't belong to lose sight of folks they depends on. Hit makes me forgit who I is. Go by the name of Clio, born in slavery, mammy I don't recollect, pappy neither, brought up and 'longs to Miss Amy Prescott, taught me manners and how nice folks feels. Don't she come back, the power in these-here knives is go'n play out."

"Clio," I called to her.

I heard her muttering protest. "Don't tell me that warn't *somebody*." Then she spoke out, "Whoever you is, present yo'self at my door wid every piece of your clothes and shoes on, wid dust on 'em got from walking 'hind a plowing mule. I don't want to talk to nobody I can see the other side of."

This was an order coming to the outside from her door.

As I started down the hall, she warned my approaching footsteps, "I got a working spell in here for strangers! Miss Amy done got *everybody* mixed up. Right in the midst of everything, she done took off to town! Something done come over her! My age, I wants folks to stay whar they belongs and be who they is."

"Clio."

I pushed the door back.

"Don't cross my threshold until I sees you."

The first thing I saw was the open scissors shining on the floor, the blades toward me.

Clio, her eyes as pointedly ready as a bird's on its nest, was lying in the middle of a white feather bed. Now a neat lace cap covered her hair. A clean white gown was fastened under her chin. The eyes in her dark face were large from illness and troubled with dread of desertion. Confinement had separated her from every familiar thing.

"*Who* you?"

She squinted at me sharply, raising her head slightly from the pillow.

"Schoolteacher," she said in a minute. "Better than nothing in a empty house." Then she asked me abruptly, "You ain't heard nobody prowling?"

Only then I noticed on the floor around her bed the circle of weapons against unnamed things: a straight razor, a piece of broken glass, the blade of a handleless knife, and a long rusty nail.

The room was pleasantly warm. A handful of red embers lay in a hollow of gray ashes on the colorless burnt-out brick of the hearth. On the narrow shelf of the little pine mantel a red glass contained a spray of paper spills. From one end hung a string of peppers, another of drying roots, curling yellow leaves and slivers of bark.

The unaired closeness of the room was pungent with oak ashes, the elusiveness of long-absorbed Negro smell. I had stepped back a century. It was hard for me to realize that this loneness was under the roof of the Prescott house. What a thin thread held Clio to the outside world! I thought of the pictureless room in which Wakefield and I had sat. On the walls around there wasn't a remembered face.

"Miss Amy fix 'em *right*, like I told her?" Clio asked me sharply.

She saw my puzzled face.

"Them things the devil won't cross."

"Miss Amy?" I asked as if I hadn't heard.

"Leaves me this way when she ain't here, like I tell her to do. Don't you tell her, hard as she's trying, but she don't know nothing at all. Look here!"

With surprising agility Clio pulled a napkin from a plate on the table at her side. There were two or three biscuits and a fried chicken leg. "Miss Amy fixing *me* something to eat! When she coming back from Warren? Ain't never cooked a day in her life till lately. Ain't et a mouthful. Go hide it somewhere before she gets back. Wisht she knowed how to fix me something *soft*. Something I kin *chew*."

Then Clio looked at me suspiciously. "Hard as she trying, don't you tell her nare word. Hide it quick!"

I asked Clio whether Miss Amy had told her where she was going.

"Warren? Gone somewhere! She ain't been like herself. Taking my job. Me lying up here in the bed, waited on!"

Then as if she just remembered, "Mr. Raleigh done it. *He* done it. Got everything turned upside down."

She looked at me. "What *ails* him? I hears Miss Amy in the kitchen clanking, rattling pots and pans like she don't know how to pick 'em up, or how to sot 'em down when she do. I has to lie up here in bed and name to myself who I is. Like I needs something to hold to. Middle of the night hit's just like I'se floating. Ain't got no edges I recognize. Floating out of I fergit what and going I don't know where. Has to say out loud to nothing but the dark, 'Go by the name of Clio. Born in slavery. Don't remember my mammy. Nor my pappy, neither. B'longs to Miss Amy Prescott.' Hearing that out loud consoles my peace of mind." Then she added with surprising thoughtfulness, "Called myself married once. I left him. He left me. Don't know which. Whichever, it was a blessing from the Lord. But that memory don't do nothing but mess me up."

I noticed the old woman's gaunt face. Since that day of

her collapse on the walk and of Tanner Haynes' old recognition of frailty, of the untiring march of time upon those around him—upon flesh and memory and aspiration—Clio's face had wasted to prominent bone and startled eyes, at home in neither the past nor the present day. I had a sense of the widening, widening distance of two boats at sea, widening beyond the carry of human voice.

The sum of her life now seemed such a weightless, such an elusive thing. The knives, the broken glass around her bed, the untasted food at her side—here were the lone threads tethering her to the life Miss Amy could give.

"Go by the name of Clio. Born in slavery. B'longs to Miss Amy Prescott. That's who I is."

Suddenly Clio raised her head up a little from the pillow. "Is she come back?"

"She?"

"Miss Amy? She ain't where she kin hear me?"

I shook my head.

"I'm go'n tell you a secret. I ain't never told a living soul."

Her eyes held me with their intensity. "She helped to ruin Mr. Raleigh. She helped to make him not to try. Her forgiving, her always looking, *always* looking 'way off, made him come to feel he weren't even there. He *talked* to me. He *talked* to me. Miss Amy don't know it."

Clio was speaking almost in a whisper. I had the feeling that she was trying to salvage something before it escaped forever, to persuade herself that something she remembered was true. "One day I told him, 'All the mean folks in the world, the Lord done blessed me to be her shadow, to follow 'hind her steps. She a good woman.' Looked at me a long time. He say, 'Clio, goodness can hurt.'"

Her head went back on her pillow. Her eyes were distant. "Hit seems to me like that's what he said. Hit seems like that is what I recollects."

For a moment I thought she was going to fall asleep.

I noticed that an old letter had been tacked to the wall just at my shoulder. In a smudged penciled hand it read:

Clio, Maid-Servant
Care, Mrs. Raleigh Prescott
Plantation, Moratuck County

"That's my letter! That's my letter," Clio spoke out.

From her quickened words I could tell that a surge of memory had seized her. "That's the letter I got. Come all the way cross the country. Wid my name written on it just as pretty as you please. Look at what that handwriting say, 'Clio, Maid-Servant.'" Her voice was bright with recollection. "Inside, written down in words for anybody that kin read, it say, 'Clio,' (calling me by my own name) 'come to the North where we's at.' Miss Amy read it to me. That's what it say. 'For Clio,' Miss Amy said, putting it in my own hand. I say, 'For me? Do the writing stand for me?' Here was me holding my name in handwriting come from a thousand miles. Bless Jesus!

"Had to go look for a mirror see my face. Face look back at me. Said right to it, 'You is Clio. That's who you is!' Was walking round on tippy-toe like I come somebody all at once. Somebody had done singled me out. Little old Flora says to me, 'Clio, what ails you, walking round, two feet off the ground?' Says right back to her, 'That letter naming me in handwriting ails me, if you wants to know.'

"Don't you tech that letter," she told me. "You leave it right whar it is."

She looked at me warningly. Then her head went back on the pillow to her private thoughts.

When I left her a minute later, I closed the door on the fan of scissors, knives, and broken glass that glittered around her bed, the sharp edges that protected her in an empty house when Miss Amy was gone and when in the dark she couldn't see the letter naming her on the wall.

CHAPTER THIRTY-ONE

From the quiet of Mr. Hornsby's window I saw Wakefield
—from the same window which had several days before
framed Pettigrew and the wide-eyed Negroes around him,
standing like figures in an album animated on the page,
arms gesticulating, pointing, making of Pettigrew's somber
face their one realized certainty of the afternoon. Now the
same wavery glass, shimmering in the slant of the sun, removed from any familiar context of landscape or time,
framed the lone figure of Wakefield.

The window where I stood, with the sour-sweet scent of
Mr. Hornsby's wine bottles around, was a forgotten, a least-
visited spot in the house. I had caught Wakefield in passage,
he'd stepped so unexpectedly into the empty frame of today's earth and sky.

There, before me, out of nowhere, he stood in the trembling light of the moment, which the narrow pane of glass
with the glitter of a diamond, borrowed briefly from a slanting ray, made sharper than life.

Wakefield was alone. Weariness weighted his shoulders,
as he hesitated in that suspended interim of time before he
knocked at the back door of the house.

The empty buggy was at the end of the walk, dropped
reins dangling, already forgotten, across the wheel. The collar of a fresh stiff shirt was white under his lean and distant
and copper face. A single shadow moved with his reluctant
approach across the yard.

All at once it came to me: Wakefield had always been
alone; since that day as a youth when he'd stepped from the
buggy in front of this very house, under old Mrs. Prescott's
furious eyes, and left his half-brother Raleigh to drive si-

lently off, he had followed his startled single way between two worlds. And Wakefield had survived. But now there was missing that defiant, proud resoluteness of privacy, which had thinned his face that afternoon at Miss Amy's door. Now his shoulders were stooped, his knock on the back door less firm.

I could not help thinking of Clio lying abandoned in her bed, watching the empty door, then turning with frantic search to the tacked-up letter nearby which named for her who she was. Was it that Wakefield, too, with the fallings away from him in years, in defeat, in frailty, had to cling to some memory of who he'd once been?

When I answered the door in the full light of the afternoon sun, I was startled. Wakefield looked like a Negro. I had forgotten that he was. It was in his eyes. His fine dark eyes under black hair were bloodshot, remote, indirect, not so much out of hesitation to confront me but out of the fatigue of his retirement from expectation. His copper skin seemed muddied. I could detect the stale scent of whiskey. Here was a face now before me that I would have passed a hundred times on a Saturday afternoon on the streets of Warren: on the streets thronged with Negroes from the country, their mules and empty wagons in the paper- and bottle-littered lots behind the stores, the Negroes not so much in the stores but on the sidewalks in front of the sun-bleached, scant, unpurchased displays, nameless unrecorded faces which to be remembered had to be looked at separately, individually, but which were passed unseen, unrestored as people from their dark anonymity, looking out with I knew not what privacies of fears and hopes. In that unidentified humanity how many Wakefields had I passed? I felt the start of recognition that this man before me now, whose story I knew, would have been lost, too, could have been anyone in the flow of Saturday crowds, forever unanswered by the denial of the search of my eyes, the nod of my head.

As I looked down at Wakefield (he was standing at the

bottom of the steps), I remembered the first night of our meeting, how during the hours of his desperate relentless recovery of his past under the flickering light of his wood stove, I'd detected a far-off dignity, a far-off strength of solitariness, that had made him neither black nor white, that had made him a man grieving for his childhood brother, for full and happy remembered times, grieving out of some still-living hope and need.

"Miss Amy?" I asked him.

A long time passed before he answered very quietly. "Ain't her I'm looking for. It's you."

In a moment he answered the perplexity on my face, as if reluctant to be the bearer of the words. "*He* wants you. Brother Raleigh."

Perhaps it was the very naturalness of the way in which he said "Brother" which shocked me. Coming from him in the full light of day, the word vibrated in a way it hadn't done in the pulsing dark of his room. Wakefield was a Negro. I could see old Mrs. Prescott at the top of the steps as she looked at her own husband's son, her eyes flashing, her anger uncontrolled. Was this, too, an anguish which Miss Amy had learned to push back and back?

Quietly Wakefield reached into his pocket. As indifferently as if it had ceased to be his concern, he handed me a folded paper.

It was a penciled note, an indefinite child-like handwriting which seemed strangely incongruous with the burden of formality it contained.

> Mr. Jones, would you do me the favor of coming to Haynes place at earli'st conve'nce? You could be of assistance to family and self. Arrangements to see me without knowledge of my wife and children would be apreciated greatly. Will trust your judgm't concerning this matter.
>
> Y'r obed't s'vant
> Raleigh Prescott

This was the first time I'd had any indication that Raleigh Prescott knew I was there.

Only hesitantly did Wakefield reveal interest. He looked at me directly. "What're you go'n tell Miss Amy?"

When I told him that all of them, except Clio, were in town, a frown came to his face. The upheaval in their lives had shaken he hadn't realized how far to the edge of things. He said, "She done lived a lifetime."

He looked at me in the doorway appraisingly. I was an outsider again whose function he hadn't determined. "Be better, let me take you back."

That I was actually going to see Raleigh Prescott in person, that he himself had sent for me, lodged in my mind like a sinking weight.

What surprised me was my realization, after the buggy was in motion, that I'd never actually expected to see Raleigh Prescott at all. Unconsciously, perhaps with a sense of relief, I'd dismissed him to an irrelevance he'd sought for himself, thankfully sparing myself any necessity for judgment. This abrupt approach to an encounter was unsettling. I felt unprepared. Having to meet Raleigh Prescott, face to face, was an—inconvenience. I'd arrived at the plantation on the afternoon of his disappearance—he already a faraway traveler walking out of my life, glimpsed from the completed perspective of time. Now Wakefield was driving me along in chilling wind, toward I knew not what. Raleigh's had been, I thought, a closed story, all of its scattered fragments assembled for me—his pride, his passion, his loss, his longing at rest. I thought of Mrs. Prescott's desperate drive to Katie Williams, of Ella Fitzpatrick's alarm on Colin Ashby's porch, of Amy's anguish, now long subdued, as she watched him leave with Wakefield in the surrey.

I turned to Wakefield. "What is there for him to see me about?"

I tried to fix the wavering, insubstantial outline of a face before my eyes.

Wakefield at my side in the buggy (the stale odor of whiskey was strong, not yet releasing him from the privacy of his last twenty-four hours) became physically present in his slept-in clothes. "What does he want to see you for?"

Out of pursuing uncertainty, "Has anything happened? *Changed?*"

"Changed?"

The word aroused him. Was that the word for whatever had compelled Raleigh Prescott to send for me?

"Folks don't change," Wakefield returned. "It just takes time to show all of what they are, what looks different. Be better, sometimes, not to live long enough to show all. Ain't no grief for some, dying young."

Wakefield's eyes were set ahead, no longer seeing the road he'd been using all of his life, across the imprisoned geography of his world.

It wasn't bitterness on his face. Nor had resolution departed. But his dark eyes were somber.

I did not know what had happened at the Haynes place, but I sensed that Wakefield was the only person in the world who did, and that he carried it alone.

The fields across which we drove were featureless in their wintry desertion. Time had stopped for them, abandoning them to chilled diminishment. Even the rim of pines on the horizon receded in this vast fallow waste. It wasn't that the land along the road to the Haynes place seemed unfamiliar. In open day, without night depths, without the glowing pinpoint of a pilot buggy ahead, you saw nothing to remind you that it was a way you'd been.

"I hope to God," Wakefield said out of his own absorption, "that don't nothing happen to Miss Amy. She been on my mind all this time. Going to Warren on bank business go'n be a lesson, a hard one, I hope she ready to take."

I knew it was Prescott land Wakefield was talking about: drained resources, depletion since the war of any timber against which money could be borrowed. I knew that Miss

Amy was driving herself finally, with a sense of relief, of longing, to know what remained concealed from her. Had she, too, during a sleepless hour, stood in front of the mirror as Clio herself had done: saying to the once-lovely, now tired disbelieving face returned to her: *I am Amy Pendleton Prescott, finally and completely now?* Perhaps, even, with a sense of relief again: *I am the Amy Pendleton my father from the very beginning feared would some day have to be?*

We had already entered the pine thicket dividing the sun-streaked open acres behind us from those ahead. Nearness to the exit—a wedge of sunshine between close-growing trees—quickened the horse's stride.

Tanner Haynes' house under moonlight had been an insubstantial luminous shell, floating in misty expanse.

"She done already had to learn a lot," Wakefield was speaking to himself. "Maybe it's go'n stand her in good stead."

It was almost as though I wasn't in the buggy at his side.

Now, in the clear, the open earth itself fell back and back. What had been a moonlit glow of a house, its windows yellow in the mist, concealing the intrigue of Tanner's youthful loves, was now a starkly reduced frame, uninhabited in the emptiness, with only a few towering stripped trees around it to mark where it was.

Wakefield jerked the reins up. "Who'h—Who'h!"

At the roadside, four or five split rails turning the corner of the pasture fence had been dislodged. They were lying at all angles in a heap, making a wide opening for cattle, mules and hogs.

"He done *tole* 'em and *tole* 'em, check that fence!" Wakefield was frowning with disgust. "Where every one of them hogs been getting out! Can't depend on nobody."

Wakefield got out of the buggy and bent over the tangle of split rails. He struggled with the top one which had been pinned under another. It surprised me to see that the exertion was too much for him. He let the weight fall, then

stood up to catch his breath. Briefly he wiped his forehead
with the back of his hand. Then he bent over again, gripped
the rail in both hands. The strain showed in his back. For
barely a second the balance swayed between two pulls.
Then, his face taut with effort, he shook free the locked
rail. It fell dryly to the ground.

When he got back into the buggy, he was still breathing
fast. His hand trembled a little on his knee. A bead or two
of perspiration shone on his upper lip.

"Giddap."

We drove on for a while quietly.

He knew that I had caught him in a moment of naked-
ness.

We had reached the lane leading up to the house before
he said to me, "Be understanding when you talk to Brother
Raleigh. He ain't himself. Him and Mr. Tanner done crossed
bad. These last two days been hell."

When he stopped in the yard under the bare trees, he
delayed. Hesitantly, almost pleadingly, he looked at me, his
eyes still a little bleary, his coffee-colored skin still flushed.

"Told you I been worrying about Miss Amy. She the one
I'm waiting for. A man got to know something's right."

He had already revealed to me, standing over the rails at
the roadside, that he had a beating heart.

CHAPTER THIRTY-TWO

"You wait in there," Wakefield whispered to me as soon as we were inside the front door. "He been sleeping half the time. Let me see is he wake."

The door to the living room, in which we'd sat around old Dr. Pitt pulling himself together in front of the fire, was open. But the room was deserted. A good crackling fire was still burning on the hearth. Freshly built, the fire leapt up against blackened brick, leaving tiny bursts of sparks in the felty soot, budding red and fading away. The yellow of the carpet and the old scarlet of the smoke-darkened portrait over the mantel quivered under hearth-brightening flame.

I'd been seated a moment or two, with the crackling and sizzling of the fire in my ears, before I heard voices from the back of the house. The door to the kitchen was ajar. The detachment, the faraway preoccupation of the speakers, was such that I knew my entrance hadn't been heard. I sat as awkwardly as an intruder with no chance of retreat.

It was the unidentified woman's voice that froze me to the silence of my heartbeat. The emerging and fading of the ancient figure over the mantel was the only life in the room. Strangely, the voices were outside the flow of my own day's time, they seemed so unrelated to the moment I was prepared for.

"How much longer has that man got to stay here?"

The pause was determined, the answering voice doggedly controlled to admit nothing of value, of feeling, "Jennie, I don't *know*. As long as he has to. Maybe a day or two."

"I knew it had to happen." They were slow words edged with desperation. "I knew something had to happen. Why in heaven's name we ever—I should have known better than try to deceive myself again."

With the same determined withdrawal, evenness: "You didn't deceive yourself *then*. I didn't deceive myself then."

Suddenly her words flared: "You act as if there'd never been *anything!* As if you didn't—" she hesitated, "*recognize* me, didn't know who I *was*. Had no—responsibility." She threw the word at him.

Tanner's voice was pained, almost hoarse. "Good God, Jennie, that's all I've ever known."

"Sometimes I think you're—afraid of—people. Afraid of yourself."

"Sometimes I am."

Then she was beseeching, imploring (I could see her standing, distraught), "Oh, Tanner, won't it be the same after *he* leaves, after he gets out of this house? Whatever it was he brought with him, it was something besides himself." She spoke angrily, "That man has changed everybody over here. Even the Negroes." Finally she added, "Is it her, Tanner? *Tell* me, is it?"

"Please, Jennie. I don't *know*. I *don't* know."

There was a long pause. "One thing you do *know*." Her voice had dropped to a whisper, dreading an answer: "What was it he *said?* Something that cut *you*."

"Mr. Prescott is not himself, Jennie. There's no good reason for you to know."

"Except," she answered, quieter this time, "if it hadn't been for me, he'd never have said *anything*."

Her voice trailed off. In withdrawing to the privacy of her own realization, she drew a space of silence behind her. With the fire still sizzling on the hearth, the old colors of the portrait still pulsing from the twisting flame, the words I'd heard seemed sourceless. Silence had swept the voices away, leaving me with the startled wonder of whether I had imagined or heard. In disbelief I had to tell myself that the anguish, so near and so far, as that of an old romance reheard, actually belonged to living people.

Then her voice was there again for nameless youth: it was a cry: "Oh, Tanner, I am afraid. You don't know what loneliness is. *Everybody* needs you."

This, too, could have been heard, could have been imagined, in the following quiet. Yet I knew that when I saw Tanner Haynes, face to face, the echo from the moment would remain in my ears.

Wakefield at my back startled me. "Brother Raleigh was sleep back there. He putting some clean clothes on."

Abruptly, "Who is that going out the back door?"

He went over to the window. I stood quietly. "About to worry him to death. Knew the minute I heard that door shut, was bound to be her." He still hadn't turned to me, was muttering to himself. "Caused all the trouble to start with. All the mess we got. Take a woman like that, think she losing him, drives for where he's weakest at, just like she put 'im together, knows exactly where he hurts. Watch. Go'n hold on to the claim she got. Go'n make him pay. Bad thing, she *got* a claim, too. She knows he human, knows it go'n pain him to cut her loose. Thing about Mr. Tanner— *main* thing—he couldn't live with himself doing what he hates in other folks."

When I asked Wakefield who she was, he looked at me absently. "Ain't telling you nothing that everybody don't know. Name of Jennie Blackstone, widow-lady with two chirrun. Husband, age of Mr. Tanner, killed in the war. Mr. Tanner been keeping her company two, three years. Just lately she took to coming *here,* claiming to see how she can ease his heavy housekeeping. Doing nothing but finding out where he been. Mr. Tanner started off enjoying her company. He fast in the corners. But, this time, look like he let his guard down more'n he meant."

Beulah, who when I'd last seen her had got a treatment from Dr. Pitt for an ailing back—a prod of his fingers into

the flesh of her ribs—was standing in the doorway, holding
a tray of half-eaten food and a crumpled white napkin. She
was looking from one to the other of us accusingly, to decide
where her annoyance should be directed. "Is that woman
gone? I heard a door shet."

"They talking in the yard."

"Wish she wouldn't leave that buggy outside the window.
Old Mr. Haynes lying up there in his bed, worried to
death about who she is. Got it in his head that Mr. Tanner
has done got married. 'When did my boy git married?' asts
me everytime I go in the room. I say, 'He *ain't* married, Mr.
Haynes.'

"But it don't do no good at all. He knows something going
on in this house, and he can't figure what. It's a weight on
his mind. Give him a minute, he'll go right back to it. 'What
did you say was her name?' Today he ain't *et* nothing, seeing her standing out there. We got enough trouble wid Mr.
Raleigh gitting well, without stirring Mr. Haynes up."

Beulah started toward the kitchen with her tray. The
laces on her shoes were dragging behind her.

At the door, she stopped abruptly and turned to Wakefield. "You know what's done hit me, Wakefield? How-come
Mr. Haynes' mind is so stirred?"

Wakefield looked at her without answering.

"It's done come to me all at once. Whilst Mr. Tanner was
in the Army, he had to live with his other son's wife. How-
come I didn't see what was worrying that poor man? Lying
up there waiting to be put out again!"

Beulah, with her understanding, went on back to the
kitchen, not even aware of the tray in her hands.

"They *still* talking," her voice came back in a minute,
"right out there in the middle of the yard where Mr. Haynes
can see."

"What she's saying is the truth," Wakefield said quietly
in a moment, "but I didn't know Beulah had sense enough
to see. Mr. Tanner been looking after him since the day he

got out of the Army. No wonder all Mr. Tanner wants is for folks to leave him alone, caught like he is."

Wakefield threw a couple of pieces of wood on the fire. With the poker he gave the logs a shake. Sparks flew up the chimney and showered the hearth.

When he turned he said, "What Beulah don't know is that woman worries Brother Raleigh more'n she worries Mr. Haynes."

Wakefield seemed genuinely perplexed. "I thought Brother Raleigh knew more about what was going on."

Looking directly at me, he said, "You know, Mr. Tanner been going with that woman two, three years. They weren't bothering nobody. Won't nobody bothering them. All he wanted, needed, was to keep it like that. Thought a heap of that woman's husband. Started out after the war trying to help her. Heard him say a dozen times, 'Roger Blackstone was a fine man. Died brave.' Mr. Tanner didn't know what this thing was turning into. I know that man has been on his mind."

Wakefield's voice, low and reflective, "Brother Raleigh had to come sleep in this house a few days, hurt like he was, to *see* things. Taking Mr. Tanner's situation the way he has, a strange thing. First time he found out who she was, that she was coming here, his face flushed all over, said, 'Wakefield, get me out of here.'"

After a moment Wakefield added, reminding himself, "Mr. Tanner's always been one of Brother Raleigh's heroes. Looks like Brother Raleigh saw what he himself hadn't been."

Then Wakefield looked at me absently.

"Brother Raleigh getting himself cleaned up now. Being under this roof for a while has got his mind going. Help him if you can. He's go'n ask you a heap of questions. So he can see where he's at. Be easier for him to say things. He don't know you."

CHAPTER THIRTY-THREE

Going from one part of the house to another was like going
to a later part of the day. With blinds nearly closed, the
room into which I was led, away from the afternoon sun,
was in semi-dark. A stuffy warmth hit me at the threshold.
A low wood heater on a square of tin was joined to the
sealed-over fireplace by a rusty, faintly smoking stove pipe.
One side of the heater held a sinking red glow pulsing
faintly on the floor.

A few seconds were needed to place the furniture: the
high dark bed with ornate headboard, mahogany grape
clusters and trailing leaves, an oversized armoire between
two windows, its top just missing the ceiling, a dresser with
a cloudy mirror, flickering as dully as a patch of water under leaves at twilight. From it two swan-neck stands were
suspended for shaving-cups. The furniture emerged so
slowly that it seemed to be wavering in dissolving gloom.

I smelled woodsmoke, turpentine, and medicine-sharp-
ened air. It was a womanless room. At first the heavy warmth
of the scent was the only evidence of life.

The breathing, the waiting, the slight stirring of two people came almost as a surprise.

A voice, unexpectedly youthful, formal, said, "Pettigrew,
give the man some light."

The silent figure of Pettigrew, a heavily aroused waiting
shadow, was bending over the table. Then, yellow light
blossomed, restoring an old drawer-dimmed photograph to
the clarity of day.

Raleigh Prescott's eyes were on me. I knew that they had
been from the instant I'd stood in his doorway. He looked

at me out of the past. I had the feeling that I'd come accidentally upon a twilight room which should have remained closed.

Raleigh Prescott was propped up in bed, two pillows at his back. He wore a clean white shirt. His hair had just been brushed. I was surprised at the tired youthfulness of his face. The yellow lamplight lay upon blond hair shining now from a wet brush. Sharp blue eyes held an intensity I wasn't prepared for. They looked at me with feverish burning. The shadow of handsome youth was still there, but youth, heavier, coarser, sensual, aged before its time in illness, dissipation, perhaps even in frightened outrage.

It was his realization that I was looking at him in the lamplight for the first time that made him turn defensively away. He knew that he was there, in a flash of exposure, inescapably, as he was. His face flushed. A man in withering embarrassment had received a child's punishment.

The long moment seemed never to pass.

Yet, even then, it was I, strangely, who had made the step back into a past which shouldn't have been opened. All the man's youthful torment seemed to have pursued him into the room. I wanted to say to him that it was he who had asked me to come.

With a flash of insight I saw there had been something there for Miss Amy to love, that there *still* was. A restless, hurt, sensual litheness was still his—life still clung-to, still pulsing in frustration and shame.

I couldn't help thinking of what Wakefield had said—*people didn't change, they used what had been there waiting, unused.*

It was only the shadow of a thought hovering there, without even the sharpness of words: *it would have been easier if Raleigh Prescott hadn't had to be dealt with any more.*

I was afraid that what I was thinking was showing upon my face.

There was a kind of petulance in his groping for authority: "Pettigrew," he said, "get the man a chair."

Pettigrew, a buttoned-up out-door man holding to his hat, was waiting in that silent depth of a Negro in a white man's house, at the beds of illness, sitting behind the stoves in the corners of kitchens, seeing and unseeing, their knees together, hands long and graceless upon their laps, the scent of outdoors clinging to them. He moved slowly, ponderously, obeying Raleigh Prescott, not even showing that he'd heard. Through his spectacles he looked at the man on the bed as distantly as at a child recovering from an illness. The straight-backed chair he placed for me near the stove was small in his hands.

I knew that from his bed Raleigh Prescott was searching me—the stranger, already accepted, already needed, under the roof of his own house. Even before I could take my seat I heard his resentful words: "I judge you think I have deserted my home and family?"

I was too surprised to answer, for I hadn't expected he'd see me as an accuser.

Then, as if he hadn't heard, he pressed for an answer: "That I have—*abandoned* my responsibility?"

The formality was unnecessarily aggressive. Lamely, I answered, "No-sir."

"I hope people are not forgetting that I'm going to be back on my feet. Shortly."

The insistent harshness was embarrassing. He himself had become uncertain of his adversary.

Pettigrew didn't even turn his head to look at him.

Wakefield who had followed me into the room and had been standing silently at my back said, "Raleigh, *you* asked this man to come here. You *sent* for him."

"Do my wife and children know you're here?"

Wakefield answered for me: "Nobody was at home."

"What do you mean that nobody is home?"

His feverish eyes, alarmed, darted from one to the other of us.

I told him I believed they'd driven to Warren.

As if I'd asserted the impossible, he said, "What in tarnation would *Amy* be doing in Warren?"

From the flushed agitation in the man's face, the willful sharpness in his voice, I wondered if he'd been drinking. Pettigrew and Wakefield were determinedly silent.

Finally Wakefield said, "This man can't tell you. He doesn't know *what* she's doing, Raleigh."

"I suppose I'm not free to make judgments any more, to make decisions? Is that it?"

He was looking at any of us who would answer.

"Nobody said that," Wakefield said.

"You don't have to say things. All you need do is *look*," Raleigh said. "What you and Pettigrew and Tanner have been doing—*looking* at me. Not saying a damn thing. Let me tell everybody I can *look* too. That's what I've been doing. Because I've been laid up in bed don't mean I can't *see*."

The undertone of threat was that of a child, appalled at abandonment.

"Has my wife been able to find something for you to do?" he asked abruptly. But behind the surliness I detected a frightened seriousness.

I hesitated for I really wasn't sure what he meant, how much my answer *did* mean to him.

Wakefield and Pettigrew were watching us both closely.

"I meant," he said, flustered, "have Amy and the children kept you *occupied*?"

I told him they hadn't, that they had been too occupied themselves.

"But they've *turned* to you?" The words were out before he thought.

"Turned to me?"

"Certainly. Don't you get paid for Latin? Haven't you got the answer to their problems in your books?"

But then I saw the man's unhappy eyes. I was sorry for him.

The presence of the Negroes in the room hadn't apparently to any degree altered his questions. I had an odd sense that he felt them deaf to his words—two silent shadows, unhearing. Or, else, that alone with them he had no need, perhaps even no ability, to conceal.

Was it here with these two Negroes that Raleigh Prescott had found the only acceptance of himself? Had they alone through the years refused to measure him, out of some need or expectation of their own? I could see the anguished old Mrs. Prescott making her appeal to Katie Williams not to deprive her of what she held and a moment later in painful recognition feeling the emptiness of her victory, the humiliation of having Katie Williams return to her what she had concealed from herself. I could see the young Amy Pendleton, after the long sheltering of her girlhood, discovering what there could never be in Raleigh to give. Was her refusal for so long to take him for what he was merely her passionate need to deny that this was all there was of the world her father had withheld from her?

I saw Raleigh Prescott in his flushed illness and frustration, obsessed by his surprise that the world he'd left hadn't changed—lying there in the bed as a used, as a broken, as a finally abandoned shell of the women's desiring.

As yet I knew at that very moment that Miss Amy, an older woman in Warren, driving herself to discover what remained, was perhaps feeling the glow of a strange gratitude for what there once had been in Raleigh to share. Only a few days before her heart had lifted to the beauty of the afternoon as she'd sat in the failing golden light so briefly there.

What Raleigh Prescott said then startled me, for his voice had become so abruptly reflective and distant. "Maybe you have stood them in good stead. Maybe you've filled a wide place. My God, how young people need somebody." The thought seemed to absorb him. After a while he turned to me thoughtfully: "Did my daughter tell you about—*herself?*"

But he didn't seem to be expecting an answer.

"You've got to know that child to understand her. One thing about it: Amy's going to get around to understanding her. She got around to me. Flora took after *me*."

Quite surprisingly there was a vague smile on his flushed face. "My little girl used to follow me around. When she couldn't follow Blunt, she'd follow me. Could read her mind like a book. Used to scare me sometimes. Would have to stop and ask myself: 'Who said that?' Said things that would carry me back twenty years. Could see myself, a tow-headed youngster, knowing the world was mine, saying what came off the top of my head, when every day was a surprise. Taught that girl child how to ride a horse down behind the barn. Amy wouldn't even know where she was."

Raleigh Prescott had sunk into the quiet of such reverie that I felt for a moment he'd forgotten I was there.

Then after a while he turned toward me again, the lamplight still faint on his brushed hair.

"You're wondering what it was I called you for. Because you came from Warren. I want to know something about the Cary boy my daughter married. I want you to tell me about his people."

I didn't know how to answer him. I wasn't sure what he wanted to hear.

The longer I delayed, the more restless his eyes became.

When I finally said that I didn't know them well, he snapped back sharply, "Knew you weren't going to say anything. *All* of you sitting around, not saying anything. Well, I already know what I need to know. The old man never had a day of education in his life. Came from nobody. Bought him a Sunday suit, a high stiff collar, and showed his face in church, his hands still shooting out from his cuffs. I know that crowd. You don't *have* to tell me. What they call coming up in the world! That's who my daughter Flora's married to. That boy—whatever his name is—is—you can't make a silk purse out of a sow's ear—not that quick."

When I looked up, a little startled, Raleigh Prescott's flushed eyes were wet.

Then, not looking at any of us, not speaking to any of us, he said, "God-dammit, why couldn't my daughter marry somebody?"

Wakefield stood up. "Wait a minute, Raleigh, that boy is all right."

"Oh, for God's sake, Wakefield, what the hell do you know?"

Wakefield turned slowly and walked out of the room.

CHAPTER THIRTY-FOUR

Wakefield's departure left a throbbing silence. It was hard to believe that the soft murmuring in the wood heater had been there all the time, so persistently there on the scorching tin—the soft murmuring of fire and dully shining white of bowl and pitcher on the dresser, the fading photograph of a young couple holding the reins of saddled horses and the cracking leather of a trunk in the corner (scuffed and frayed from whose forgotten travels?), half-yellowed now by a blade-like slant of afternoon sun. This was the room in its timeless abandonment into which the intrusion of our voices, our presences, seemed so transient, so brief.

I looked at Raleigh Prescott lying there in the destroying silence: a face flushed, ill and sullen. Was this, finally, the youth of old Mrs. Prescott's pain, of Katie Williams' romance, of Amy Pendleton's first knowledge of the world? Those shadowy, early years seemed a misty storybook memory, barely remembered and faraway.

This was the face of Raleigh Prescott I was watching. It was at *this* moment that he was speaking, out of an old, old depth of pride and anguish which I realized no other could ever know. A voice, once oddly silenced for me, was speaking to Pettigrew defensively, accusingly: "What does *he* know about who my daughter ought to marry? I know who is fit to come into my family and who isn't. That girl belongs to *me!*"

And Pettigrew said, "Mr. Raleigh, you ought not to a-said that to Wakefield." His voice was final and hard and without charity. His gaze was direct.

Raleigh Prescott looked at the black man in amazement.

Pettigrew sat there, unmoving, unapologizing. The reflection from the lamp was steady on his spectacles.

"Why?" Raleigh said. His forehead had reddened.

I thought that Pettigrew had closed his eyes, that he had not heard.

"I asked you why."

In the silence as though within a suspended moment related to no presence, no voice, I saw the faint shining of the pitcher and bowl, the lightness of whirling motes in a prison of slanting light, and the arrested riderless horses in the old photograph.

Finally Pettigrew spoke bitterly, out of an old passion long denied, "It ain't none of my business. It ain't none of my business at all." He was looking down at the stove, heavy annoyance on his face.

Raleigh Prescott watched him uncertainly. An assertion had come from some depth in Pettigrew which astounded him.

In disbelief Raleigh pressed him: "I asked you why."

The pulsing light on the floor at Pettigrew's feet marked the passage of seconds in the room.

Pettigrew's face was concentrated in pain. The black skin of his forehead beneath graying wool shone faintly with wet.

"Don't make me say nothing, Mr. Raleigh. Don't make me say nothing. Not this late. What I said weren't none of my business. I ought to know to keep my mouf shet."

He sat there in his rigid isolation, his thick chest rising and falling, barely concealing a painful and wild surge.

"I ain't got any right to tell Wakefield to keep out of my business, to tell him that who my daughter marries don't concern him? Is that it?"

Pettigrew's eyes briefly flared. I never thought I'd detect hostility toward Raleigh Prescott in that somber face.

"Mr. Raleigh, you knows your rights better than I do." He was looking directly at him. "One time, you got to be the judge."

Raleigh's face was strained with disbelief, his voice low, hoarse. "You ain't acting like yourself. All this time you been living on my place."

Pettigrew was still looking into Raleigh's eyes: "Comes a time when every man living got to be who he is. Black folks included. You want me to get off your place?"

I knew that both men had forgotten me.

"What in the hell ails you?"

"Don't nothing ail me 'cept all at once I knows right from wrong. When I can't help being who I is any more. You want me to get off your place?"

Raleigh Prescott didn't answer him. He hadn't heard Pettigrew. In stupefaction he looked at the solid, unflinching black face.

He went on: "Wakefield got 'tachment for you. Wakefield's got claim. If I done said too much, it's cause I got to be who I is. One time, Mr. Raleigh, you got to judge."

He was speaking unheatedly, implacably, as though pursued to reveal finally, in some undreamed-of chance, this hard core of himself, erasing years of deception, the token surface ties of white and black man, abandoning Raleigh Prescott ever so briefly, and defining, for once, some inexorable urgency within himself.

"And you been living close to me all your life," Raleigh said hoarsely, not believing it was Pettigrew he was talking to now, not believing his own words.

"Everybody been living close to you," Pettigrew spoke coldly. "Me, Wakefield, Miss Amy been living close to you. Close as she could. Close as you let her."

"I know how close I been living to my wife! That ain't your damn business to say." His face was red with fury. "Jones!"

It took me a second to realize he had turned toward me; that it was my name he'd shouted.

"I want you to find me some transportation! I want you to get me out of here!"

"Dr. Pitt go'n move you." Pettigrew said. "Dr. Pitt go'n move you when the time come. Said hold you till he come back." His voice was still cold, still uncompromising.

"One way or another, I'm going to leave this house!"

Raleigh Prescott had raised up from his pillows, using his elbows as props. A pair of crutches which I saw for the first time leaned against the chair at the bedside. With a sharp sweep of his hand Raleigh grasped for them. They slid and clattered to the floor far beyond his reach. Dust rose where they fell. He looked down at them in bewilderment, as if it had been *their* willful rejection of his reach.

Pettigrew stood up. His face twitched. I wanted to look away. "For God's sake, Mr. Raleigh," he burst out, "don't let me and you say nothing else to each other. I'm too old to be carrying weight. You the last man in the world I got reason to hurt. Can't nothing look right to you laying up there in the bed like you is. I ought to a-had that much sense."

Pettigrew picked up the crutches, sat down again. He rested a trembling hand on his knee.

Raleigh Prescott's weight went back to his pillow. He was breathing heavily from exertion, from the discovery of treachery so near his side.

From the depth of his pillow he spoke in a moment: "You said all you could say."

Pettigrew's hand was still trembling on his knee. He rose up heavily, slowly, from the little chair that was too small for him.

He bent over and picked up his round hat that had been on the floor at his feet. And without saying a word to either of us, he walked out of the room.

CHAPTER THIRTY-FIVE

I thought that Mr. Prescott wanted to be left to himself. I got up from my chair.

"Don't you leave here."

He raised up from his pillows, looked pleadingly at me. Lamplight caught the beads of perspiration on his forehead, the startled shine of his eyes. His hand was trembling. I could see just above him the dull mahogany gleaming of the grapes, the festive twining of leaves. Without Pettigrew, without Wakefield. At this very moment, his wife, his children, were on separate new-found missions of their own.

I thought of Clio in her bed groping for the people around her, tantalizing her in her frailty, appearing, disappearing: familiar faces, only in whose affections she saw herself.

As Raleigh Prescott looked at me: *"Don't leave me. Don't leave me in this room,"* his illness seemed to lie between us, giving to anybody who walked into the room the advantage of life.

He passed the back of his hand across his forehead.

Oh, what was it he'd sought? Not this!

A little tremor passed over his aged-youthful face, the innocent sensuality that had been his to give the world: for which the world had used him and left him. For a second he was a youth again: a physique of open fields and fast horses, blond hair burned in the sun, the princely heir, the pride, the world all his for the asking.

He looked at the crutches where Pettigrew had placed them: they were a monstrous intrusion at his side. He seemed not to know what they were.

Don't leave me. This is not what I sought. Not this.

I was held there by the plea in his eyes.

I could see him in that tangle of woods: Tanner Haynes and Wakefield bending over a crumpled figure in the briars and cockleburs, looking down at him, so abruptly a stranger as he lay there in an old familiar hunting coat, its big pockets blood-stained and sagging from the limp, lifeless weight of rabbits, his boots mud-caked, his arm flung out in the collapse of a child's exhaustion. I could see the two men looking into the stricken, flushed face, breathing heavily, in an urgency of need, alien to their own—a face which had now achieved a separation, an anonymity, a strange, proud, almost triumphant, declaration of himself.

Raleigh kept looking at me with such absorption that it seemed that the human countenance had just become for him a mystery beyond exploring. I don't believe I'd ever felt the pressure of such scrutiny: my face, my body, my deformed foot.

After a while he said with breathless fatigue, dropping his head back to his pillow. "Jones, sit down near my bed."

I took the chair, still warm from Pettigrew's body, still holding the weight of his despairing judgment. I felt that I saw him with Pettigrew's eyes.

The sheet over Raleigh Prescott's chest perceptibly rose and fell.

"You've been living in Warren all your life," he said, the thought, the words too much of an effort for him. "Seven miles away. I'd never heard your name."

He looked at me a second time, at my whole person, my unknown past. "If you don't mind me saying it—I mean: have things gone *hard* for you?" Then he added, "Sometimes you got to talk to somebody. Sometimes—

"Lay up here in the bed for two weeks—the way I have—nothing looks right."

Then he brought it out—"Everybody round you starts talking to you like you haven't grown up, or your hearing isn't right. It doesn't make any difference what I think any more? Is that it? Is that what they're all thinking? Everybody whispering outside my door—that's all I've heard—whispering. Sick people got sense left—even if nobody thinks they have!"

Raleigh Prescott's voice was hoarse, his eyes still feverish. He seemed to be finding his way ever so slowly over unfamiliar ground.

The thought flashed through my mind: Could people ever return to what they left?

"You know, it's a strange thing talking to somebody you don't know like this. Easier than talking to Amy or Pettigrew or any of them. When they come in the room, I—" he left it unfinished.

I remembered then that this was the first time that his bed hadn't been surrounded by familiar faces—all too patiently waiting, too patiently understanding—none of them releasing him from himself, from what they remembered, from what they'd hoped.

"I get tired of trying. And now I don't know what to do." He said it as innocently, as simply, as a bewildered child, "I don't know what *they* want me to do."

He'd thrown back the sheet from his white shirt which he'd put on for my coming. His fists, nervous, tense, folded and unfolded on his chest.

"Found that out yesterday when that woman came in here—not even knocking, coming in my bedroom just like she belonged here. Like I didn't make any difference any more. Do women go to a man's house like that now? What's happened to everybody? God knows! That woman isn't any friend of mine. Not a friend of any of my family's. I didn't have half my clothes on. She was standing at the foot of my bed with a piece of cake she'd brought over here, telling me she was going to get me well, was going to have me out of here in a day or two. And Tanner standing in the

door behind her, not even wanting to look at me, not wanting to see my face."

Once more, for himself, I could tell that Raleigh was
measuring the scene, measuring every word, for every stray,
disturbing value the visit had had. He was retracing his
steps, warily, cautiously, afraid the ground would disappear
underfoot.

"It bothered me: looking at Tanner. Was that how far it
had gone between them? He'd lost his—right to—be himself?"

Raleigh was looking at me, his eyes big with unnatural
luster, asking me to help him know.

"I couldn't help thinking with that widow woman standing at the foot of my bed: I'd never seen my own mother in
a petticoat, not after Pheebe turned me loose from her
apron."

It is difficult for me now to record what happened. But a
quiet came over the room as if we'd both heard a call from
far in the distance. The words he'd spoken aloud seemed to
hang with a strange kind of resonance. Raleigh Prescott
rose up slowly in his bed. What had been the aging face
of despairing, bewildered and weary youth was now con-
stricted with fear: still nameless, still unspoken.

He turned to me beseechingly, knowing I'd read his
thought, seen his far-off glimpse.

"Is that what it is: people don't think that I make any
difference? That I haven't got any pride? That I lost my
right to feel? You got to pay *all* your life?"

His head went back on his pillow, and his eyes were wet.

CHAPTER THIRTY-SIX

The low fire in the stove was still sizzling. The window beyond Raleigh Prescott's bed was dark. I realized that by now the lamp's settled glow was returning light to the outside—pulling into the yard for the night the scattered little outhouses, reaching out with ghost-like beckoning to a buggy down the road, to a lone Negro taking a short cut home across a cold field.

Here was Raleigh Prescott lying in a bed in this luminous shell of a house which had become for the darkening countryside their one nightly returning ship to their closed-in sea.

And Raleigh Prescott, released from the others, was talking to a stranger.

He turned to me, spoke so quietly that I felt I was the only person left in the world to hear: "Has Amy been talking to you?"

I nodded my head.

"You ever know her daddy?"

I told him I hadn't.

After a while he said, "He taught her to expect so damn much. God knows." He was looking up at the ceiling, his hands unmoving on his chest. "Thought I was somebody." He spoke so impersonally that it made it difficult to believe he wasn't talking about a mutual acquaintance of years past. "Wanted to make her safe—on paper. I didn't understand."

His reflection was as persistent as if a younger Raleigh Prescott had returned.

"Just loving somebody ain't enough. Amy didn't know

anything. Mr. Will Pendleton wasn't any perfect man. My mother wasn't perfect."

His eyes steadily watched the ceiling. "I reckon my mother got what she was looking for. Me and Amy."

After a while he brought himself back: "Seems like what I wanted to ask you"—he rubbed his hands over his forehead—"seems like I got off the track. Don't even know how to ask you." He hesitated. "Amy heard about the letter. You might as well tell me the truth."

I told him that she had.

Finally he said, "I already know the answer. You don't have to tell me. That letter didn't even make any difference any more. Didn't make any difference, one way or the other. There wasn't anything left to change. Was there?

"My God," he said after a while, "why couldn't Flora marry like she ought to? God knows. I wish she'd done it for Amy's sake."

Looking into the gathering dark outside, he asked himself in barely a whisper: "Hasn't *anybody* ever thought I loved Amy?"

I didn't know how to answer.

He twisted around toward me.

"You mean, nobody ever thought I did?" The color in his face was rising.

It was as if *I* had spoken the words.

"What *Louisa* has thought? *All* of them? I've had nightmares every night I've been in this place. I've hated to go to sleep. Even in the daytime, I haven't known what I dreamed, what was true. God knows when you're sick, nobody understands you. You don't understand anybody else!

"I could see everyone of them!"

The frantic, feverish surging of his thoughts distorted his face.

"I was calling them, calling them—one after the other— Amy, Louisa, Flora, Otway, Wakefield—one right after the other—nobody could hear, nobody would answer. Every last one of them were looking me straight through."

He was rubbing his hands over his face, dispelling the lingering force of the dream. "Jones, you ain't known what it is, not knowing where you are, just knowing inside of you, you don't make any difference, nobody cares any more. Dammit, Jones, I *need* people. *I* can't live without them."

He raised on his elbow. His search of my face was as pressing as if he'd gripped me physically by the shoulder.

"Don't tell me they haven't *talked* to you since I've been gone! Amy, the children—*all* of them. God knows what people have said! No matter what happens: I told you the truth."

Getting it out seemed to compose him a little. He threw back the sheet from his white shirt which he'd put on for my coming. Two fists, firm, tense, rose and fell on his chest.

It was his profile I saw now. In that light, illness hadn't aged him. This was the man that had been the father of Blunt—the one possession Miss Amy had made her own.

"Have you talked to my daughter Louisa?" he asked, this time not turning to look at me.

"Has *she* talked to you about—me?"

I told him that she had.

"*She* thinks I don't make any difference? *She* thinks I'm through?"

His was a frantic, feverish need to know.

When I looked at the man I felt obliged to speak: "That girl loves you. She doesn't know how to tell you. How to say—"

"Louisa?" he said vaguely, turned slightly to look at me, not quite believing me.

"Louisa," I repeated.

I could see the film over his eyes, the unconscious tightening of his fist.

He was speaking slowly, "I was afraid of what they thought of me. My God," he said.

After a moment he said, "I didn't know how to talk to Louisa. She and Amy were born knowing what folks ought to be. They were born to get hurt."

Raleigh Prescott lapsed into a long silence. Firm, long, fingers folded and unfolded.

"Jones," Raleigh Prescott said. I noticed the change in his voice. "Do you know what's going on in this house?"

I was baffled. "Going on?"

"Do you know about Tanner Haynes?"

I was looking away, but I could tell that Raleigh's eyes were on me.

Of course I knew about Tanner Haynes. On my first night at the plantation everybody had turned to him.

He didn't seem to hear me. He said simply, "My daughter Louisa is in love with that man. All women are. He was Blunt's friend. Somebody she's had to look up to. God knows," Raleigh Prescott said to himself, "she was right. They *were* men. I was their age, it didn't cross my mind I could hurt. Something that Tanner Haynes knew about himself, he was a boy.

"Let me tell you something, Jones: I'm not through. I'm not through. I'm going back home. Amy Pendleton trembles at the sight of that man."

He startled me so that I wondered if I'd heard him.

His repetition was an echo from a depthless source. "Amy Pendleton trembles at the sight of that man."

Pendleton, Pendleton. Not Prescott.

"That girl is leaving this God-forsaken country. Louisa."

Raleigh Prescott was sitting up in bed. In the flash of a second I thought he'd forgotten that he needed his crutches to get to the floor.

"Tanner Haynes has been living with that woman, that Jennie Blackstone. You saw her out there yourself. You know what I'm talking about. Not a morning passed I haven't heard her drive up in that buggy. Wants me away from here. Dammit, don't anybody think I got any pride?"

Raleigh's face was red, trembling.

"I have! I have! I'm go'n tell Tanner Haynes—"

His voice cut off as sharply as if it had been sliced. I hadn't realized until the silence how loud he'd been talking.

Looking at Raleigh Prescott's face, I knew without turning that Tanner Haynes was in the door.

"Mr. Raleigh, what are you going to tell Tanner Haynes?"

His voice was so low that I wasn't sure I'd understood him.

"What are you going to tell Tanner Haynes?"

I dreaded to turn. The man's physical presence filled the door. Hatless, his hair was black over his fine dark eyes, the compassionate eyes that had taken the measure of so many others on breaking Virginia hillsides. The firm, sensitive, splendid features of his face struck me at the moment as almost ascetic, remote. I saw him bending over the body of the prostrate Clio, recognizing again the waste of human spirit, human flesh. This was the solitary man who had been the soldier, the lonesome warrior both here and there.

Now—he and Raleigh Prescott were looking into each other's eyes, as though neither of the men had ever seen the other before.

In the entire room there wasn't the sound of a breath.

Their eyes were unflinching, unwavering. Was it that in this fraction of a second each of them saw in the anguish of the other, something of himself?

"Tanner Haynes," Raleigh Prescott said, but his voice was a plea, beseeching, out of recognition in a stranger of the sureness of being understood. "Please leave my daughter alone. For Amy's sake, please let Louisa go."

Tears were coming down his cheeks.

I didn't look at Tanner Haynes. Without saying a word, he turned and closed the door.

CHAPTER THIRTY-SEVEN

When I left Raleigh Prescott's room a while later, no lamp was burning in the rest of the house. The fire in the living room had been forgotten. Old firebrick held more warmth than did the weightless ashen log under a single curl of smoke. Cold from outdoors, from flat stretches of wind-swept fields, was driving the circle of heat back to the hearth itself for the night. Already, it was a midnight room.

Then I heard voices in the kitchen, saw the knife-thin shine of light framing the ill-fitting door.

I could smell the salty sharpness of ham frying, the pungent thickness of baking bread, the aroma of coffee. Voices inside were soft in the lamp-lit air.

"Wakefield, you had done ought to get married. It ain't according to nature to live by yourself."

When I pushed the door open, steamy warmth enveloped me.

Her back to me, Beulah was standing over the wood range. A good pine fire cracking inside made red rings of the black stove "eyes," and quivered at the door of the firebox, slightly ajar. A steaming pot kept a thinning cloud of vapor suspended over the stove, frosted the cold panes of uncovered windows.

Wakefield, looking down at a cup of coffee, was sitting at the kitchen table, listening to Beulah, not listening.

"Ain't no lonesomer part of the day than wintertime twilight. Outdoors, all you kin hear is a axe way off, a dog bark. See the world drop away from around you, leaving you right where you'se at, wid whatever you got at your feet."

Wakefield, at the table, lamplight throwing a long shadow across the bleached, lye-scrubbed floor, was stirring his coffee, not tasting, not knowing Beulah was watching his lone figure in a way she'd never done. For her, all the years of his life could have followed him into the room and stopped at his feet.

I could see the nameless Negroes, hats in hand, who had stood in the light of kitchen windows at the houses of white people in town when I was a child, and who for the labor of a few pieces of split wood were served plates of left-over supper on the backsteps or, on cold nights, were brought into the kitchen near the stove, heads bared, hats on the floor beneath them, big hands inching over knee-stretched thinness of overalls, rusty ankles stockingless under cord-tied shoes, sometimes ankles circled with a dirty string and a dangling coin to ward off evil spells, stepping into the light out of back alleys and, in a few minutes, returning to obliterating darkness.

Beulah stopped and looked at him.

"Wakefield, you ain't never took up wid nobody!" The thought was abruptly disturbing.

"Trouble is, take something ain't made yet to fit you." She was explaining him to herself. "What other folks do *is* you. I'd been in a fix, bless Jesus, if I'd a-had to wait on Lonnie Gee. One thing I done learned early, had to, was, don't no one thing kill you. Did, all of us be dead."

She bent over, started shaking clinkers in the firebox, assaulting the stove with Wakefield's plight.

Brushing the explosion of ashes from her apron, she said, "They's worse things than feeding folks."

Wakefield saw me. He started up from his chair.

I knew the search in his eyes was for what I'd left in Raleigh's room.

Wakefield was to drive me home. His untasted coffee was still smoking, waiting, the spoon in the cup. "He *through?*" Still looking for what my face revealed.

Beulah, without surprise, apology, turned. "Might as well set, drink you some coffee. Warn't my business to ask howcome, but it look like you caught in the midst of things, aimed to or not."

Wakefield overcame his hesitation, indicated a chair at his table.

Placing a cup in front of me, Beulah said, "What's Mr. Raleigh done *said* to Mr. Tanner? Making him walk past me and Wakefield like we was kitchen chairs? E'm had Pettigrew walking out, hat pulled down on his head, bent on saving a soul."

I asked Beulah where Mr. Tanner was.

"By hisself. Without knowing, is all I kin tell you. Marching as straight away from folks as he kin. Daytime, I'd say he was on his horse. God knows he got plenty to walk away from.

"Raleigh say something to him?" Wakefield was still watching my face.

When I nodded, Wakefield pushed back his cup. His face was mottled. "Good God, what's Raleigh going to do?"

Beulah and I both knew no answer was expected.

"Who know what is going on in a ailing mind?" she answered.

Wakefield, his face drawn, turned to Beulah, giving her unexpected attention. I knew her question had lodged something he'd wanted to resist.

"That man ain't hisself."

Wakefield kept looking at her.

"Look at old Mr. Haynes laying up there in his bed, mind going and coming, trying to hold on to Mr. Tanner. Seeing Miss Jennie out his window 'bout to worry him to death. For all *he* know, she the one he lived with during the war— the one that got shet of him. Sick folks git one-track minded."

"Raleigh ought to go home," Wakefield said. "Ought to get well at home."

"Sho he had. Laying up there, *left out*. Finding out they ain't nobody living that don't git left out."

Beulah started to the woodbox, turned abruptly to face Wakefield. "How-come Miss Jennie worries him so? He been knowing two years her and Mr. Tanner was courting. We was making out over here, some fashion, till he come. Now Miss Jennie ain't herself. Mr. Tanner ain't hisself. Wakefield, you tell *me* something. Is the trouble *Miss Louisa?* Don't a day pass, Miss Jennie don't ask me when she been here."

When Wakefield didn't answer, she said: "*You* ain't go'n tell me nothing. Might as well not ask. You loves 'em both so good—Mr. Tanner and Mr. Raleigh—you ain't go'n say nothing. Carry their troubles locked inside you, just like they your'n."

She stopped, looked at Wakefield getting up wearily. "Wakefield, I reckon they *is*. I reckon they what you got."

Wakefield's figure, his back to us, was framed in the steam-frosted window. Sight of him startled me. I remembered the glimpse I'd had of Colin Ashby through the wavy glass of the office window in town, seeing that his life had been lived.

Presently Wakefield was speaking to me, not turning his back, "Should I say something to Raleigh before I drive you home? Anything he *wants* me to say?"

I told him he hadn't been talking when I left.

"You see Mr. Tanner—Jesus knows where he at—tell him come eat some supper. Tell him there ain't nothing here to worry him. Tell him to come on back."

She was calling to us across the yard near the buggy.

Leaving the warm steaming kitchen, I felt the chill of the fall night. A new moon low over the far pines had just lost its lifeless transparency and begun a luminous spread-sail trip across the night.

The stall where Tanner Haynes' horse was kept was empty. The saddle was gone from the rack.

Somewhere across the fields we didn't yet know, the first

tentative waves of moonlight would be touching the solitary horseman, gleaming on the metal of the stirrups, the harness, outlining his firm lone face.

"Told you one time," Wakefield said when we were seated in the creaking buggy, "that I was go'n tell you about that man."

I said to Wakefield that Tanner Haynes could have been married a dozen times.

"Could-a," Wakefield answered, "but that ain't saying nothing at all. Half of him would a-satisfied most women, been pleased to git. Onliest one that's done come close to knowing what's hidden is Miss Louisa. Trouble now—it ain't never happened before. He ain't never seen anybody like her. With what he been through, he don't quite believe she was real. How-come she couldn't a grown up sooner? How-come he had to see her so late?"

Wakefield had picked up the reins. The wheels of the buggy were grinding in the dry, hard earth.

As we left the yard behind us, under flooding moonlight, the roofs of all the outhouses, the spokes of wagon-wheels, the metal of forgotten farm tools leaning against sheds, began, one by one, to appear and take their places for the night.

Ahead of us stretched a now-uncharted misty somnolence which was like the breathing of the earth itself. The misty way opened up for us and closed behind our wheels.

I remembered what Beulah had said about Tanner. It was strange to think that at this very moment he was riding out somewhere by himself—we didn't know how close or far!

I asked Wakefield why Tanner had never married. Since my first sight of him, a lone figure across the fields, he'd remained, for me, elusive, remote.

It took Wakefield a long time to answer.

"By himself in the midst of people all his life," he said. "Told you once I was going to tell you about that man."

The reins in his hands were dangling between his spread knees. He was leaning forward, as though he sat in front of a fire.

Then he told me that Tanner's mother, a great beauty, died when Tanner was born. In a womanless house, except for Negro cooks and nurses, he'd been brought up by two elder brothers—Hunter and Stuart. The three of them had lived in an outdoor world.

They'd taught the boy to ride, hunt, swim. In those days Moratuck River lowland was great country for game—squirrels, rabbits, deer, occasionally bear. Rock fish came up the river every year to spawn. It was old Indian country, where springs, creeks, forests still kept Indian names—Roanoke, Potecasi, Conacanarra, Chockoyotte.

Tanner's father, born to be taken care of himself, was bereft, bewildered, after the loss of his wife. He'd adored the woman. For a long time he lost interest in life. Perhaps he resented Tanner—perhaps not. But he abandoned him to the older brothers—the Negroes. Half the time he didn't know or, apparently didn't care, where they were.

It was Hunter, the oldest of the sons, who was Tanner's guide and mentor. Hunter, rather than Stuart, replaced the boy's father.

Every spring, Wakefield said, the waters of the Moratuck River, after winter rains, rose over its banks and flooded the lowlands for miles around, leaving a red mineral deposit ankle-deep, sticky and rich enough to grow cotton head-high.

One of the worst of the floods he remembered like yesterday. The reddish-yellow water was creeping out into all the low spots, sending long snaking fingers into the ditches and gullies covered over by lush growth. Nearby fields had already turned to shimmering mirrors reaching to the tips of last year's stalks. Except for string-like cracks in the surface which the tips made, you couldn't tell the water was moving at all—a relentless, ominous flow from a hundred miles upstream.

Wakefield had gone out with the Haynes boys to round up stray cattle, to drive them to high ground. Smaller animals, snakes, toads, even birds, had already fled. Tanner was hardly old enough to go.

It was on a wedge-like rise thick with cypress trees that they heard the calf bleating. The three boys spotted him, Wakefield said, in a minute. A red calf was standing on a little rise no higher than a worn down haystack, already surrounded by swirling water. You could almost see the little hill shrinking in front of your eyes.

Between the spot where the boys stood and the calf's slowly sinking island, water was rushing into a wide ravine, carrying broken branches, stripped leaves, a stray log or two, rolling over and over.

The calf across the swirling rush would put a front foot in the lapping water and then pull back.

Hunter, Stuart, and Tanner just stood there, looking.

Wakefield said Hunter took his young brother by the shoulders, looked down at him and said, "Tanner, don't you *move* from this spot. Do, I'm go'n whip your hide."

Then Hunter and Stuart stripped naked and plunged into the stream. Both disappeared, shot up a minute or two later half-way across, shaking water from hair-plastered heads.

"Don't you move, Tanner. Hear what I say?" Hunter was shouting. But now there was a dead-serious strain in his voice.

Wakefield said that Tanner had been seeing his older brothers disappearing in the Moratuck River ever since he could remember, but that, this time, Tanner, his clothes on, moved a little closer to the edge. Wakefield said he himself wasn't worried, for he saw their naked bodies, shining, streaming with water, grasping for the overhanging brush on the other side. Before he knew it, Hunter and

Stuart, pushing and tugging, had the calf between them. Then all of them together, the boys and the calf, shining arms, legs, hoofs, made a terrific scramble and splash—the calf was kicking, bleating, almost went under. Arms were flailing, water swirling around them.

They heard Hunter's cry, "Stuart, *you* get out of here. Tanner, don't you move."

Then Hunter and the calf went under.

Stuart had already broken away. "God-dammit, Hunter, let the damn calf go!"

When Hunter came up his face was distorted with pain.

Wakefield said that he himself was wearing high laced-up boots, with extra lengths of string wound round the tops and tied in double knots.

He sank to his knees, began tugging at the wet, hopeless knots. He saw that Stuart was already knee-deep out.

Then, without believing it, he saw the calf free of Hunter's body. The space was widening between them. Hunter's body was giving to the current like a string straightening out. Wakefield said that what caught him with the horror of a nightmare was sight of the calf scraping and clawing up the bank.

It was while he stood there, frozen, watching this, that Tanner jumped in. Saw his arms swing clear of the water, saw his hand reaching for Hunter's dangling hand, heard Stuart yelling at him, throwing him a rope of twisted vine.

Wakefield said there hadn't been time for thinking. What he remembered next was the icy water dividing his hair, splitting his own skull, the heavy trousers and boots like bags of stones, pulling him back, dragging him, not letting him go. He said that he went down in the muddy stinging water and that when he came up he couldn't see.

It was a floating log that saved him and another vine rope thrown from the other bank.

What Tanner had done had already been done.

The boy was on his knees, yellow mud running, streaking

his face, his chest, water dripping from his nose. He was
bending over the naked body of his brother. Hunter's mouth
was parted. Hair had matted on his forehead. A trickle of
water came from his nose. In disbelief, the boy touched
the swollen, bleeding cut beneath his brother's ear.

Wakefield said, "Stuart was standing back. Hunter belonged to Tanner. Stuart knew that."

Then Wakefield added, "If I live to be a thousand, I
won't ever forget that boy's eyes. He turned to look at me
and Stuart to see if *we* were living. He couldn't believe
we were alive.

"I had to look away. I couldn't face him. Not right then.
Seems like I've owed him something all my life. Stuart,
too, for being the ones to live."

After a while Wakefield said, "What happened then was
the calf. She was red, slick with mud, dripping. Her wet
flank pressed against Tanner's side. She was eating grass."

Tanner looked at her vaguely, distantly, not believing
what he saw. Quietly, slowly, the calf went on grazing. The
boy's eyes followed her. He could hear the snapping of the
blue-green grass. A fresh little half-circle, like a hoof print,
had already been eaten at Tanner's feet.

"But I've always known that what mattered was that
Stuart, that *I* wasn't there. I knew talking was no good
about heavy boots, about near drowning. For him, I was
a grown man he'd looked up to, and I wasn't there."

CHAPTER THIRTY-EIGHT

We drove in silence before Wakefield spoke again. So often during the past days I'd been aware of the man's separateness. Even at the time, with Wakefield close at my side (a chill blade of cold had cut under the worn horsehair blanket over our laps; the remaining glass eye of a pony, whose once-bright figure had dissolved into the dust-heavy cloth, was a pin-point of cold under my hand), I had an odd sense that our proximity itself was unbridgeable, so much that he carried, still living for him, was past, so much of it long ago. My momentary nearness seemed only the narrowest of chance meetings of two widely-separated ways. I had first seen him so short a time ago. I knew that he and the glimpse of others I'd had through him would at a time not far away be only a memory.

But this man had, somehow, shattered the confines of my sheltered years in Warren.

It was with the sense of excitement, of heightened alertness, with which you hear the distant roar of the sea before it appears in its unfathomable blueness before your eyes, that I rode with him through the early night fog. It was the fog that made our way seem uncharted, our buggy adrift, the land itself featureless, concealing familiar field, hedgerow and split-rail fence. Only the snorting of the horse, the hanging of foam from the bit, the slick lashing of harness against straining muscles, led us on.

Unaccountably, the ride had become for me an exploration of the past. What had already been, had become for me a landscape over the horizon, still waiting, still unencountered ahead.

I suppose I felt this because of the fresh wonder Wake-field had lodged in my mind about himself, about the others. So much about them seemed unspoken, withheld. Those people, I felt, were unlike those I'd known in Warren. It had given me a lift of spirits to catch the glimpse of the far-off things they'd sought: Miss Amy and Blunt, Tanner and Wakefield himself.

The jolting of the buggy, the tingling cold of my body in misty silence made me think of the sheltered tree-lined streets of Warren. The people here seemed to have lived in a way town people I knew had never done. It was as if they'd lived closer to life itself—were more vulnerable, more exposed to cold and heat, the never-ending spectacle of change in the racing skies, the falling leaves, the returning green and the mysterious disappearing stars. Distances here were greater, roads primitive and rough, freezes seemed harder, the silences of cold more awesome, and the all-night-long *knocking, knocking* upon shutters and doors unsettling for the heart. Clinging-together little houses along the walked-on streets of Warren were faraway. And, somehow, the human needs, the longing, the loneliness, the courage of far-off search, seemed to be sharper, stronger, as though the people here had been doomed to this lonely countryside upon some punitive quest.

Perhaps this was all my fancy, but so they seemed that night on that strange ride. I was a long way from the book-lined, low-ceilinged office where my horizon through sedate old windows was the courthouse, the town pump, the unimpassioned faces that every day passed from door to familiar door.

Finally Wakefield leaned forward in the buggy, held the reins tighter in his hands. The horse-hair blanket had slipped from his spread knees.

"What he says, this late, to Pettigrew and me don't make any difference. But the way Mr. Tanner came out of that room won't right. Even if he ain't himself, Raleigh's done wrong." Wakefield thought for a minute: "What in God's name is Raleigh go'n do? Mr. Tanner got enough quirks of human nature to put up with. It don't seem right. Ain't nothing Mr. Tanner asked for. Folks drains him to death."

I asked Wakefield whether Tanner would ever marry Louisa.

After a while he turned to me. "You ain't been here long enough to see he got more respect for Miss Amy than anybody in the world, for what she did with what she had."

I told him I knew what respect Miss Amy had for Tanner.

This time he said without turning, "And it scares her just to look at him."

For the first time we came to a turn in the road leading away from Tanner Haynes' house. Mist obscuring the ground had begun to thin. Great clear patches opened up around us.

"Trouble is," Wakefield said, "Raleigh got it in his head he owe it to somebody to set things right."

It was at that moment in the clearing that I saw, before Wakefield did (he was looking straight ahead), the faint reddish glow. We were, after the sharp turn in the road, facing west. I looked at the flattened, vaguely pulsing glow over the trees a little absently. It was what was left of an already forgotten sunset, sinking under the spreading luminous weight of the climbing moon. The dark forest, separating us from the Prescott plantation, made a wide basin. Into this, the glowing seemed to be sinking, dissolving, pulling behind it the last light of day.

It didn't even seem necessary to call Wakefield's attention to what seemed so persistently lingering ahead.

But in a minute or two he stopped the buggy. He was looking out directly between the horse's pointed, slightly raised ears. He said to me as if I had already spoken: "That ain't no setting sun."

Now there was a returning, mounting flare over the line

of trees, a rebellious flare contesting the spread, the weight of the consuming moon.

Not even then had I thought of the Prescott plantation, for the directions of the field-squared roads at night meant nothing to me.

Only when the reins went taut, snapped in his hands, and he grasped, without looking, for the whip which I'd never seen him take from its leather pocket at his side, did the possibility strike me.

Wakefield's delay appalled me. He sat there in a paralyzed moment of outrage, disbelief. I was conscious, as I had been when he'd tugged at the fallen rails, of his quickened breathing, of his physical aging which seemed, almost perceptibly, to be leaving him in a struggle, uneven in his own eyes, with the exhausting hours of the day. His eyes were weary. Unconsciously he was gritting his teeth.

"She don't deserve this. She ain't even home."

I asked Wakefield whether he knew it was the house.

"Could be anything. Country fires, one broken down shed can feed a dozen. At the mercy of God and the wind. Had nightmares about 'em all my life."

Something in the man's face caused me to look at him. His hand trembled. In utter astonishment I saw that he was afraid. "God knows," he said, "there's so much a man can't do."

The despair of a lifetime seemed to clutch him to the spot. His breathing was labored. "So much that your doing can't change. Your color, where your heart goes, what folks can and can't give."

What he had said would have startled me, but I knew that he'd forgotten I was there, no longer cared that I was there. The uncertainty of the night was a closer presence than mine.

"God help poor Raleigh," he said. "He go'n think it's a

curse on him. He ain't *ever* been able to straighten his Lord out."

Only later, when I looked back upon that night, did I realize I never knew at what point the horse broke from his statue-like trance in that suspended moment which held him and Wakefield together, only the thinnest quiver of the reins binding them, flesh to flesh. Nor did I realize until much later how quick our passage was through the woods. What had earlier seemed an interminable lurching and jolting and by-passing of hub-deep ruts, which the fragile spokes of the wheels seemed barely to withstand, passed in a kind of timeless, unmeasured silence between us, with only the lashing out of reaching branches, stinging to arms and legs, clocking for us the pine-fragrant distance consumed. I do remember that the ride was a confusing confrontation with light and dark. The moon was high enough to send down shafts of light through the leafless branches of the trees, beckoning toward what appeared to be passages through and shadowing the curves where the real tracks lay. But always ahead, as if it were coming toward us, hung the pulsing red glowing of that false sunset, reaching out with the strange vibrancy of a second burst of fall color through the treetops.

It was when we approached the clearing on the other side and could look out across open space that the sourceless smoke seemed to come from a spot of unmoving ground, the red center of awakened fields looking on.

"Five times in my life I've seen the sky light up like a carnival."

There was an unfamiliar bitterness in Wakefield's voice. What he saw ahead had become a personal affront to him, an unnecessary assault upon privacy of memory.

"One thing about it, there ain't no horses. Miss Amy and the children have gone to town."

This was the first time that I knew it wasn't the house itself. How Wakefield knew at such distance I couldn't tell.

I remembered that the barn I'd looked into on my walk around the plantation was a few hundred yards from the main house, but not too far for sparks on a windy night, not too far for the grass on the hard dry ground. Only this morning I'd scraped the dry earth with my shoe.

I told him I didn't know they stabled horses there any more.

"Do, Miss Amy's buggy horse, Raleigh's riding horse. Mules down in the lot. Trouble is, they panics. See flame, they ain't got no sense. Snort and scream, fight right there and burn to death."

We were as far away now as the burning barn had reached out to light, showing individually in the fields the broken stalks of last year's corn in a kind of eerie twilight.

"That black smoke boiling up out of flame. Barn built out of heart pine hunnerd years ago. Same as burning tar, pitch, and turpentine."

Only then was I conscious of the roar. Billowing red and yellow flame bursting through the dry cypress shingles of the roof had created a suction like a waterfall, carrying with it litters of paper, corn shucks, handfuls of straw, drowning out every human sound. The cavernous mouth of the barn was a tunnel reaching, snatching, consuming from the outside. It even snatched the voice from my side.

The flaming roof had thrown a circle of pulsing light over the yard—an orange glowing over a semicircle of people standing back, looking oddly like miniature people, voiceless and anonymous, in some strange pantomime.

I remember that I was then not even surprised at the number of people, white and black, making that living circle. Nor did I wonder then where they had all come from, from what distance over fields and trees the billowing red cloud in the sky had drawn them. But they were standing there, black women holding children, dogs close to their legs, their faces aglow, casting long shadows behind them, like the spokes of a great wheel. And in wider circles behind them every building on the plantation, every fence post and roof, stood up in its own flickering light, as if each of them had been summoned for counting, had actually been drawn closer in.

The flaming pine timbers inside the cavernous shell of a barn outlined its height and width and depth against the sky. There wasn't a window, a slit between boards, a crack in the roof that didn't have its pinpoint or its knife blade of light. It looked like a multi-lit ship on a dark sea at night.

Just as we drove into the yard (close enough for our horse to lurch sideways: he began to quiver in the harness), an acrid tar-burning scent enveloped us, stinging to the eyes and flesh. Some of the rafters high under the roof, pulling great flaming banners behind them crashed down to the earthen floor. A shower of sparks, like a monstrous blossoming, shot up through the collapsing roof, briefly held an expanding umbrella over the barn, the yard, the nearby houses, pushing the circle of onlookers back, drawing their lit-up faces upward to the sky. Then the sparks floated downward and were dissolved one by one in the darkness around.

I didn't know when Wakefield left the buggy. He was already silhouetted in front of me, holding our rearing horse.

"Git out the buggy! Git out the buggy!" he was shouting straight ahead, but I knew the words were meant for me. "Good God, them horses in that barn. Both of 'em! Miss Amy's back!"

I hadn't seen the little group before, gesticulating, indistinguishable still, framed now within the reddish glow of a side door to the barn.

Now I was at Wakefield's side. With one hand he was working feverishly at the harness, with the other stroking the trembling horse's side.

"Told you! Look! They goes wild! Fire in their eyes. Turn

this one loose, he run straight toward it. Heard of 'em running 'cross a lot to git in a burning barn."

He'd unharnessed the horse, turned him around. "Git him out of sight of fire." Pulling at the bit, he was leading the horse back.

"You go over there! See that nobody don't go in that barn! Horses in there or no. Better burn them up than folks. Good God, they all too close!"

At first I couldn't make out what the wildly pointing little group was doing. All of them had an odd thinness about them like pasteboard figures that would in a moment burst into flame.

Then I recognized Pettigrew bending over a barrel. From it in a minute he pulled a soaked, dripping blanket.

Then I recognized the strangely wrapped figures: Miss Amy, Otway, Louisa, shawls, coats thrown about their shoulders, their hats on.

"All of you get back, get back from the door! Dammit, Louisa, get back!"

A single figure, standing at the door, a long chain in his hand, was shouting back at them.

Somehow the voices were divorced from what I saw.

Suddenly Miss Amy, a coat hanging from one shoulder, moved out.

"Good God, Miss Amy, get back."

"Tanner, Tanner," she was crying out. "Just Raleigh's horse! He knows me. He'll come!"

"Good God, Miss Amy, get back."

Both Louisa and Otway clutched at her arms.

Then it happened so quickly I was only later to remember and try to believe what I saw.

There was a frenzy of flattened figures pulled by unseen strings in an explosion of pantomime, black whirling smoke, licking flame, and shouting voices unrelated to any recognizable form.

What I saw then always seemed to me later only what I conjured in a sickened fancy.

Pettigrew dropped the blanket over the head and shoulders of Tanner Haynes. In a second Tanner had disappeared within the glowing framework of the door.

Miss Amy's single figure was silhouetted just outside within the light. Then they were all thrown together: Miss Amy, Pettigrew, Louisa, and Otway.

All I heard were the words: "Raleigh's horse!"

I don't know how long it was before Tanner appeared. The blanket still over his head, shoulders, he was backing out, bent double. Two loops of chains were cutting at the necks of the wild, screaming horses. It lasted only a second, but the horses' wild pawing of the earth and Tanner's forward pull held them together for a suspended frozen moment within the bursting energy of an equestrian statue.

The balance swayed, the heavy figure of Pettigrew was there beside Tanner, now within the door.

In a second of disbelief the horses were outside.

And all the group were around them, separating the horses, around Tanner. Louisa was lifting the blanket from the dripping, smoke-blackened figure. Miss Amy was throwing her own coat around Tanner's shoulders. The horses, now away from the door, still pitching, rearing, were in Otway's and Pettigrew's hands, still pulling away from the chains looped around their necks.

A second rafter crashed downward in the interior behind them, sending out another explosive, sky-reaching spray of sparks, lighting once more the disbelieving startled faces of the Negroes now watching the whirling, smoke-blackened little circle of horses and men.

And, once again, I heard Tanner's shout coming from no face I recognized, "Good God, Miss Amy. You ought not to be here. Miss Amy, get back!"

I didn't even know that Wakefield was at my side. "You

know," he said, "one time, I could a-done what he did. One time, I would a-tried."

There was no vainglory in his voice or eyes. There was merely a memory of youth.

CHAPTER THIRTY-NINE

Blackened heaps of smoldering timbers, lit by scattered bursts of flames, kept up a constant sizzling where buckets of water had been thrown around the edges of glowing embers. The sizzling was like a persistently urgent flight of bees in mass frightened exodus. Languishing black smoke, thin and patchy, hung over the piles of charred wreckage. Every now and then a heap of smoking lumber would collapse, send up a quick spurt of flame, bright enough to pick out figures lingering beyond the heat. Seen from a distance, the smoldering, bursting flames could have been a site of deserted, nearly extinguished, camp fires.

Upright timbers, left standing, rising with tatters of clinging smoke, gave the odd appearance of the framework of a structure only sketchily begun.

Everywhere around clung the unrelieved pressure of the scent: the scent of charred wood that is lastingly present, absorbed in clothes, the hair and skin, that lingers in closets, in the forgotten places of a house, returning when least expected, a never-defeated ghost of the past.

Then I noticed the sky. Great black clouds, high overhead, had already set off on their missions across the world. But a thin murkiness remained, veiling the stars themselves, arresting the moon in the eerie light of an eclipse. We below stood in strange twilight, isolating a closest neighbor into an elusive, never-to-be recaptured identity.

When I went toward the dwindled group still waiting (the circle of Negroes, children, and dogs had broken), a kind of lassitude, as palpable as the odor of charred wood, hung over them. The silent crowd, gazing separately in disbelief at the smoldering fires, was still held there, not yet released from the enormity of what it had commonly endured, bound from this moment on by a single doom.

Even physically they seemed at first to have been disfigured, to have escaped narrowly with what they once had been. It was almost with a sense of supplication that they looked at me to accept what remained.

I was conscious, first, of Miss Amy.

In the light of the fitful flares, the unnatural haze of strained moonlight above, she was standing alone. Her dress was wet, disarrayed, smoke-stained.

She was hatless. The wave of gray-black hair so carefully prepared for her first groping encounter with me was pressed thinly to the crown of her head. Her dark eyes were unnaturally large. Sputtering light into which she was separately gazing caught the tired lines of her face. As I watched her, without coat, without hat, looking into the finally meaningless fires, her solitary figure put a lifetime between this eerie night and the image of the shy longing girl about to go out from her father's home. Was it that she now saw in this rushing wave of time that Blunt had been her one legacy, her one gift to the world? Was it that there was no more for her to be? Weariness weighted the handful of people round her, kept them all apart.

What I saw then—an indecisive scene of half-dream—was Wakefield standing at a distance, watching her, of his going with hesitant step toward her, approaching a lonely presence he'd never approached, and of her turning toward him, the light on her face, and of his ever so beseechingly offering his hand. The two of them alone were standing there, the light from the smoldering fires flickering at their feet. Miss Amy's fragile white hand was in his. For a moment she held it, clung to it, looked up into the man's eyes. And he was gone. Miss Amy had turned away.

I heard Otway's voice then. (For the first time voices seemed not so much to break the weariness, which was like the smoke itself hanging over them, but to reveal the depth of weariness from which they had come.) Exhaustion disfigured him. His smooth face was sunken and smeared, his eyes large. His frail shoulders were outlined under his hanging dripping shirt. His wrists stretched from sleeves too short. Frightened eyes sought those of his mother, asking in incredulity: *What was it he'd done?*

Turning in stupefaction from the charred heaps around him, he looked pleadingly at them all.

Over and over he said, "Fire I built wasn't bigger than your hand. Have seen Daddy do it a thousand times. Cold days—to keep his hands warm. Edge of that field over there. First thing I knew, it got away—"

His shoes and trousers were blackened from stamping on the blazing grass.

"Good Lord, Mama, what have I done? Telling you the truth! I saw Daddy do it a hundred times."

Otway smeared his face again with a smoke-stained hand.

"Oh, son, son," Miss Amy said to him. "It's nothing *you've* done. You had no way of knowing. No way of knowing. You did only what you knew, only what you'd seen him do."

But beneath the weariness, there was a firmness about her voice that surprised me. "For heaven's sakes, son, go take that wet shirt off. You'll catch your death of cold."

"My Lord, Mama, you haven't even got on a coat!"

I remembered then that it was her coat that she'd thrown over the soaked shoulders of Tanner Haynes.

With dripping jacket in his hand, Pettigrew was standing in front of Miss Amy. I was seeing him for the first time without his round hat. But his spectacles caught flashes of flame.

Miss Amy was telling him, "Pettigrew, please see that Raleigh's horse gets some water. Please see that those horses are watered and fed. Promise me that you'll look after Raleigh's horse."

But Pettigrew was shaking his head, saying over and over, "Done tried. Done tried. Horse won't let me git near him! Wild as a streak of lightning. Won't let me get near him. That horse is scared."

He paused for breath. "Tried to come up on him from ever' direction, holding the water out front so he could see. Starts bucking and kicking, to knock the fence down. Just like he trying to get back to the fire we pulled him out of. Like it was appointed for him."

He put the bucket of water down on the ground and wiped his forehead with his hand.

"Mama," Otway looked at her pleadingly. "Let me try! Let me try! Let me do this!"

"Stay way from that horse, boy!" Pettigrew said. "He bust you wide open, thin as you is."

Miss Amy just stood there, looking from one to the other of them, the fire catching her exhausted face. Then she spoke as simply, as directly, as a child. "Raleigh's horse knows me. He'd let me come to him. I'm sure he would."

"No, ma'am, no ma'am, you ain't going near that horse." Again Pettigrew was shaking his head.

Louisa looked at her mother in astonishment, as if she wasn't sure that it was she who had spoken.

Tanner Haynes, flattening a mound of burning trash with a rake handle, stopped abruptly, turned to look at Miss Amy. He threw the handle to the ground, walked over to her. He had never looked at her so before: had never heard that voice which came from her tired face.

Tanner's handsome features were blackened. His black hair over dark eyes showed an edge of singe as did his eyebrows. A wet smoke-gray shirt clung to his chest. Arms and hands were black with soot.

They looked into each other's eyes firmly, directly. He made a tentative gesture to put his hand on her frail un-covered shoulder.

He said, "No, ma'am. You can't go."

Still looking at her, he took her coat, which was merely a shawl for him, from his shoulders. "I didn't know until this minute that I had it on." As gently as if he were draping a child he returned the coat to her shoulders. "No, ma'am," he said. "You can't go."

Tanner picked up the bucket.

Miss Amy said, "You've done enough, Tanner Haynes."

Tanner hesitated. Her voice held compelling quiet.

They were all looking at her: at the weariness, at the endurance in her face that had been as great as theirs, that came from older reserve, from they knew not what faraway source.

The firelight seemed to hang separately upon her face.

"Little Man can do it," she said. "He has a way with animals. There's something about him. They can sense his touch."

Silence fell round her. Each of them seemed to draw back.

She looked at them in the circle, one at the time.

Nobody spoke.

"What is it you're not telling me?"

For the first time Miss Amy made a gesture of pain. "You don't need to tell me. Little Man and Sis Hannah have gone." Not looking at any of them.

Pettigrew nodded his head.

"Oh, my God in heaven," she said, "who is going to look after them?"

I hadn't realized that Wakefield was standing so near me.

"Don't know what I been thinking all my life. Right here at me. That woman. One time, I got something to carry with me long as I live. Brave folks twist my heart."

The sputtering failing fires had about gone, had almost dropped the circle of people back into darkness again.

Waiting there, I didn't know in what short time I would be leaving the plantation, nor did I know that I had heard the last words I was ever to hear Wakefield speak.

CHAPTER FORTY

When I went into the living room about an hour later, Miss Amy was by herself. She was sitting in the same chair at the fireplace from which she'd formally received me that cold drizzly afternoon when Raleigh Prescott had not come home.

Now the room was almost dark. A single lamp on the desk at her back cast her lone shadow across the hearth. The assembly of pictures behind her—of her father, of Blunt, of others I didn't know—were in shadow. The low fire was withdrawing a weakly pulsing glow from her feet, the embers of a fire returned to after the house is asleep.

My first glimpse of Miss Amy from the doorway rather startled me. I had the feeling that the solitary figure, the dimly lit room itself, were dissolving before my eyes, that I had really never known this woman at all, but had had only glimpses of a story heard in childhood, unrelated to visible people or any landscape that I knew.

I remembered with what nervous expectancy I had been driven in the wagon through the desolate war-deserted countryside: the empty windowless Negro shacks, the unplowed fields, the choked paths and pine forests devastated, with the unimpressed and uncommunicative Pettigrew, carrying the separate heaviness of his aging life, at my side, a suitcase at my feet, a volume of Caesar's *Gallic Wars* in my lap. That ride itself seemed a trip of my fancy. What far-off purpose were the *Gallic Wars* to have served? The book hadn't been opened since I'd been here: it had been added to the forgotten and unopened ones left on Mr. Jasper Hornsby's shelf in the room smelling vaguely of wine, in which the wasp buzzed its sole, separate clocking of time.

It came to me with a little twist of surprise that this woman had thought it *would* serve. What?

My abruptly pressing awareness of the book wouldn't release me. Such a short while ago it had had a significance for me, for her, which I now couldn't locate, couldn't define. It was almost as if what had been sought so short a time ago had vanished from the horizon itself.

I looked at Miss Amy's graying hair. (Her back was to me: her face toward the fire.) Even *she* didn't remember that I had brought the book. Had the reason for my coming to the plantation already escaped *her?* Had the *Gallic Wars,* a last hopeful vision so quickly lost, already become as distant as innocence itself?

It flashed through my mind as I stood there that the book, lying where I wasn't even sure, would not be opened again, not even by myself. Nor was the survival of those disappearing penciled lines *Louisa Tanner amat* written for Mr. Hornsby's drowsing eyes even known by any in the house.

I said, "Miss Amy, you wanted to see me," feeling even as I spoke that I was stepping from a remote world outside, across a threshold into a depthless privacy only partly re-coverable even for her.

Miss Amy's movement to look at me in the failing light of the room was hardly more than the stirring of a figure in an old tapestry, submerged, fading in color, only one of many shadier, darker figures in deeper background.

She said, "Come sit with me for a few minutes, Geoffrey. How little did I think that what I've got to say to you would have to be said tonight. The fire has cheated us of time, has moved us so far, so soon."

Since she'd left the rest of us at the smoldering rim of embers, she'd changed her clothes, brushed her hair, as she would have done after a long, exhausting journey. There

was even some semblance now of the early image of her I'd
carried long before I'd come to the plantation and looked
at her, face to face—the image which had continued to
hover in the background, a half-remembered, half imagined
shadowy thing, whenever I sat in her presence: often the
remembered, the shadowy image had been stronger than
her presence itself: the young woman riding in the surrey
through the streets of Warren with her adored father, the
two of them, out of gentleness, out of an unworldliness
really, who had somehow reminded the people they passed
of their own mortality, the mortality of all perishable things:
the young woman of dark eyes, of dark hair, of richly
glowing skin, a transplanted figure, not quite native to
Warren streets. Was it the evanescence of loveliness that
made it seem such a rarity there, there and wherever it
appeared? It was the image, too, of her as a girl sitting
on the steps of her father's house, hearing for the first time
in a kind of speechless wonder the reluctant words of her
father about the little Mr. Whittington who after all his
quiet years in Warren had gone suddenly back home. It
was the image that had so agitated Ella Fitzpatrick on that
summer night in Colin Ashby's porch: the picture of her
friend Amy, so quietly endowed in a manner Ella had
never been, suddenly upsetting all that Ella knew of the
world, by asking Ella for help: the stricken beauty, in
disbelief and unutterable pain, asking Ella to fetch her
bridal clothes, hanging so recently in their closets, from
the Prescott plantation. And Ella's later shock at Amy's
determined stricken face as she'd stood at old Mrs. Prescott's
graveside, with the flushed, defeated youthful Raleigh at
her side, asking so pleadingly of her for whatever there was
of strength and understanding to give, knowing at the moment that he was lost with her and lost without her. And
there was the later, much later, image of the woman sitting
closeted, alone in her room, not eating, not sleeping, having
stood on the steps so bravely the day before, waving good-

bye to her own, her one true child and saying to the others of the family that just this one time to leave her, that she was tired, tired. And, finally there were always in my mind the glimpses of Miss Amy through the years, watching the buggy disappearing down the driveway, leaving her, carrying Wakefield and Raleigh upon his awkward, poorly contrived journeys, in painful loyalty and painfully uncertain love even, to Katie Williams, the mother of his first son, leaving Miss Amy with the throbbing ache of an emptiness, knowledge of unutterable loneliness, that was to become for her the scar of living, the scar of time.

And it had been such a short time ago that she'd sat in that same chair in front of me—only a few days ago—her hands tense in her lap, hearing my words and not hearing, postponing for one more moment, one moment longer, what her mind had already accepted, what she couldn't have prepared for, what she hadn't known she'd ever have to assemble her courage for: Raleigh Prescott had finally denied her, Raleigh Prescott had gone. It was the only leave-taking that remained: she had learned all others.

And this leave-taking was for her, for them both. The years of their lives were gone.

Now as I watched Miss Amy sitting there, the weariness, the exhaustion on her face put a lifetime between us and that cold afternoon a few days ago.

I saw with an understanding that had never come to me before how thinly transparent is the present moment of time.

At Miss Amy's back were the pictures of her father, of her son, of the others I didn't know. I knew that she wasn't aware of them in the shadow behind her.

I remembered the impression I'd had of her that first afternoon: dressed for me, sitting so formally at the edge of her chair, as if prepared for leaving, a visitor here in the Prescott home, surrounded by worn, now-cracked leather furniture, brought over rutted roads by wagons at a time

long before her memory, before Raleigh's memory, to a
house envisioned on a Caribbean island by one of Raleigh's
ancestors that even he couldn't name.

And I remembered that this house had been old Mrs.
Prescott's castle, that, out of her own anguish in her own
time, she had bequeathed it to the son who was exclusively
hers, just as Blunt had been Amy's son.

It was upon Miss Amy's face that all of the past, the
layers of time, seemed to be attending.

The calm now, the weariness, the acceptance, the absence
of seeking—was this finally now the woman she'd been
foredestined to become? Was this courage of solitude the
bequest that her father would have recognized in his
daughter, that would have warmed his heart to see across
the years? She was not aware of his picture at her back, of
his gentle courageous blood in her veins. This courage of
solitude was in the order of her time. It had always been
secretly coursing there, waiting, waiting.

There seemed to me then to be no beginning, no ending
to any life. It was as if I saw in Miss Amy a never-inter-
rupted, never-ending *becoming:* a becoming to what there'd
been in her to be. Only the flow of the years were to reveal
the secret places, to uncover the reserves of strength and
courage and acceptance that she drew from back and back.

I didn't know when Miss Amy's story had begun, nor
could I see the end of the far shadow it had already
cast: in Otway and Louisa, even in Flora, looking at times
so uncertainly at her husband, and in Wakefield himself
who had finally, so briefly and yet so lastingly, held her
hand.

And I knew that Miss Amy had had to call me to the
plantation, that for her the vision of the *Gallic Wars* had
had to be summoned once more, that the force of memory
had kept alive for her a far-off vision which had made
all the difference in life for her, which had made her and

Wakefield and Tanner Haynes lonely watchers in the world, doomed to silence and to grief.

The calm of weariness with which she spoke to me now was not surprising when it came. There was a directness about her that was as simple as that of a child.

It is even difficult for me, looking back, to place what now happened in its proper sequence in time. It seemed as I sat there that I had already lived through it, had already known that it would come, and that I only caught the echoes of what had happened long ago. The weight of the consuming past seemed to devour the moment itself. The moment belonged to what level of time? When was it decreed?

"Geoffrey," she said, speaking with that now unburdened directness of a child: "It is hard for me to have to tell you what I'm going to say."

She looked at me calmly, frankly, wearily, "But there is no other way."

Her hands were perfectly quiet in her lap. Her lovely dark eyes in her tired face were looking at me, at my deformity, at all my early lonely ambitious years, saying to me: *You learned so early: there's nothing from you I can hide.* And I knew that there was a compassion in that woman that I should never see again.

"I'm not going to try to tell you how much your being here has meant."

She stopped abruptly.

"Geoffrey, my father was a great Latin scholar. When I was a girl I took it as a matter of course. But he could read Latin as well as English. Latin and Greek. My father was a most accomplished man." She hesitated, looking into what was left of the fire. Then she added, "It took a lifetime for me to understand what I took as a matter of course.

"Oh, Geoffrey," she said in a moment, this time gripping the arm of her chair, "you've got talent. Colin Ashby told me so. Can't you pursue it? Can't you get out of Warren where it matters? Can't you—?"

She halted so abruptly short of what she intended to say that the word "escape" rang in my ears.

Still clutching at the arm of the chair, "What a tragedy it is not to use talent. Sometimes it seems to me the only real waste."

She lapsed into silence.

She looked back at me finally and spoke so quietly that her words even then seemed an echo of what I'd somewhere heard long before.

"My father had a sister, my Aunt Caroline—they were talented people—who had a beautiful, beautiful voice. She left Warren after her marriage to live in New Orleans. She married a brigadier general—a man with a brilliant career. But Aunt Caroline gave up hers. I've never forgotten it. I've never ceased to wonder what she could have become. Maybe it's just as well," she added, "that I don't know."

It even seemed at the time that Miss Amy had forgotten what she'd called me for.

But finally she said, with that directness, unembarrassed, no longer encumbered, "I've come a long way around to tell you, Geoffrey, that I'm not going to be able to keep you here. I had so wanted the chance for my children. But now—you can tell as well as I can that it won't work.

"What's happened, and what's happened today, makes my asking you to come here look like such an empty, such a foolish gesture. I found that out this afternoon—how futile, how out-of-touch, I must have seemed. But—" she paused for a long time, "it was something I wanted to do. I felt I owed it to myself to try—for the children's sake."

Silence settled between us. The failing light of the tapestry seemed to absorb her figure, to claim her within the passionless silence of its own.

Then she was saying what she herself couldn't quite believe. "The way I was treated in Warren this afternoon was an experience I'd never had. Never thought I would have."

There was no rancor, no bitterness in her voice, merely disbelief. "There's no reason for me not to tell you. Frankly, Geoffrey, it helps me for somebody to know.

"I had to go to the bank. There was nobody else to go. Raleigh had borrowed, and borrowed, and borrowed on this place. I'd never dreamed. It didn't help to find out that others have done the same thing. That really didn't help."

She was still not believing, still repeating the scene for herself.

"Maybe it was harder for me than it should have been. But it was hard. I could have wept for my father.

"If Mr. Harvey Berkley had been there, what a difference it would have made! He was a great admirer of my father. You remember, for years and years he was president of the bank. Do you know that I thought he *still* was?"

I told Miss Amy that he had retired after the war.

"It's no wonder what they thought," she said, "when I asked for him!"

"There's a new man there," I told her.

"Heavens knows I found that out! What a shocking thing for me. He didn't even know who I was. I asked for Mr. Harvey Berkley. They thought I was out of my mind."

She went on shortly, "My father left me some property, Geoffrey, down on Halifax Street. I've kept it all these years. That was what I was going to use.

"That man looked at me—I can't tell you how. 'Madam,' he said, 'do you know what *little* that's worth?'

"Heaven knows, Geoffrey, I didn't know. All I knew was that I'd held to it through all the years.

"But what it *was* worth," she said, "will serve for the time being. It will serve a purpose now. All I could think at the time was what I would have given to see Mr. Harvey

Berkley's face. That man didn't even know my name. I felt
that I'd give every cent I had to see a familiar face.

"But do you know," she told me, "as I sat there looking
at that man, saying to me how little it was worth, knowing
that he didn't even know me, had never heard my father's
name, I felt a kind of numbness. It was a strange experience. It shocked me to realize: *he doesn't know me.
But it doesn't matter any more.* I remember saying that to
myself: *It doesn't matter any more.* That man didn't even
know that my son Blunt had lived and died. I didn't even
want to tell him that Blunt had been mine."

Miss Amy was looking into the fire now. I wondered
whether she'd forgotten that I was there.

"It's what happened the other afternoon when I was sitting under the trees. It seemed to come to me all at once
how beautiful the earth was, how much I'd never seen. I
felt that I never wanted to go into a house again. For all
that was left, there seemed so little time. Every golden leaf
was a separate falling thing."

She wasn't looking at me now. I could see the flashes of
late sun through the bare trees, the separately falling
leaves about her chair.

It was then that Louisa's voice startled us.

"Mother, are you and Geoffrey still talking?"

Miss Amy and I both turned.

Louisa and Tanner Haynes had come into the room.

Both of them were disheveled. Neither of them had
changed clothes. Both of them seemed to have just left
the half acre of glowing ashes where the old barn had
stood.

Louisa brushed her hair back from her forehead. She was
looking at her mother as if she had yet to discover what
the fire had done, what of her mother she remembered.
But her own sensitive gentle face was tired.

Tanner Haynes standing behind her seemed to have
brought all the outdoors with him into the house. A damp

shirt still clinging to his chest, his face and hands still blackened, his dark handsome eyes intent under his heavy singed brows. His had been a separate battle during the burning of the barn, the rescue of the horses. I remembered what they'd said of him during the war. It was he others had followed—he who'd learned so early that he was alone. Even now about him there was the smell of charred burning wood.

Now it was he who spoke, looking at Miss Amy with a directness which had become for him during the last hour all that mattered.

"Miss Amy, may I talk to you?"

Louisa was at his side, looking into Tanner's face. She, too, had aged.

If Miss Amy had been waiting for him she couldn't have revealed less surprise.

The urgencies of the last hours had for them bypassed time.

"Will you sit here, Tanner," Miss Amy said.

"No, ma'am. I'll stand.

"Miss Amy, you've always known me."

"Always, always."

"Louisa is younger than I am. There are years between us."

"I know."

"I want to marry Louisa. Today I felt that the time had come."

Miss Amy repeated the words softly: *Tanner Haynes.* It was as though it didn't involve her decision, her thinking. It was something that had already happened, that she had merely to look back upon, to assign its place in time.

What others had said: *that she had once trembled at sight of that man* was no longer revealed in her waiting, tired, expressionless face.

She made no answer. None seemed necessary.

But Tanner said, searching her face now, "You know I've

lived in a womanless house. You know what people have said of me—" He hesitated: "About my affairs?"

Miss Amy barely nodded her head.

The hardly perceptible rise and fall of his chest revealed the relentlessness of purpose which was driving him. He had arrived at the moment by his own separate lonely way.

"But there is something, I must tell you, that it wouldn't be right to conceal."

Miss Amy looked directly at him: *What did she know of this man?* Her large weary eyes held him steadily.

"Mr. Raleigh will not accept me. Mr. Raleigh has asked me to leave Louisa alone."

Miss Amy got up from her chair. For a second her hand went to her forehead.

"Poor Raleigh," she said. "It doesn't matter. That was something that he had to say. But it doesn't matter. Be understanding, Tanner. Try to understand him now. I wish in God's name there was something I could do for him."

Her voice was utterly weary, but completely controlled.

Louisa was looking at Tanner with speechless, worshipful eyes.

Then I saw that Miss Amy's eyes were wet.

She went toward Louisa, took her daughter in her arms. "My dear, dear child."

Then looking at them both, she said, "You both learned *so* early. You both know that life can hurt. No more blessing than that do I have to give."

The tears fell from her eyes now, as she stood there alone.

Louisa said, "Oh, Mother, this *isn't* going to be the same. This is *not* the same at all."

She threw her arms about her mother, embracing her with youthful passionate love.

Then through her tears Miss Amy was looking at Tanner.

The youthful fragile figure was between them.

Neither of them said a word.

BOOK FIVE

BOOK FIVE

I had been back in Warren for about a month (Judge Whitaker had taken me into his office to "read" law and serve as clerk) when I got a surprising note from Miss Amy saying she and Otway and Louisa were coming to town that night, that they were in fact going to spend the night at the old Warren Hotel. What was surprising about the note was that it was for a supper party for Flora and Alex Cary that she was coming. Colin Ashby, she said, had wanted to honor the recently married daughter of his old friends. Miss Amy added that she especially wanted me there. She had already explained to Mr. Ashby about my stay at the plantation: how much it had meant to all of them for me to be there during those days. She'd come to regard me as a member of the family.

She concluded by saying that she'd seen Dr. Pitt the day before. Raleigh had progressed well enough and could be brought home from the Haynes place within a few days.

Would I meet them at the hotel that night at seven o'clock?

I must admit that it was with a real sense of *their* need that I got ready. What an effort this party was going to be for Miss Amy I felt I alone knew. It rather startled me to realize that it was my familiar face she'd seek. So short a time ago she'd been only a legendary name.

I already knew that Mr. Colin Ashby was a generous and thoughtful man. What combination of people this strange occasion would bring together, there was no way on earth to tell.

It was long after dark on that short day in December

when I started the drive across town in a hired surrey to the Warren Hotel. The sky had been a somber gray since morning. It was particularly cold.

Just as the surrey turned from my house into the wide rutted street, a few hesitant flakes of snow began to fall. The first flakes lay uncertainly in the air, melting even before they hit the warm straining flanks of the horse, disappearing at touch upon the rough surface of the buggy blanket, and delaying, as fatally as moths around a light, about the yellow glow of the surrey lantern. But the traceable and individually dissolving flakes within the moving warmth of the carriage acquired in the distance the thinness of a white blown veil, concealing uncertainly the already darkened houses along the street, and separating us from the way we had come.

But for a block around the hotel, which had been built near the depot for overnight train passengers, the air was heavy and damp with stinging smoke which made a great ballooning cover for the depot and hotel yard, destroying the tentative fall from above before it reached the earth. The hotel porch had long ago been stained a dirty gray. Even the red cannas out front stayed blackened in the summertime with soot. I could see the lighted windows in the hotel glowing like a row of oranges behind the trapped smoke. For winter, the rocking chairs on the porch were turned around and tilted against the wall.

Before I could see them, I heard the horses stamping and shifting restlessly, straining in harness, in a surprisingly crowded yard. Buggy wheels jerked and clicked on the hard earth.

Three Negro boys, falling in and out of the light from the windows, turned like tumbling black shadows at the sound of my surrey.

The biggest was racing toward us, arms outstretched, jerking up the smaller one like the tail of a kite behind.

"Lemme tote yo' suitcase! Lemme tote yo' suitcase!"

"Get away, boy, that horse stomp you flat!" the driver shouted.

"One penny! One penny!" the little ones cried.

"Ain't got no suitcase! Get out from under that horse's foot!"

"Horse sinking in the middle! He sinking in the middle! Look at him sink!"

Arms waving, they were off in a streak to another buggy coming into the light behind us.

Ecstatic voices filled the air: "Hish yo' big mouf! Yon' some *snow* falling! Yon' some *snow* falling! Hish yo' big mouf!"

Had these little beggars, I wondered, come from a plantation? I remembered the picture of the boys, wide-eyed and frightened, looking out at me from tied-up furniture in the wagon behind Sis Hannah and Little Man. Perhaps Little Man, with his powers and one eye cocked toward the sky, had already found customers in the tumble-down shacks around town, amid the chicken-coops, pig-pens, and wet clothes on sagging lines.

It was then I heard the strains of a fiddle cutting through the murky damp outside. It startled me. It didn't seem possible that Amy Prescott could be physically present here. Already the plantation seemed years and miles away.

The big lobby behind frosted glass doors was dimly lit. Walls and ceilings seemed to have been smoked in a long-ago fire. Unused chairs pushed against the walls gave to the room the lull of an emptiness that follows a just-departed train. A few "sample" bags were piled near an unattended desk with a clap-bell and a single lamp. Behind it were a couple of rows of pigeon-hole mailboxes—empty, except for an unasked-for letter.

In the middle of the room a brown-stained iron stove in a sandbox showed the dull-reddish glowing of a sinking coal fire. Its door was cracked open. Flame flashing on a brass spittoon made a lonely signaling.

A scattering of on-lookers near the dining room door told me where the party was. The double-doors stood open a little, letting out the strains of the fiddle, excited voices, flashes of bright dresses.

I knew that after a while these train-weary watchers would be gone: they would be trying to sleep upstairs, with shifting train lights over their beds, and the sound in their ears, half in wakefulness, half in fitful dream, of bursts of laughter, of clanking boxcars and hissing engines, stopping and starting, rolling on finally across flat and deserted countryside, where only the stars saw the moving pin-points of light.

The humming of voices behind the doors, with their green shades half-down, struck me as a ghostly, not-quite-believed, intrusion into these nearly emptied halls—a brief unaccountable returning from former days. As a child before the war, I had heard so many stories about the balls and the festive dinners in the old Warren Hotel.

The men looking on waited in stiff weariness—shreds of tobacco smoke clinging round them as a sign of their exclusion.

Looking at me in my white shirt, my pressed blue suit and polished shoes, they stepped back uncertainly, making a passage for me out of their lives.

The dining room inside was brighter. Candles burned upon a dozen or more glowing tables, upon silver and sparkling glass. Across the room a trestle table covered with shining linen, a crystal punch bowl in the center, had been set up as a serving board.

Only Colin Ashby, astride the town, could have brought these same people together.

The fiddler's music floated over them, around them, toward me: it was lost upon them. The fiddler, an old colored man, gray-haired, a pitcher of water at his feet, sat off by himself. The strings of his bow, up and down, up and down, caught the light of the lamp. It flashed upon

me: how briefly were they all together: how briefly were
these strangers met. I felt I was withholding something
from them.

Not yet included, I saw Otway coming toward me across
the empty span of floor: "Geoffrey, Geoffrey, Mama's waiting for you!"

There was a shadowing, haunting familiarity about him.
For the first time I saw him dressed for an evening: blond
hair brushed, dark suit, white shirt and tie. He was Raleigh
Prescott twenty-five years ago.

Genuine relief raised the boy's voice. I *was* included. I
belonged to them.

Otway, his innocence claiming me, was the youngest of
them all. He still looked on from the outside.

"Grown folks are so damn silly when they get a little
liquor in 'em!" he said to me. "Talk to folks they been
looking at all day like they haven't seen 'em in a week."

Beyond Otway's wet brushed hair, in the half-light between the scattered islands of flaming candles, I saw faces
I'd been seeing all my life on the streets of Warren, but
faces I'd never placed together in the flickering light of a
single room. I had to remind myself why they'd assembled.
Already seated, there were Mr. and Mrs. Courtney Wayne,
Colin Ashby's friends. (They both traveled two or three
times a year to Missouri for horses and mules. With his
whiskey toddies and black cigars, he gave us a glimpse of
the outside world.) The young new clergyman in white
collar and black coat was standing at their table, showing
Mrs. Wayne something on an envelope. The Clerk of the
Court, Mr. Willie T. Pegram, in a cloud of smoke, was
telling something to listening faces. A burst of laughter
came from them. They were off from the crowd. And there
was Mr. Ashby's strong gray face. He was seated, undisturbed, in the middle of youth and age around him. He'd
taken Alex's parents, Mr. and Mrs. Cary, under his care.
The plain, Sunday-dressed, middle-aged couple were listen-

ing to every word. Intent young faces circled Flora's curled head. Candlelight caught her anxious eyes. She was watching a back door. And there was the widower, Mr. Harvey Russell. (His children were grown. People had been saying for twenty years he was going to marry again.) Ella Fitzpatrick in a shiny yellow dress had a finger going in his face.

I asked Otway where Tanner Haynes was.

"Couldn't come. His daddy's sick. Louisa might as well not of come. What being in love does to you, I've seen enough! Leave yourself behind, wherever you go!"

I could tell I was the first partner Otway had found.

I asked him how his daddy was.

"Lord-amighty, Geoffrey. You left at the wrong time! Me and Louisa just been sitting there, waiting, being polite to Mama, just like she was going somewhere."

Then he looked at me. "Geoffrey, you *live* in Warren. Ain't this a *mixed-up* crowd? Know what I mean? *Mixed-up?* Never saw Mama in a crowd like this. Boy, has she put up a *front!*"

Otway hated to release me.

Even the chattering, the laughter there, was a stray ghostly current about to pull me in. I felt I'd caught the town—unexpected, half-glimpsed faces fractured in candlelight—in some hurried passage to—I didn't know where.

"Ought to seen Mama, speaking to those people. Alex's folks. Dog, if she didn't go to *them*. Mr. Ashby took her to 'em. He watched her face every second. Mama wouldn't a-known 'em if she'd met 'em in the street."

Otway was releasing to me everything he'd taken in, "Geoffrey, I don't believe Flora's got good sense. Somebody told her about Tanner and Louisa. Looked like she'd been hit. Mad, anyhow, because Alex's drunk. Everybody feeding him liquor. Back of the hotel right now, trying to sober him up."

Then Otway said, "I got to take you to Mama. You the

one she wants to see. 'Cept that woman, Ella somebody, talking her to death."

Nobody noticed us at first. I had a moment to find Miss Amy. Her back to me, she was already seated at a smaller table. I knew that the jeweled hands across the table belonged to Ella Fitzpatrick. Mr. Harvey Russell had gotten away.

"Mama wants you to sit at her table. She meant it," Otway said.

Some of the people were looking curiously at us. They didn't know where I belonged. I wasn't even surprised any more to see Cora Finch—maybe she was Alex's cousin—or Bessie Boyd, or Carter Jones who was a distant cousin of my own. We looked at each other briefly. I knew what Carter thought: how far we'd come.

I looked at Mr. Ashby again, talking so patiently to Alex's parents. Time had brought them together, whatever barriers there had ever been. Mr. Ashby no longer cared. He'd known too long who he was. Age had removed him from the expectant, seeking faces around him.

I followed Otway toward Miss Amy.

Ella Fitzpatrick was wearing a long, shimmering yellow dress. Her dyed hair was the color of fading straw. Coats of powder had given the thickness of a mask to her skin. Circles beneath her eyes were those of an aging woman. The sag of skin beneath her bare arms did not belong to the Ella Fitzpatrick I remembered. Her nose and ears had grown larger. There was something unsettling about her desperation to conceal her age: the jewelry, the comb in her parched hair, the dark penciled lines of her brows. I thought of an old actress waiting to be called on stage.

Mr. Ashby had once said that Ella was the kindest person in the world, but as shallow as a pie pan. Wide eyes and open mouth were waiting for their word.

"Amy, you've been a *recluse!* Now you listen, you're *my* age. I'll not have you acting—Amy, *tell* me something? Were

you *prepared* for this? I'm glad she *did* get married, if it
was just to bring *you* out. Bless you, my *dear* friend."

Her jeweled fingers went across the table, patted Miss
Amy's wrist.

Seeing us, Ella's hand flew up. "Of *all* people, Geoffrey
Jones."

Miss Amy turned toward me, "Geoffrey?"

She *was* glad to see me. She held to my hand. Through
the ring of voices, the clatter of plates, the sharp burst of
steam from the depot yard, we looked at each other pri-
vately, for a brief moment. But the exchange was enough.
She assured me that she *was* the Amy Prescott I knew, that
the Amy of those exhausting days had become a memory
for her as well. Now she seemed rested. Her dark eyes were
not restless, searching, merely a little sad, a little absent.
But *this* was the secret we carried between us which the
others needn't know. She was wearing a dark blue silk dress,
a string of pearls. Her up-swept graying hair had been
freshly brushed. But she knew I'd seen her on that cold
afternoon. She was saying: *Do you remember? Do you remember: You and I know that life is passing.* She pressed
my hand. In this room of chattering people it seemed that
Miss Amy and I were alone.

I asked her: "How is Mr. Raleigh?"

"Dear Raleigh," she said. "Dr. Pitt has told him he can
travel this week."

"Amy," Ella burst out, "that was such a *distressing* thing.
Didn't know *one* word about it, *one* word, till Colin Ashby
told me last week. A *hunting* accident. Why, the poor thing
could have *killed* himself."

"Geoffrey," Miss Amy said, "sit here with us. I need support in Warren now. I know so few faces. I feel like a
stranger in town."

"What *friends* you and Geoffrey have become, for
heaven's sakes! When Geoffrey was a little boy he used to
sit on Colin Ashby's porch, listen to us talk and talk. The

Lord only knows what he *heard!* Amy! Tell me what Raleigh *did!* Get shot in the *leg?* Poor, *poor* thing! What a *burden* that's going to be for *you!* The *older* you get, things don't get *easier*. They get *worse!*"

"Otway," Miss Amy said, "find you some young people. Aren't there some young people here you can make friends with?"

"Ought to be!" Ella said. "If Colin—bless his heart—left *anybody* out, I don't know who it *is!* Business connections! Sometimes I think you have to pay too high a price to *be* a success."

She paused for a minute, staring at the window. Her mouth dropped open. "Oh, my God!"

"Ella," Miss Amy exclaimed.

"Look!"

Three little black faces, like Halloween masks, were pressed flat against the porch window, looking in.

Ella's fingertips touched her chin. "Those little *niggers* out there! Thought I'd seen a *ghost*. Amy, why did Colin come to *this* dismal place? Drummers looking in one way, little niggers the other!"

"Mama," Otway said, "you're gonna have to say something to Flora. She's mad with Alex."

"Why, son?"

"He's had too much to drink. He's sick!"

"Poor dear," Ella said, "young couples in love are so *tiresome!* They think there's *nobody* in the world but them. After a certain age it gets *tiresome*. I've seen too *much!* I've *buried* two husbands!"

"Son, where is Louisa?" Miss Amy asked. "Go find her! Don't leave her by herself."

"Mama, she's talking to people!"

"Is she *talking?*"

"Yes'm."

"Amy, I know its *none* of my business. But as long as I've

known you, I feel like I can ask you *anything!* Don't tell
me you were *prepared* for this!"

Miss Amy looked at her with a vague smile.

"I *knew* you weren't. All your *life* you've been able to
keep up such a *front!* I don't mind *telling* you! Amy, *you
bury* things! *I* know when you're *hurt. I* know. Your daddy,
bless his wise heart, would *never* let you run wild with the
rest of us. But you *wanted* to. I could tell. Underneath you
were just like us. Sitting here as *controlled* as you please,
just like you've *known* those Cary's all your life."

I saw Miss Amy's sad eyes looking at Ella—her old friend,
thoughtfully, even tenderly. She didn't know what to say.

"You were as *cordial* to that woman as if you felt *sorry*
for her. I *saw* you. Life does *strange* things! There's nothing
wrong with them. They're all right! But, Amy, you can't
tell me—look at 'em—that *they* aren't out-of-*place!*"

"Oh, Ella, Ella," Miss Amy said, a frown of pain on her
face.

Ella was looking at Mrs. Cary, flushed, listening to Colin
Ashby's patient words. Her dark hair was parted in the middle and held at the back with a brown comb. She was wearing a plain gray dress. She'd pinned a gold watch, taken
from a treasured drawer, high on her waist.

Ella said, "I've been *dressing* up for parties *all* my life.
This time, I over*did* it! My dear mama used to say, 'Ella,
that thing you've got on is too *tight.* You don't think you're
dressed up unless you *hurt!*' Poor dear Mama! I know I
drove her *wild!* Amy! I was talking to Louisa a little while
ago. A lovely, sweet girl! So *mature* for her age. *Just* like
you!"

Then she blurted out after a minute, "*Geoffrey,* they tell
me you've been out to the plantation teaching *Latin!* What
in *heaven's* name *for?*"

CHAPTER FORTY-TWO

Swinging doors to the kitchen had been propped open with a straight-back chair. A wave of smoky heat, flickers of firelight from the black kitchen range, the smell of roasted turkey, muffled sounds of Negro voices (unintelligible, strangely alien), flooded over the heads of the shifting waiting crowd. Faces turned. From the semi-dark of the dining room, we looked into the oily heated flare of the kitchen. Conversation round us dropped. Strains of the fiddler's bow filled the emptying air. The old Negro in the corner had been fiddling all the time.

Ella Fitzpatrick was looking vaguely at the crowd as if she'd just realized where she was. "Life is a *strange* thing," she said. "Right here in the *middle* of this crowd I feel so *lonesome.* Amy, don't *you* get away from me. All of a *sudden* I feel like *you* are my *only* friend. The *only* one I can *depend* on."

She was carrying a full plate just served from the buffet. As she put it down on the table her hand quivered. "Get your plate. You and Geoffrey, but *don't* get away from me."

A hesitant line of people were already holding their plates. Colin Ashby, standing, had caught Miss Amy's attention, was motioning to the table.

Two of the cooks from the kitchen, changed into fresh white coats as stiff as shingles, stood at the covered table over the platters of food. The browned turkey with parsley and baked apples oozed beads of hot juice. A flat silver tray was covered with thin red slices of old ham. Identical pickle and celery dishes made a widely stretched chain. One waiter presided over a big casserole of smoking baked oysters crusted with bread crumbs. His gleaming face above the steaming dish was set in a fixed smile at the comments of the guests. At the end of the board, golden rolls dripped with butter.

Colin Ashby was standing back seeing that the others were served. He had his hand on Mr. Cary's back, pushing the hesitant couple into line.

The little crowd around Flora was still holding back, all eyes on the door leading to the alley outside.

"All right, come on, everybody," Colin Ashby was saying. "You young folks over there!"

"Amy!" Ella was calling out. "Bring your plate back here! You've *got* to sit with me."

For a moment between the faces of the others, through the sounds of the voices, Miss Amy and Colin Ashby were looking at each other. Briefly I felt that they were alone in the room. She was looking at their old loyal friend, still alive, still dispensing to others from the full measure of his understanding and patient heart. *Do you remember me? Do you remember me?* she was saying.

I looked at Colin Ashby, his absent face gray under heavy brows. Candlelight from the table below set his face apart, apart from Mr. and Mrs. Cary, Willie T. Pegram, still holding his glass, Cora Finch looking desperately about for somebody to sit with, the widower, Harvey Russell, bending over the turkey, Mr. Courtney Wayne crushing out his cigar in a saucer, from the shining expectant faces around Flora, alarmed and angry at Alex's delay in returning: Mr. Ashby saw nothing. *Was this where the years had carried Raleigh and Amy? Was this where the years had carried them all?*

It was almost as if the two looked at each other across widening distance and were afraid they would never see each other again.

"Mama, me and Louisa are going to eat over there where Flora is. They *put* us over there," Otway was saying into her ear. "You go ahead and *eat*. Enjoy yourself."

Ella Fitzpatrick, waiting for us at a smaller table, seemed surprisingly agitated. "Some people you can't talk to," she said before we sat down. "I don't mean a thing in the world by it," she spoke wearily as if the party had just become a disappointment to her, "but it's *wearing*. The conversations I've had with *this* crowd!" She cast a quick look back over her shoulder. "Where did Colin Ashby *find* these people? Business will make you do *anything*."

"Ella," Miss Amy said, "I'm the one. I feel like I've been out of Warren for a century!"

The candle had begun to sputter, dripping a trickle of wax into the saucer.

Ella was trying to fold her full rustling skirt beneath the table. "I don't mean to offend you at Flora's party, but I *wore* the wrong thing. That old souse over there! That old— *rooster!* The one I was *trying* to *talk* to! Charlie Buell. So full of *punch* he can *hardly* stand. Right *wall*eyed. Some little snippet—some little *nobody*—told him he ought to *dance*. Every minute I was talking to him, all he could *say* was, 'Young people are *wunnerful*. I *love* young people! Young people are *wunnerful!*' I thought if he said that to me *once more* I was going to throw a glass of water in his face."

Ella was visibly upset.

From the far corner of the room above the scraping of chairs, we heard a burst of voices. "There he is! Hurrah for Alex!"

All the guests, even the waiters, with suspended knives and spoons, turned to look at the boy's entrance. The slender bridegroom came in guiltily. His face was white, his hair disheveled. Two attending friends walked cautiously a step or two behind him. He gave a weak smile to the hailing voices.

"Poor thing," Ella said. "He won't be able to *stand* the sight of *food!* Amy, did you know the boy at *all?*"

Miss Amy was looking at Alex. He could have stepped into

the range of her vision for the first time. To Ella's question she shook her head.

Flora, already seated, was watching every step Alex made. Then she turned abruptly, refusing for a while his apology.

"Put the poor thing where his mama and daddy can't see him," Ella murmured to herself.

There was a flurry around Alex. Somebody placed his chair, filled his coffee cup.

"Amy, you know what this reminds me of? About the little boy and the birthday party."

I could tell that Miss Amy wasn't sure what Ella had said.

"Amy, you're not even *listening*."

Then Miss Amy was looking at Ella's powdered face, covering the large pores on her nose, the poorly concealed penciling of her brows, the restless flash of her jewelry. Ella had been going to parties all her life, looking year after year at younger and younger faces.

"Lily Pender used to tell it. Little boy every day asked his mama: 'Is it time for the party? Time for the party?' 'No, son, I've told you fifty times you're *not* invited until next week!' Same thing next day. 'Today, Mama?' 'No, no, no, no.' But the day did come. Dressed up, slick and shiny, the little boy went off. Twenty minutes later, mama looked out and there before her eyes he was. 'Son, what on earth?' He looked up with tears pouring from his eyes. 'I throwed up!'"

"Oh, Ella."

"Didn't you ever hear Lily Pender tell that?"

Over the sound of voices, the scraping of chairs, came the insistent ring of a knife striking a glass. Voices died down around the room. The fiddler rested his bow. Murmurings from the kitchen, the slamming of a door somewhere inside the hotel invaded the room.

Faces turned to Colin Ashby, standing. Candlelight below him threw his shadow to the wall.

Somebody beating on a table was saying, "Hear, hear!"

Colin Ashby was looking thoughtfully, a little absently, at the upturned faces around him. Finally he said, "I was just thinking a minute ago when I was looking around this room at all these young faces. To tell you the truth, I almost forgot where I was—"

A glass was knocked over at a table nearby. Water was spilling to the floor. A voice said, "Be quiet back there!"

Colin Ashby turned absently and looked. The disturbance didn't bother him at all.

"I tell you one thing. You young people round here are coming up too fast. When I made up my mind to have a little supper for my old friends' daughter, married right here in Warren under my nose, the only place came to me was the Warren Hotel. I just made out a little list of people on an envelope, and I tell you it opened my eyes. Ella and Amy sitting over there know what I'm talking about. Willie Pegram, *you* know. Just try making out a list. Well, that's not what we've come for—"

Colin Ashby hesitated, took a sip of water. His voice was surprisingly tired. His glass hit the table too hard when he put it down.

Ella Fitzpatrick winced, put down her fork. "For heaven's *sakes*," she said, "what does Colin think this *is?*"

I watched Miss Amy's attentive face. Colin Ashby had always been there, had always been exempt from the infirmities and frailties of others, from the wear of time.

In a moment he went on, "I'm going to tell you younger people the truth. When I had this little party tonight I was thinking about one of the prettiest girls that ever grew up in this town."

Ella Fitzpatrick said, "I wish he'd *hush*."

"I can see that girl right now. Tell you all a secret. *I* was go'n court her. Mr. Will scared me off. If he'd had two, three more, it would have been a different tale. Take my word for it. All the men *looked* at her. Now you young folks let me tell *you* something. A lady if there ever was one.

Amy Pendleton, stand up over there. I just want 'em to look at you."

A wave of silence swept the room.

I watched Miss Amy's face go white, her chin set. Clinched fingers supporting her on the table, she rose slowly and faced the room.

There was a moment of real silence, *Amy Pendleton, Amy Pendleton,* as all the young faces turned to look at her.

Candlelight flickered upon her quiet face, her gray hair, the blue silk of her dress, the shining string of pearls. Her eyes misted over.

Would any of them, except Colin Ashby and Ella, ever know how lonely she'd been?

There was a dignity, a loneliness, there in this confusion that they weren't prepared for. Who was this woman who had stepped out so suddenly before them, who had been living out her life in the vague countryside beyond their town? She was already a memory, a voice from an already forgotten past.

Slowly, about the room, feet shuffled, chairs scraped. One by one, people stood. Then, slowly, thoughtfully, the clapping began. The clapping filled the room.

Even in my own eyes the faces were blurred in the crowd: those of Louisa and Otway, Colin Ashby nodding his head, Flora and Alex, Willie T. Pegram, Ella Fitzpatrick biting her lip.

Behind them all, the old colored man had stood. His arm was working away at the fiddle, but nobody could hear the music he made.

CHAPTER FORTY-THREE

"For heaven's sake, Amy. You and Colin Ashby have got me so upset I can't *eat*."

Ella was wiping her eyes with a lace handkerchief, already knotted and wet.

"I came to a *party!* You two have gone and stirred up *everybody's* life. I don't *want* mine stirred up. I don't want to *look* at it."

The guests, once more seated, had resumed eating. Lowered voices, the subdued clink of china and silver filled the room. Two Negro waiters, perspiring over the steaming dishes, were taking a moment's respite. They were wiping wet foreheads with the corners of long aprons. The fiddler, his fiddle and bow crossed on his chair, stood behind them drinking a cup of punch.

"What did they *put* in that punch? It went to my *head*."

Just as Ella was about to pick up another roll, the persistent ringing tap of a glass spread through the room.

"Quiet, everybody! Quiet."

A shattering clatter of pans came from the kitchen.

"Quiet!"

A heavy set, middle-aged man, his face flushed, his coat open over a wrinkled shirt, was getting to his feet. He seemed to be steadying himself on a slightly swaying floor.

Faces at the tables around him were set in alarm.

"Hold it, Charlie," Mr. Courtney Wayne, half-rising, spoke out.

"Oh, my God, it's Charlie Buell!" Ella Fitzpatrick put down her roll. "What in *God's* name is he going to say?"

She turned deliberately in her chair to look at him. Her agitated powdered face was already offended.

"Easy, Charlie."

Charlie Buell was gripping the back of his chair, nodding his head emphatically. "Now one thing I wanna say." He looked out severely at the crowd.

"Say it."

"Now Miss Amy Prescott is aw—right. She's awright. Colin, you tole the truf. Now Raleigh Prescott's awright. Been knowing him all my life. It makes me—*proud*—to add my praise." He took a determined swallow of water, raised his hand. "But these young folks here tonight are *wunnerful.* I just want you all to know that I *love* these young folks. Tell you the truf. Be around 'em is *wunnerful!* Now, let everybody drink a little toast!"

"Sit down, Charlie, that's all right. Everybody's eating turkey now."

"That old *rooster,*" Ella Fitzpatrick said. "I wish I was close enough to crack his skull!"

Miss Amy's face caught my attention. She had put down her knife and fork. Quietly, thoughtfully, she was looking at the tottering figure. "Ella," she said, "do you remember that when we were young Charlie Buell was one of the beaux?"

"Amy, you *amaze* me. You never *looked* at Charlie Buell. And you *know* it. Your *Papa* wouldn't have let Charlie Buell come within a *mile* of your *house.* Why can't we talk about something *pleasant?*"

Ella began to eat her turkey as if she'd just discovered it.

"Mother, are you all right? Are Geoffrey and Miss Ella taking good care of you?"

It was Louisa. She put her hand on her mother's shoulder. The two looked into each other's eyes.

"Have you *enjoyed* it, daughter? Have you had a good time?"

There was tense searching in Miss Amy's eyes. "Who are the people you are talking to?"

Louisa was not as pretty as her mother had been at her age. But her brown hair, her sensitive intelligent eyes caught my attention. This was the first time I had seen her free of the strain and the painful dismay of those days at the plantation. The anguished traveling, back and forth, between the two houses seemed a long time ago. A glimpse of Raleigh Prescott came back to me, his flushed uncertain face against the white pillows, his Negro companions, faithful, patient, standing so silently at his bedside. It struck me all at once: had Jennie Blackstone returned? It was odd: the intimacy the desperate woman had claimed had been a final offense, impossible for him to bear.

There was a radiance about Louisa's face now, a separateness: she was going to marry Tanner Haynes. The younger and older woman looked into each other's eyes. It was an act of embracing, an act of parting. I could hear Louisa's assurance: *it isn't going to be the same. Not the same at all.*

"Now, Mother," Louisa said, "aren't you glad you came?"

Miss Amy answered, "Ella has reminded me of everything. I'd forgotten how Warren used to be."

"Because I'm *old* Warren," Ella broke in. "That's all I've heard tonight. *Nobody* will let me forget it. Colin Ashby *annoys* me. He's not that *old*. Standing there positively *doting*." Ella pushed at the straw colored hair over her ears.

Then she looked at Louisa as if the thought had just come to her: "*Louisa,* didn't I hear something about *you?*"

Louisa flushed.

"You and Tanner *Haynes!* Of all *people!* I didn't *dream* it. *Somebody told me.*"

She hesitated, looked at Louisa with freshened interest. "You and *Amy* will never cease to *amaze* me. All I've heard since the war, *any* young woman in the country would marry *that* man at the drop of a *hat*. Well, Louisa, let me tell *you* something. I think it's wonderful. I *do*. But there's not one blessed thing *anybody* can *tell* you." She raised her hand warningly. "Don't ever *listen!* I've had *two* husbands. I *needed* them. Didn't have the sense or *anything* to live by myself. My poor papa used to say, 'Ella, who in *God's* name is going to take care of *you!*' Child, don't think I didn't *wonder* myself. It scares me right now."

She started to pick up her coffee cup, then put it down.

"But you and *Amy!* When *we* were girls, I didn't even put *Amy* in my class. Let me tell you, child. Your mother had—*character*. We stood in *awe* of her. But *Amy* has put up with—*things* just like everybody else. Better! Tonight, she has been almost like she *used* to be. Amy," she burst out (her eyes misted over), "I have *thought* about you and *thought* about you."

Miss Amy smiled quietly at her old friend.

"Ella," she said in a minute. "You told that little story about Lily Pender. Do you ever hear anything about her?"

"Lily *Pender?* My God, Amy, is *that* what you've had on your mind? Heavens, Amy, *everybody* knows about Lily," she said reproachfully. "Where *have* you been? It's—*tragic*. That's what it is."

"Why?"

Louisa watched her mother's hand suddenly fold and unfold on the table. Her big dark eyes were searching Ella's face.

"Why?" she said again.

"I know *I* haven't got much sense! But *who* in heaven's *name* did her papa think he *was?* In this world you have to *do* with what there *is*. Married twice, I *know*. Letting the bars down will *not* kill you! Look at that poor cracked *lonesome* Eva Birdsong walking up and down the street, just *begging* for somebody to *talk* to. Makes *me* shudder. What if *I* was in *her* place?"

"But, Ella, I want to know about Lily." She was hesitating to bring out the question: "Didn't Lily *marry* well?" Then she said impulsively (I felt she hadn't intended to say it), "I've been so far out of the world."

Only Louisa and I noticed what had escaped her lips.

"Depends on what you mean by *well*. I wish those loud people back there would *hush*. I'm *trying* to *think*. Money, my God, yes. But you *know*"—the thought just struck her—"nothing in this *world* is exactly right or wrong. What I've been through with ten thousand kin people, I'm *still* confused. Amy, you've made me lose my appetite."

But as soon as she put her fork down, she picked it up again and absently began to eat her oysters.

"My stars in heaven. Somebody back there is trying to sing *Lorena*. I'll bet my hat it's Charlie Buell."

Miss Amy said, "Ella, I want to know why Lily's marriage has been tragic?"

"Geoffrey, *you* tell her. *You're* a Latin scholar. I don't even know what the word *means*."

But she put down her fork.

"That man isn't what anybody *expected* for Lily, Amy. Sweet and innocent as *she* was, she didn't *deserve* him. Lily's daddy pushed the *whole* thing. Thought Lily was too good for *anybody* around here."

"Lily never comes back, does she, Ella?"

Miss Amy's frank insistence caught Ella's attention. "*Honestly*, Amy, I feel like I'm *corrupting* you. Lily Pender was just the right kind of *furniture* for that man to put in his house."

A whiff of burnt grease floated over the dining room from the kitchen.

"My heavens," Ella said, "we might as well go in the *kitchen* and eat."

Then she went on: "Behind her back that man has lived lives—not one but *lives*—that poor Lily will *never* know about. And he's used that poor thing for *business*, for *society*. Lily *looks* like somebody. Amy, Lily *reminded* me a little of you! But, *why*, when anybody would have married him for his *money*, did he have to go *deliberately* and pick out the most *innocent* person in the world? I hope her *papa* was *satisfied*. *Died* and left *Lily* to live it out. And that is exactly what she's *done*. What people *won't* do for appearances! Eat their *hearts* out. *Appearances*." She threw the word out. "I'm tired of them, Amy! When I married Carter Fitzpatrick, I reckon everybody realized I was."

Ella had lost interest in her food. She gave an exasperated push to her plate.

"But *one* thing, with *Carter* there wasn't a *day* that I didn't *know* where he was—either playing poker with Johnny Moore and Tom Beckwith at the livery stable or burying some *cousin* I didn't know he had. I do *honestly* believe that I have babbled my *whole* life's story. Heavens, it doesn't sound like much!"

After a moment she added: "I declare I believe I understand why Lily used to tell that little story."

Ella was taxed by this review of her past. The powder on her long face was splotched.

"Amy, it just doesn't *pay* to look back."

It came as a surprise to us that the guests were already getting up from the other tables.

Some had circled around the fiddler who was playing a livelier tune. Some stood in the doorway to the lobby, pulling on coats. A group of young faces had crowded around Flora and Alex's table. Colin Ashby was shaking hands with Mr. and Mrs. Cary. Charlie Buell had gone back to the punch bowl. I could see the smoke from Mr. Courtney Wayne's black cigar.

Waiters, holding big trays, loaded with stacked dishes, made their way in and out through the crowd.

"Mother," Louisa said, "you and Ella and Geoffrey wait here. Alex's parents are leaving. I'd better speak to them. Mr. Ashby has had them all night."

Miss Amy stood up from the table. The candlelight was shining on her silk dress.

"Louisa, Louisa," she said, "hold them! I want to tell them goodbye!"

I noticed that her hand trembled, as she clinched the beaded bag at her plate.

"Oh, Amy! Amy!"

There were tears in her eyes as Ella Fitzpatrick came round the table. Her lips quivered.

She threw her arms around her old friend's neck and held her. "Oh, Amy, my dear girlhood friend, I just understand it. You have been just as *human* as I have been all these years."

Miss Amy patted her sobbing friend's shoulder and smiled into her face.

A little while later I was driving home in the surrey under a steadily falling snow. The white veil between us and the hotel thickened at every turn of the wheel. In the middle of the wide white street, the surrey was leaving a deep trail. The comfortable old houses along the way, behind their yard shade trees, had drawn back from the road. Their lights were gone. The houses were dissolving in night and falling snow.

The horse was shaking flying snow from his head. The Negro driver had brushed it from the sagging leather seats.

Our one yellow light, glowing softly in the silence, made of us a tiny moving island in the white expanse. Falling flakes hovered separately, briefly, about the lantern, and then we left them behind.

I knew that the hotel under its failing smoke, blocks away across town, contained by now a nearly emptied room. The soft warm candles were already extinguished. Trays of unscraped plates still waited in the kitchen. Waiters were yanking stained cloths from the tables which they would set once more for the breakfasts for the lonely occupants in the locked rooms above. I could see the Negro cooks, their aprons off, revealing glistening black arms, sitting for a moment, elbows on knees, resting their feet. And under the obscuring white fall outside, the last of the guests, delaying in conversations at the steps of their buggies and surreys, were about to go their separate ways. I knew that they would never be together again. Already the scene was far away. It had already been caught in the current of time.

Perhaps it was the silencing snow that kept me from going to sleep that night. There was, outside, such an unnatural stillness. From my bedroom window, where I watched, the thickening fall of white had already cut off from me the lonely darkened houses in the neighboring yards. The snow had made a shining crusted mound on my window-sill. Sparkling little stars of frost had begun to fracture the cold glass of the panes.

The old hotel where Miss Amy and Otway and Louisa were sleeping was separated from me now by trackless silent space.

I knew that at this hour only one lamp would be burning in the deserted cold lobby of the hotel. Perhaps the old stove, with its shaky, rusty pipes hanging from wires under the ceiling, still held a handful of sinking red embers, still signaled feebly to the brass of the spittoons.

How strange it seemed that Miss Amy and her children were sleeping in the drafty comfortless rooms upstairs, surrounded by a scattering of strangers. Miss Amy was sleeping now—for the first time in how many years?—in the town in which her father and mother lay buried. Unknown to her parents, she had returned.

Her presence in Warren on this quiet night seemed strange, a violation of time. Her presence here almost removed from me my belief in the plantation itself.

Raleigh Prescott, the stricken man, had not yet returned to his mother's house. Supported by his devoted attendants —Pettigrew and Wakefield—he was still waiting within reach of his crutches to salvage what remained for him of time.

Who was in that cold empty house with Clio? With Miss Amy and the others beyond the reach of her voice, was she turning in frantic alarm toward the tacked-up letter on her wall, the letter that named for her who she was? I was confident that Miss Amy had not abandoned her to the separation that would so soon be hers. I could see on the floor around her bed the glitter of the metal from the low fire: the knives, the scissors, the broken glass, protecting her from the unnamed evils of the night.

And I could see the lonely room where I had so briefly stayed: the old schoolmaster's room, with Shakespeare and Cicero's *Orations*, unread, on the shelf over his desk, the old copy-book sheets in the drawer with their Latin conjugations in childish fading print. Were the imprisoned wasps at the cold windows still clocking the lonely passage of the night?

Mr. Jasper Hornsby was lying now in the snow covered earth in the graveyard beyond the grove. I had visited it only a day or two before I left.

Far from Warren, far over the deserted countryside under the blinding snow, the little graveyard now was almost obliterated. Only the wrought-iron railing around sinking anonymous graves reached above the crusting expanse of white. The gate with its delicate scroll was locked in cold and ice. Three cedars, three silent sentinels, stood watch in this vast space over the spot of earth where old Mrs. Prescott; her husband, Wakefield's father; Mr. Hornsby; and earlier generations of forgotten, nameless kin lay buried. The cotton and corn fields around, where for over a hundred years the slaves had trod, were now silent and white, and unvisited by any step.